NEW YORK TIMES AND USA TODAY BESTSELLING AUTHOR
VICTORIA ASHLEY

Royal Savage

Copyright © 2015 Victoria Ashley

Cover design by CT Cover Creations

Cover Photography: Lane Dorsey

Model: Josh Mario John

Edited by Charisse Spiers

Edited by Virginia Tesi Carey

Formated by N. E. Henderson

PROLOGUE

ROYAL

I CAN'T CLOSE MY EYES.... I refuse to. Every time I do, all I see is blood, death, and pain. I can feel it—almost taste it.

It doesn't matter that I'm still breathing; I no longer need it, I no longer want it. I despise it along with everything else around me.

The only thing I long for is to fucking fade away and pretend as if I'm not standing here covered in blood; crimson fucking red from head to toe, with my heart pounding so viciously that my chest feels as if it's going to burst the fuck open.

My lungs burn as I inhale another long drag from the cigarette I've been holding. The smoke fills my lungs, expanding them and sending a cooling sensation throughout my shaking body. I long for some kind of relief, but it fucking brings none. I take another drag anyway, waiting for what's to come next. I know what's coming, because I called them: red and blue flashing lights.

I stand frozen in the window, numbly watching as they

grow near, the sounds of sirens getting louder with each passing second.

Taking one last drag, I toss the cigarette at the glass and turn away. I couldn't care less if this motherfucker burns down. There's nothing left here for me. Not anymore.

My body starts moving, mindlessly checked out and lost somewhere in this never-ending nightmare of my world at its end. I feel the hatred start to build, the animosity of the night overwhelming me.

I bring my blood-covered hands up to rub my face as I growl out, releasing some of my pent-up anger. I growl out until my throat feels raw, but just like the cigarette, it does shit to relieve this pain that is slowly killing me.

I walk slowly and in a daze, passing three breathless bodies before I stop in front of... her. Blood covers her blonde hair and her once pink, plump lips are now ice fucking blue. I reach over to pull her into my arms, feeling my heart die a little more with each breath that she doesn't take.

That's when the door flies open and I hear them piling in. Heavy footsteps take over until that's all I can hear, besides the erratic beating of my dead fucking heart.

A buzzing fills my ears, my heartbeat speeds up at an uncontrollable rate, and all I see is red as I'm yanked to my feet, two officers fighting to restrain me. I don't care if they fucking take me away. I will rot in fucking hell for her, but I'm not done saying goodbye yet.

I feel the cuffs snap around my wrists, hard; too fucking hard. My hands may not be free, but that won't stop me. Rotating my shoulders, I swing my head back as hard as I can, slamming it into a nose that I hear crack. That shit is broken. I know that for sure, and so does he by the way he curses and steps away to hold his bleeding nose.

Another set of hands attempt to grab me from behind as I make my way down to the ground, on my knees, burying my face into her lifeless neck. I kiss it gently for the last time, before my head is yanked backward and I'm torn away from her. I'm pushed down to my face and a knee digs into my neck.

This is where my world ends. This is where I stop wanting to live. This is where I lose her...

CHAPTER 1

AVALON

TWENTY MONTHS LATER...

I LOOK MYSELF OVER IN the full-length mirror one more time before turning to Madison and gesturing to my outfit. It's a black form-fitting skirt that stops just below my ass, paired off with a low-cut silver blouse and black stiletto boots. It's been sitting in my closet since I bought it over a year ago.

"There. You happy I squeezed my huge ass into this just for you?" She nods and rubs her hands together, showing her excitement. "Yeah, you better damn well be, Madi. My plan was to own this sexy shit but never *ever* wear it. You just ruined that for me and I have a feeling that if I bend in any way, my ass is going to rip right through this stupid, over-priced fabric."

"Oh, shush it." Madison bumps me out of the view of the mirror so she can get a look at herself. Her strawberry blonde curls are pulled up into a loose ponytail and her curvy body is wrapped in a little black dress, hugging her perfectly. She's stunning in it. Apparently, every girl should own one. I don't, but whatever.

"That's what I'm here for, Ava; to ruin your plans, because frankly, they all suck ass and involve boring shit lately. Oh, and by the way, your ass looks fantastic in that skirt. There's nothing wrong with a voluptuous ass. If I were a dude, I'd be all over it, trying to bite it. Just saying." She smacks her red lips together and grabs her little, red handbag. "Let's go. The cab is waiting."

"Yes, Master Madi," I tease as I shove my phone into my purse and switch off the light on my way out the door behind her.

Apparently Jax, this guy I've never met, has this huge, all out party at his house once every month, and finally, I have let Madison talk me into going. I work long hours at *Stylin'*—the hair salon, and by the time I get home the last thing I'm worried about is partying it up and getting wasted out of my mind.

We're in the cab for about twenty minutes before we pull into what seems like a mile-long driveway. I look at Madison, who seems giddy as can be and then back beside me out the window. It's already dark, so there's not really much that I can see besides trees, bushes, and statues. I can tell that it's beautiful though, and well-kept. Whoever owns this place pays good money to keep it looking nice.

"Look, if we don't pull up at this house in the next two seconds I'm tapping out. Seriously, who needs a whole block as their driveway? It's insane. Maybe we should just go to *Flynn's*, get some beer, and play some pool instead."

Madison grins like a maniac as we pull up in front of what looks like a fucking brick mansion. It's insanely huge. Okay, so I may be exaggerating a bit, but it still looks like three of our houses put into one. It's lit up by some kind of blue lighting in the front and has a huge fountain off to the right side of the door that people are standing around, with drinks in hand.

There's at least a hundred or more cars and motorcycles parked in various spots in front of the house.

"I need a drink and fast. Our boss is a grade-A-bitch and I still want to choke her over what happened this morning. Fucking old, stuck up cunt." She tosses the elderly cab driver a twenty-dollar bill, blows him a kiss, and gets out of the cab. I shake my head at the guy and hurry out of the cab as he looks me up and down and wiggles his bushy eyebrows.

Trying not to fall, I jog up the pathway to catch up with Madison. "Nice, Madi. I think the driver just ejaculated on himself while looking at my tits." I shake in disgust and let out a small breath to calm myself. "If we get stuck with him when we leave, my ass is walking."

"Hey, old men need release too," she teases. "Don't be so selfish." I slap her arm and she laughs before throwing her arms up and swaying her hips to the small group of people gathered around the fountain talking. "Just promise me you'll try to have fun. I know this isn't your thing, but I swear it will be fun. There's a good chance that you will meet some cool, laid-back guy and forget about Colton and his small dick."

I can't hold back the laughter that erupts when she calls Colton's dick small. I told her that *one* time when we were both trashed. I never for one second thought that she'd remember that night. I've spent the last six months hoping that she won't get pissed at me and out me to Colton. I seriously have to kiss major ass every so often and butter her up a bit.

"Thanks for the reminder." I hold up my pinky and wiggle it around. "Thank God for fucking vibrators." Hey... I might as well have a little fun out of the situation. Colton *can* be an ass sometimes.

"Hell yes! Exactly!" She presses a hard kiss to my forehead, no doubt leaving her big red lip prints. "Screw Colton. Thank fucking God for vibrators and let's have fun."

I grab her arm, slowing her down as she begins walking

away. "That doesn't mean I'm here for guys. He's still my boyfriend. I promise I will have fun tonight, but no guys for me. Just drinks. Got it?"

She rolls her eyes. "Oh, honey. Colton is temporary. He's already been around for six months too long if you ask me. If he were doing it for you, then his size wouldn't even bother you. It's how he works it that should matter, so I'm guessing he's falling short in that department too."

I open my mouth in surprise, but close it when I realize that I really don't want to get into this conversation tonight; not when I'm stuck here with her for who knows how long.

I met Colton six months ago when he came into the salon for a haircut. He spent the first two months making me feel special and wanted, until he got me right where he wanted me, and now the last four months have been spent with him working what seems like twenty-four hours a day, seven days a week. If I'm being honest, no, he doesn't satisfy my sexual needs...not even close. Does that give me a reason to dump him? Madison seems to think so.

She pushes the enormous blue door open and pulls me into the foggy, dim house. The music blasts through the rooms, mixed with shouting and laughter as Madison dances her way through the crowd, bumping people with her hips to get through. Some people look back at her with glares, while others just ignore her and move out of the way. That's what I love about her. She doesn't give a shit, and usually, I don't either.

We push our way through two large rooms until we finally find our way into the kitchen. We stop in front of what appears to be a drink buffet. "Drink choice for the night, sweetness?" Madison asks loud enough for me to hear her over the fast beat of the blaring speakers.

"Vodka and anything," I scream back. "I don't really care as long as it's strong enough to make me forget about tomorrow altogether."

"Gotcha, honey." Madison reaches for two red plastic cups and searches through the various bottles of liquor for any kind of vodka she can find. She holds a bottle up in the air and winks when she finds it. Then she walks over to the table covered with pops and juices and snatches up the bottle of lemonade right before some uptight chick with too much makeup reaches for it.

The girl rolls her eyes at Madison and places her hand to her hip.

"Calm your tits, sweets. I'll be done in a sec," Madison says with a careless smirk.

I watch as Madison pours our drinks, making mine a double. "So do you actually know anyone here?" I move in closer to her as more people push their way into the kitchen in search of fresh drinks. I feel suffocated now, as bodies bump into me and stand all over me, acting as if I'm not even there. Someone even tries dancing behind me, bumping me with his crotch repeatedly.

"Jax." She pushes my drink into my hand before looping her arm through mine and passing the lemonade over to the other girl. "I met Jax a few weeks ago when I was on that date with that loser Gage. He took me to that fancy restaurant and bored me to death. Remember that?"

We push our way outside to the back of the house and walk over to stand next to the gigantic pool. It's definitely a lot quieter out here and I can actually breathe. It's a little chilly for an August night, so no one seems to be interested in swimming besides a small group of half-naked partiers in the hot tub that are drowning in drinks and getting fresh, sharing each other's girls.

Note to self: stay the fuck out of the hot tub.

"Yeah, but I don't remember you telling me that you actually met Jax. I thought you just knew of him and his parties through one of your friends."

She takes a sip of her drink and licks her lips. "Oh I met him alright and he is one fine piece of man. The finest. Let me tell you." She smiles and nods to someone behind me, before biting her lip playfully.

I look over my shoulder to see a handsome guy with dark, styled hair and a short beard, dressed in a white Henley with dark jeans. You can see his sleeve of tattoos through the white fabric. He winks at Madison before going back to talking to his group of friends.

I turn back to Madison to see her face red and her drink now almost completely gone as she chews on her straw playfully. "I'm going to take a wild guess here and say that hot guy back there with the twitching eye is Jax."

Madison nods her head and her smile broadens.

"You ladies talking about me over here?" a voice says from behind me, scaring me. "I promise whatever it is, I didn't do it; not yet at least."

I step to the side to see the dark-haired guy—Jax —now standing beside me. He smiles at Madison before turning to me and lifting a brow. "Long, brown hair, nice curves, and big hazel eyes with fuckable lips. Avalon, I presume." He laughs and nods to Madison. "Her words, not mine; although I must agree."

Madison shrugs when I turn to her, my face now red. "What, honey? I'm all about the truth. You should be thankful. There are many others that aren't so lucky. Just saying."

I take a sip of my drink, smirk at Madison, and look Jax up and down, taking in his muscular frame. He's definitely sexy. I can see why Madison has practically been begging me to come for the last two months. She wants to talk truth and run her mouth, I can do the same. "You plan on fucking my friend here tonight, Jax? You better have a big dick, because that's how she likes them. Rough too, and preferably in every hole."

Madison spits out her drink, almost spewing it all over some girl as she walks past. The tall blonde throws her arms up in disgust and gives Jax a glare before walking off.

Jax just smiles in amusement as if he doesn't give a shit, checking Madison out. "That would definitely be a bonus," he says, not hiding his excitement at the idea. He turns to me and nods. "Nice to meet you." He then turns back to Madison. "Find me in a bit, yeah?" He winks before walking off to talk to another small crowd that is calling him over.

"Holy fuck, Ava." She pinches my arm really hard and pushes me back into the house so she can make a new drink. "I haven't even gotten to that part with him yet. We're not talking like that! Well I want to, but shit. Now he knows that I want into those sexy ass jeans of his; not to mention that I'm a kinky bitch."

I smile big and laugh under my breath as she tries to fight back her smile. She loves me for what I just did and she knows it. She'll be thanking me later. "You're welcome." I glance around me in search of the bathroom. "Hey, I have to use the bathroom. Do you need to go?"

She grabs my drink out of my hand and waves some girl over that she must know. "No, I'm fine for a while. I don't want to break the seal. I'm not spending all my time in the bathroom. I've waited for weeks to get my ass here." I get ready to walk away, but she grabs my arm, stopping me. "Oh, and I was told not to go downstairs. His friend is hiding out for the night. I guess he had a shitty day and told everyone to stay the fuck upstairs. There has to be at least two bathrooms upstairs and probably one or two on this floor, so take your pick, babes. Got it?"

"Nice to know," I say before walking away as Madison starts talking to the short brunette she waved over.

Once I get upstairs, it's easy to spot which rooms are the bathrooms. There are lines to every single one. Seriously! Why do women always have to pee? You give them a few alcoholic beverages and they're in the bathroom every five minutes instead of actually enjoying the party. I knew I should've used the bathroom before I left. I was just about to go before Madison announced that the cab was there.

After walking around to every single bathroom, which there are three by the way—one off of the master bedroom, which had a threesome going on in it, so we won't even talk about that —I take a spot in line at the end of the shortest one and that still has like ten or so women and a couple of guys before me.

I remember seeing a bathroom on the main floor on the way up here, but that had an even longer line because people were either too lazy or too drunk to climb the long staircase.

Fuck my life... and my bladder.

After about twenty minutes of waiting in line, listening to gossip, and which guys to fuck and which ones not to, I feel like I'm about to burst. I have to pee so badly that I'm becoming desperate. I'm not above begging someone to switch places. Wait, yeah, maybe I am.

I glance around at all the girls partnered up with their friends. This shit is ridiculous. It takes one girl to pee. One. I don't need someone to wipe my vagina for me. I'm a big girl.

I look around me to try to get a glimpse of the other line, but it seems to be at a standstill as well. Maybe if I go down-stairs he won't even notice; the friend I mean. There are prob-ably like three rooms down there anyway. Why not just let me use one? I'm quick, really quick. I promise.

Making a hasty decision, I turn for the staircase and make my way back down to the main floor. I glance around, but don't see Madison or Jax anywhere in sight, so I look around for the stairs leading down to the basement while pushing my way through the crowd.

I go down a couple of halls, see one more line to a bathroom and finally turn down another hall that leads to a staircase. I notice that no one is around it. Like at all. I don't know if everyone knows the warning to stay away or if no one knows it exists back here. Either way, it's a better chance that I won't get caught using the bathroom down here and risk getting kicked out. The last thing I want to do is embarrass Madison and have her hate me. A pissed off Madison is never a good one. That bitch is crazy.

Taking a long, deep breath, I exhale slowly and follow the staircase down. It's dark down here, and quiet. I also notice a temperature change. It feels about ten degrees cooler, but honestly, I love the way it feels on my heated skin. I almost just want to stay downstairs and have my own party. Screw all the crotch bumpers upstairs.

Once I get to the bottom of the stairs, I look around to see that every door in the hallway is closed. There doesn't seem to be any light coming from under the cracks of any of the doors. My bladder just can't catch a damn break.

Is anyone even down here?

Concentrating as hard as I can to hold my pee, I walk down the hall, attempting to be as quiet as my stupid stilettos will allow. It's either take a wild guess and choose a random room or open every single damn door and hope that 'the friend' is gone.

I look around me and pick a random room. Maybe the last door on the left? That looks good. I walk down the hall and place my hand to the door, pressing my ear against it to listen for any sound. Nothing, so I push the door open to find nothing but a dark, large bedroom.

Closing the door, I walk over to the one before it and am about to waste my time listening first, but decide against it. Every room down here is dark and quiet, and the longer I wait, the closer I get to peeing in my pants. There is no way anyone is here.

I push the door open and holy hell was I wrong. I freeze at the sight before me, not sure what the hell to do. Do I run? Close my mouth maybe? Yeah, that might be a start.

A man is hanging upside down on a bar, his arms crossed over his chest, doing sit ups. He's shirtless and full of tattoos, his defined muscles flexing as he moves with little effort. I can't make out what he looks like, except that his body is lean, muscular, and splattered in ink; every exposed inch of it, only stopping at his neck.

There's a small lamp on a table in the corner, giving off just enough light to see that he's there and covered in sweat.

He stops mid lift and growls when he notices the door is open. Every muscle in his body stiffens, and before I know it he maneuvers his way off the bar and jumps down to his feet.

He stands up straight, his sweats hanging low off his slender waist as his muscles tense up again. He clenches his jaw, before taking a step toward me and stopping, just close enough for me to see his face.

My breath hitches in my throat at his beauty and becomes even harder to catch when I look into his pale gray eyes. All that reflects there is pain and darkness. It gives me a chill that runs all throughout my body, but makes my legs quiver with desire at the same time.

His head is slightly tilted forward, allowing a strand of his blond hair to fall into his eyes as they slowly roam up my body, stopping on my face. He doesn't say a word. He just looks into my eyes, making my blood run cold. He looks deadly; like a fucking lethal machine ready to strike. His arms are flexed by his sides with his hands clenched into fists. He's at least six-foot-one.

I don't know whether I want to run away or into his bed, wherever that may be. His eyes are so powerful and demanding that I can't even talk. It's like he has some kind of power over me. I just stare back like a fool and hope that I won't fall to my knees.

That is until I feel a hand on my shoulder, shaking me out of my revelry. I jump and a small scream escapes my throat as I turn around to see Jax. He looks pissed and I know that I'm in trouble.

"What are you doing down here, Avalon? Didn't Madison tell you to stay the fuck upstairs? Fucking shit." He looks past me at his friend that is still looking at me; his eyes cold, dark, and demanding. "Sorry, Royal. It won't happen again. I told everyone to fucking stay upstairs."

I see Royal swallow before he pulls his eyes away from me and sets them on Jax. He doesn't speak though. He just nods his head as Jax pushes me out of the room and into the hall. "Shit, Avalon. What the fuck are you doing down here? Now is not the time to fuck with him."

I swallow hard and look back and forth between him and the door, just wanting to get one more glimpse at Royal. "I had to use the bathroom and all the ones upstairs were full. I didn't mean to disturb him. I'm sorry."

He pushes me down the hall a couple of doors down and points. "That's the bathroom. Go quickly and I'll stay here. I think it's best that Madison takes you home for the night. I'm sorry, but this shit is not cool."

I apologize to him one more time before disappearing into the bathroom and finally catching my breath. When I do, all I smell is man; pure, sexy, masculine man, and my heart goes crazy all over again. What the fuck was that and what the hell did I get myself into?

Madison is going to kill me...

CHAPTER 2

ROYAL

I COULDN'T TURN MY EYES away. I wanted her, needed her... and desired her. One glimpse into her big, curious eyes and my cock twitched, wanting a fucking taste.

When I saw her watching me, I wanted to rip that tight little skirt off of her and tie her to the wall as I bury myself deep between those trembling thighs. I want her to *feel* me; every fucking inch of me.

Feeling the madness build up inside of me, I walk back over to the bar, grab it, and do pull ups until my arms are shaking so hard that I can no longer hold on.

The music has since faded out upstairs, letting me know that it's well into the night now. This is when I know it's okay to come out of this cage I've put myself in. Avoiding people at all costs was my damn plan tonight, but someone decided to fuck that up, and now I need some fresh air to breathe.

Reaching for my leather jacket, I throw it on and pull out a cigarette, before shoving the rest of the pack into my pocket.

I light the cigarette, taking a long drag as I make my way through the dark house and outside to where my Harley is parked out back.

Letting the smoke fill my lungs for the first time in twelve hours, I walk around my bike and inspect it for damage. I have zero trust for the assholes that come into *my* home, but I allow it for Jax.

He can be reckless sometimes, but he's done a decent job with keeping my shit together, both here and at the bar. I have to be thankful for that shit.

Seeing that there's no damage, I toss my cigarette aside and straddle my bike, speeding off into the dark night. Feeling the wind on my face is one of the only two good feelings that I have left. The other one is fucking, and even that I don't enjoy sometimes. I do it as a quick escape from my fucked up head.

Pulling up at my bar, *Savage & Ink*, I park my bike and pull out my key, letting myself in through the back door.

The place smells of old cigarette smoke and a freshly smoked blunt. I can hear Blaine, along with at least four other voices as I make my way past the tattoo shop and into the bar.

Blaine nods his head in my direction when he notices that I've now joined them. "Hey, Royal. What's good, motherfucker?"

I nod my head in greeting and take a seat on one of the old, leather stools. I empty out my jacket pocket onto the stool next to me and get comfortable. "Whiskey. A whole fucking bottle."

The bar closed about forty minutes ago, yet three guys and some blonde female in a small, skintight dress are occupying one of the tables, looking baked out of their damn minds. I was expecting the place to be empty. I can't deal with people today. All I wanted was one fucking night to grieve for Riley and I can't even get that shit; not in my own home or my own damn bar.

"Who the fuck are they?" I question Blaine when he returns with a bottle of whiskey and an empty glass.

He walks around the bar and answers me as I pour myself a much-needed glass. "My guy Jake and a few of his friends. I told them it was cool to hang out as long as they were paying for shit and not messing anything up. They're good business, man. I didn't think you'd be coming in tonight. Sorry."

I raise a brow and throw back my glass of whiskey, almost emptying it completely. "I want them out by the time I leave tonight. No more of the shit like last time."

"I know, man. They're cool. I promise. Just enjoy that fucking whiskey and chill."

I lean back in my stool and watch them, not trusting them for shit. I've never seen them in my life. That makes it pretty obvious that they have no fucking clue who I am, and I don't like that one bit; not when in my place of business so late at night.

The blonde female looks my way and bites her bottom lip, as if just noticing me. Her legs slightly part and she sits up straight, as if trying to push her tits out.

"Damn," Blaine hisses. "Looks like Kellie has you in her sights now. That bitch can give a mean blow job and she's picky as fuck about who she gives them to." He pushes my arm and adjusts his dick, while watching her lick her lips. "I blew my shit within three minutes the other night. That's unheard of for me."

I don't say anything. I just watch her, watching me as if she wants to eat me for a fucking midnight snack.

Getting bored with her, I turn around in my stool and pour myself another glass. Just as I pick up the glass and bring it to my lips, I feel a hand touch my arm and gently caress it.

Fuck...

I keep my head straight, but turn my eyes to my left, looking her up and down. She may not be as hot as the beautiful brunette that barged her way into my room tonight, but she's definitely doable, and I need all the stress relief I can get right now.

Cutting straight past the bullshit, I stand, look her in the eyes, and then start walking while tilting back my drink to get to the right amount of numbness that I need.

Cracking my neck, I set my empty glass down on the nearest table and disappear into the office, knowing that she'll fucking follow. They always do.

When I turn around, Kellie, as Blaine called her, is walking through the door with a seductive ass look in her eyes.

"Close it," I demand. "But don't fucking lock it." I hate locked doors. I like to have easy access in case there's ever a problem I need to deal with.

She does as told and walks over to stand in front of me as I lean against my desk and light a cigarette.

Taking a drag, I place my hand on her throat and squeeze. She lets out a surprised gasp and then smiles, as she looks me in the eyes.

Not wanting to start up a conversation and have fucking small talk, I push down on her head until she's on her knees in front of me, reaching for my belt.

After the way I was left feeling a couple of hours ago, I need this shit right now.

I grip the desk with one hand and hold my cigarette to my mouth with the other as I feel her tongue swirl around my tip, before she takes me into her mouth, gagging as she adjusts to my size.

Blaine was right. She does give a mean blow job, but there's no way this chick will have me blowing anytime soon.

Twenty minutes of her mouth on my cock and I'm still not relieved. She keeps going faster and harder, taking me deeper until she's choking and digging her nails into my thighs. It's still not doing what I need.

Without a knock the door flings open and Blaine pokes his head inside. "Dude, what the fuck? It's been like twenty minutes."

I grab the back of Kellie's head and take charge myself, holding her head still as I thrust into her mouth.

"Get the fuck out, asshole. Now."

Blaine takes a second to watch us and moans, before finally shutting the door and disappearing. He always finds some kind of fucking excuse to barge in when I'm getting off in my damn office. Horny little shit. He takes advantage of the fact that I hate locked doors.

Right after he closes the door, I stand up straight and tangle my hands into her hair, thrusting one more time before holding her still as I shoot my hot cum down her throat.

She swallows and wipes her mouth off as she stands up and fixes her now wild hair. "Fuck... my mouth is numb," she complains.

"Yeah, and so is my dick."

She smiles, ignoring my comment, and runs her hands down my thighs seductively. "How long do you need before we *fuck*? I can go all night, babe."

I tilt my head toward the door. "I'll be out in a few minutes. Tell Blaine I said to make you a fucking drink on me," I say in dismissal.

A flash of disappointment crosses her face as she fixes her hair one last time, and then walks out the door mumbling.

I sit in the dark for a good fifteen minutes before washing up and joining Blaine and the others back in the bar. I don't really want them here, but I'll deal for as long as I can.

Blaine is too busy talking to his guy Jake behind the bar to notice what's going on over at the table, but it's the first thing my eyes land on.

Lines of blow cover the table, accompanied by a pile of cash and a little plastic bag.

The guy with a green flannel is leaning over the table, getting ready to sample the goods.

"Get your trash the fuck out of here," I say firmly. "Do that shit somewhere else."

I don't trust fuckers that I don't know.

The guy in the flannel laughs and says, "Fuck off," before leaning completely over and snorting the whole line. He stands up when done and smirks. "Don't know who the fuck you are."

I hear Blaine stammer, "Oh shit," at the same time that I make my way over to the table and grab the asshole by the back of the neck, hard.

Clenching my jaw, I move my hand up to the back of his head and slam it into the table, repeatedly, until all of their merchandise is scattered around the table and floor, his face covered in blood.

One of his friends comes at me, but I pull out my knife and place the blade against his throbbing neck.

I feel Blaine grip my shoulder, but I ignore him, pressing my lips beside the little bitch's ear, letting him know that he's fucked with the wrong person tonight. "This is *my* fucking bar, and I said get your trash the fuck out. Don't make me repeat myself again. I hate repeating myself."

I slam his head into the table one last time to make sure he gets the message, before releasing him and turning to his friend, who is now standing with his hands up.

"Get the fuck out of here." I point to the table and start walking over to pour myself another drink, before I end up killing one of these assholes. "Clean that shit up first."

Blaine approaches me, but I throw him a look that tells him he's about to lose his life if he takes another step. Tonight is not the fucking night to cross me.

He backs off, knowing not to push me right now. I know it's not his fault, but he knows how I feel about strangers dealing drugs in my motherfucking bar.

That shit has already fucked me over once. It's what got me here in the first place...

CHAPTER 3

AVALON

I SEND A TEXT TO MADISON for the third time today since I've left the house. Twenty minutes later and I still have no response from her overdramatic ass. I've been looking at my phone like an idiot for most of the day now, just hoping she'd cool off by this point. She barely even spoke to me before I left this morning to go to Colton's; pretty much just said *good fucking morning* and *have a fantastic time at the boring dinner party tonight*. I feel really bad about what I did, but I seriously had to go. I couldn't help it. Maybe next time I should just pop a squat in a nearby flowerpot. I just hope she gets over it soon. I hate a pissy Madison.

Colton is having a party at his house tonight; more like a business dinner to show appreciation and hopefully draw more people in. All of his top clients as well as their friends and family will be showing up any minute now for overly priced food and wine. Honestly, most of it looks unsatisfying and sort of gross to me.

I feel completely out of place here, but Colton suggested

that I help set up and stick around for the party. I only agreed since I haven't seen him in practically three damn days, *and* because Madison spent most of the morning shooting daggers my way. Plus, I thought maybe it would feel nice to spend some time with him and do something as a team, but he's been uptight and on edge all day.

"Hey, Marie, baby." I look up from the bowl of fruit salad that I'm picking at and exhale, annoyed. "Mind giving me a hand with these glasses and plates? We need to hurry. A car just pulled up out front and I don't want to keep anyone waiting."

Colton barely even looks at me when I make my way over to him and reach for a stack of plates. "Stop calling me that," I complain. "I don't like being called by my middle name and you know it."

"Well, it's a lot classier than Avalon, babe." He flashes me a stiff smile. "So around my clients I'll call you Marie. Avalon just sounds awkward to introduce people to. It's not a big deal, but this party is to me." He gives me a quick kiss on the cheek. "Come on."

I grind my jaw in distaste and follow him outside and over to the large table, setting down the stack of plates as perfectly organized and in place as I can. I would argue with him more on this matter, but I honestly don't have the energy today. I just want to get this party over with so I can go home, crawl in bed, and watch some quality TV by myself. I honestly probably should've just stayed in bed all day to begin with. Today has been hell.

It's well into the party now and I have spent most of it hiding out by the food table, stuffing my face with any fried foods that I can find.

Colton has apparently already introduced me to all the clients that he plans to for the night, so I really don't see why I'm still hanging around anyway. I've never seen so many stiff

VICTORIA ASHLEY

people in my life and it's making me extremely anxious and uncomfortable.

"Babe." I force a smile when Colton suddenly appears next to me, walking with a pretty brunette in a white, zip-front pencil skirt. "I want to introduce you to my new investment partner; the one I've been telling you about. Misty..." He points to the leggy bombshell beside him and then points to me. "This is my girlfriend Marie. She helped me set up the dinner for tonight."

I reach out to shake her hand when she holds hers out, and then flash my friendliest smile. "Avalon," I say with pride. "Marie is my middle name. Only Colton calls me that."

Colton gives me a dirty look, but replaces it with a sincere smile when Misty glances his way and raises a brow.

"Well, it's very nice to meet you, Avalon. Colton here is the best partner I've ever had the pleasure of working with; very professional and always knows what he's doing." She releases my hand and looks me up and down, taking in my black skinny jeans and teal blouse. "You're one lucky lady."

She clears her throat and turns back to Colton with a small smile. "I should get back to my friends now. Thanks for having us. They're having a wonderful time and the food is delicious."

He places his hand on her shoulder and nods his head. "Thanks for coming and I look forward to hopefully having your friends as potential clients. I'll be over to thank them personally."

She nods her head, smiles, and then walks away.

Colton is in Real Estate. He's very good at what he does. I don't disagree with her there, but I still don't like her much. She's definitely a lot *different* from what I pictured and hoped in my mind that she would look like. He never once mentioned that she looked like she just walked out of a damn fashion magazine.

"You look bored," Colton says disapprovingly, as I rub my

26

forehead and yawn. "Could you try to look a little happier to be here? Please. I've worked hard for this."

I reach for the glass of beer that I set down when I started stuffing my face. I've been hiding and drinking them all night. "Sorry, but it's hard to pretend that I'm having fun when I'm not. I've been standing in a corner by myself for most of the party. How excited should I pretend to be?" I take a swig of my beer and Colton's eyes widen when he gets a whiff.

"Are you drinking beer?" He reaches for my glass and looks into it. "That's what the wine is for. I'm trying to have a classy dinner, babe. These are my clients and hopefully potential clients that I'm entertaining; not a frat party with strippers."

My heart speeds up with sudden anger. "Oh really. Sorry that my drink of choice isn't good enough for your clientele." I release an exasperated breath and get ready to give him a piece of my mind. He always has a good way of making people feel shitty and I'm beginning to really see it.

I open my mouth and get ready to speak again, but stop when the sound of motorcycles have us all looking toward the driveway in curiosity. They're loud and powerful, causing people to watch in confusion as both men climb off of their bikes and kill the engines.

"Fucking shit. Not now," Colton grinds out, gripping his hair. "What the hell is he doing here?"

My eyes widen and my mouth drops open when the guy on the first motorcycle pulls his helmet off and sets it on his bike, looking directly at me.

Those eyes. I would recognize that set of eyes anywhere. His long hair is now pulled into a bun, his tattoos covered by a leather jacket, but there's no question that it's him. Those insanely beautiful eyes give him away. My heart pounds when I remember the look in his eyes last night when I barged into his room, unwanted.

"Who?" I question in a daze.

"My brother Royal."

My eyes widen. "Since when have you had a brother?"

"Twenty-five damn years; too long if you ask me. And he's my half-brother. There is a difference."

Before I can say anything and complain about not knowing this little detail, he stalks over to the driveway and grabs Royal's arm, pulling him closer to the front of the house and out of view.

People start whispering, talking shit about how 'dangerous' the two men look, but I ignore them all. Who the hell are they to judge? Stuck up assholes. Now, I really want to get out of here and away from this party.

I slam my empty beer cup down and take off in the direction of our uninvited guests. I'm both curious as to why Royal is here and why the hell Colton never told me he had a brother to begin with.

Colton turns to me and scrunches his forehead in annoyance when I approach him, Royal, and Jax in the driveway. I hadn't even known it was Jax until now. He surprisingly smiles at me and lifts an eyebrow, before setting his helmet down as if he didn't just have to kick me out of his house last night. "Stay with the party please. Tell them that I'm taking care of something and I'll be right back. It will only take a minute. Just let me get rid of them."

Jax and Royal both watch me as I brush my hair behind my ear and growl under my breath.

I swear my heart stops. It's as if I've just walked into tattooed, bearded, man-bun heaven, and I'm hoping there isn't an exit. I can't help but to watch them watch me.

"Basement girl," Jax says with a smirk, not hiding the fact that he's surprised to see me here. "Sorry about the party. Next time, babe."

Royal looks me up and down, but doesn't say a word. His eyes cause shivers to run up my spine, chilling me to the bone.

"Oh great," Colton complains. "It was their party you were at last night? Big surprise."

I tilt my head and turn to face Colton. He's really testing me today and I'm not beyond making a fool of myself in front of all of his fancy guests. "And what the hell is that supposed to mean, Colton?"

"Nothing," Colton snaps, regretfully. "I didn't mean it. This is just a big fucking deal for me, and these assholes showing up with their tattoos and motorcycles aren't making me look good. To my guests they are viewed as uncivilized troublemakers. Royal has a bad image and reputation, and I don't want that brought here."

"So you need someone else making you look good?" I question, now completely pissed off by his disrespect. "I hardly think them showing up is going to ruin your chances with potential clients. They haven't done anything disrespectful. What is your deal? I can't stand it when you're like this, which is happening more and more frequently."

Royal smirks and leans against his bike, pulling out a cigarette. He seems pleased with my response. "Calm down big brother. No need to piss your fucking fancy slacks." He lights his cigarette and takes a long drag from it, slowly blowing the smoke back out. "I just came to tell you that Riley fucking died yesterday. Thought you might want to know. Didn't come to crash your little wine party."

Colton throws his arms up and shakes his head, as if he's just ready to get back to his guests. "Yeah, well I'm not surprised. That's what happens when you live his lifestyle, and I won't be surprised if you end up like him soon."

Pissed off and looking as if he's about to lose it, Royal tosses his cigarette down and steps up to Colton, getting in his face. "You've known Riley since you were in fucking diapers and that's the kind of disrespect you show?" His jaw tightens as he wraps his tatted up fingers around Colton's neck and squeezes.

"You're a real piece of shit, *brother*." He shoves him back, causing Colton to gasp and lose his balance.

I've known Colton to be a dick, but this is on a whole new level. I can't even look at him right now without being disgusted. I feel like choking him my damn self, so I don't blame Royal or feel pity for Colton one bit. Someone he knows just died and he shows no emotion, nothing at all. All he cares about is his stupid perfect life. "Colton, you're an asshole. This is unbelievable. Un-fucking believable. I'm out."

"Just great," Colton yells out, running a hand through his perfectly styled, blond hair, and rubbing his pink neck. He backs away from Royal and grunts, while looking over at me. "Why don't you just leave with my brother here then? Go ahead." He crosses his arms and watches me, testing me. "There's plenty of room on the back of his bike."

"Fine." Clearly not thinking straight, I walk over to Royal's bike and stop, swallowing hard as I look him in the face. Royal instantly grabs for his helmet and places it on my head, looking me in the eyes the whole damn time. He's good with those damn things; too good. I pull my eyes away from his, clear my throat, and turn to Colton. "Enjoy your little party. I know you'll show them more respect than you've clearly just shown your own damn brother. The one that I never even knew you had, by the way."

"Marie..." he scolds, as if I'm a child. "I was joking. Don't leave." He clenches his fists at his sides as he watches me hop onto the back of Royal's bike and scoot up behind him. "Get off my brother's bike. It's dangerous. He's dangerous and careless."

I suck in a deep breath as Royal starts his bike and grabs my arms, wrapping them around his waist with force. His hands feel rough against my skin, the total opposite of Colton's smooth fingers. "Hold on tight, Darlin', and don't fucking let go."

Colton's eyes land on my arms around Royal's waist and he grinds his jaw in disapproval. "Off. Now."

I place the exposed skin of my cheek against Royal's hard back, facing Colton. I'm doing this now. No turning back. "No," I growl up at him, wrapping my arms tighter around Royal. "And my name is Avalon for the last damn time. Goodbye, Colton. Don't call me until you're done being an ass."

Jax laughs from beside us and then hops on his bike, flicking his cigarette at Colton. "Later, bitch."

Colton watches in disbelief as Royal takes off with me on the back of his bike. It seems his friends look just as confused as their eyes land on us.

I allow myself to watch his shocked reaction for a few seconds, before turning away and holding on for dear life. I've never been on a motorcycle and I can't deny that I'm scared shitless right now.

Somehow escaping Colton seemed worth the risk. If there's one thing that I hate, it's judgmental assholes that think they're too good for others, and that's all Colton has been all day. I'm over it right now.

WE PULL UP BEHIND A bar called *Savage & Ink,* and Royal kills the engine, reaching behind him to help me off his bike. He's rough, yet careful not to hurt me at the same time.

Smirking, he climbs off his bike and reaches over to take his helmet off my head. "Your first time on a bike?"

I nod my head and work on fixing my wild hair. "Yeah. You could tell?"

"From your death grip... yeah." He lifts his eyebrows at Jax as he pulls up beside us, and parks.

I feel a bit uncomfortable standing here with two guys I

don't even know, but oddly more welcome than I felt at Colton's party.

"Sorry about that," I say with a sigh. "And I'm sorry about last—"

"Shit happens," Royal says, cutting me off.

"Come on." He reaches for my hand and starts pulling me behind him, while reaching into his pocket with his free hand. "I've got to check on these dicks, and since you hopped on my bike... I guess you're my responsibility for the night."

After a few seconds of digging, he pulls out a key and unlocks the door, guiding me inside and past what looks to be a tattoo shop. "Is this your place?" I ask, while looking around at the hand drawn art on the walls. "It's amazing and stunning. Such beautiful artwork."

"Yeah," he responds, but doesn't offer anything else.

We walk down the hall a little further, until Jax pushes past us and opens the door to a bar. He turns back to me and eyes me up and down. "Stay close to Royal. If he gets called away, then stay by me. These assholes are ruthless and will try to *fuck* you if they see an opening."

My heart speeds up from nerves as I'm guided into a room full of tatted up men playing pool, darts, and drinking beer.

They're loud and rowdy, not giving a shit about what anyone else thinks and they all seem to look as if they feel at home here. Seeing the proud look on Royal's face makes me smile. It's crazy to see just how opposite he is from his brother. Amazing really.

Royal encloses his hand around mine again and pulls me through the room, keeping me close by his side. He steps behind the bar, keeping me with him. "What do you drink?"

I look over my shoulder at the guys shouting and whistling, calling out Royal's name, but Royal grabs my chin, pulling my attention back to him. "What will it be, babe?"

"A beer please. A nice, big, cold beer."

Royal sucks his bottom lip into his mouth as if I've just turned him on, *and* oddly... that turns me on.

"Sexy as hell and drinks beer. Well shit..." He shakes his head, while reaching for two beers and twisting the caps off. "Definitely not my brother's type."

I watch him, but don't say anything as he hands me the beer. Holding the cold bottle to my lips, I tilt it back and take what must be the longest drink of my life. It tastes and feels so good right now.

"Yup... definitely too good for my brother." Out of the corner of my eye, I notice Royal adjust the crotch of his faded jeans, before grabbing my hand and pulling me around the bar and to the back of the room, where two pool tables are set up.

He stops in front of the unoccupied one. "You into pool, *Avalon*? That's a sexy as fuck name, by the way. Don't let my dick brother say otherwise." He pauses to take a swig of his beer. "You look like you could use a little game or two to loosen you up. I think I can help with that."

I smile big against the top of the beer bottle, stopping mid-drink. "I'm not very good, so chances are it's not going to be very fun for you."

Royal yanks his jacket off and throws it over an empty chair, exposing his beautiful body art that I love so much. "I'm sure I can find a lot of ways to make things with you fun. Don't worry about that, Darlin'."

I jump away as some random arm flings around my shoulder, pulling me against a hard body. It smells good too...

It's some guy in his mid-twenties with short, dark hair and amber eyes with both of his arms covered in a sleeve of tattoos. The sides of his head are shaved and covered in tattoos as well, the top of it longer. He's definitely attractive. A little drunk but attractive. "Who's this beautiful girl?" He looks down at me and lifts a brow, cupping my chin. That's when I notice his nose is pierced. "They call me, Blaine, babe, but you can call me anything as long as you're screaming it on top of me. Hell... even below me is good. I work hard either way."

Royal looks up from racking the balls and grips the edge of the table. "Seriously, motherfucker. Don't you have shit to do?"

Blaine releases my chin and I oddly find myself smiling. "Avalon," I say, answering his previous question. I look around at all the people dressed in leather jackets. You can tell the majority of them came on bikes. "Are you part of a motorcycle club or something?" I ask hesitantly.

Royal pulls me away from Blaine and in front of him, handing me a cue stick. He helps me aim it at the cue ball and then leans in next to my ear. "Nah... it's just a place where other *uncivilized* people like myself can come and feel at home; a place that Colton will never have the balls to step foot in."

He backs away from me and I take my shot, breaking the balls. None of them go in, so I hand my stick to Royal. "And you do tattoos here too?"

"Yeah..." He takes his shot, followed by two more, sinking three striped balls in a row. "A lot of the bikers that come here get work done from me or Blaine. Jax helps run the bar, but can't tattoo for shit."

I notice how Royal watches me when it's my turn. For some reason... having his eyes on me gives me a little bit of excitement. It's not the fact that he's watching me, but more of *how* he watches me that gets me. He's so damn intense.

A few beers later, I'm having fun and laughing with Royal and a few of his friends. I sort of gave up on pool after the second game, when realizing that Royal is a damn pro. He even managed to hit the balls when he had his eyes on me. I can't compete with that.

My phone buzzes in my pocket for the fifth time in the last hour, but I hit ignore and fall back into conversation with the guys.

There's no way that Colton is over being a dick. He didn't

even bother to try calling me until at least two hours after I left, so I'm guessing his precious little party was over by that time.

"I love this song," I say, temporarily interrupting the guys.

Royal watches me carefully as I walk over to the middle of the bar and start dancing. With his lips against his beer bottle, he smirks, right before I turn away.

Now that it's later into the night, a mix of a different crowd has joined our little party. A group of girls are dancing around me, pulling either guys that they came here with or random guys out onto the floor with them. The longer I'm here, the more I realize what Royal said. This place is for anyone who accepts it and wants to have fun.

I've been dancing for no longer than two minutes and I've already gotten not one, but two offers for a dancing partner. Jax wasn't kidding about the guys in here. I politely decline, just enjoying my moment of freedom, but another guy that I've never spoken to grabs onto me, not even bothering to ask.

"I'm good." I grab his arm and pull it away from my waist. "I don't want to dance."

It looks as if he's about to pull me to him again, ignoring my request, but Royal stands up, giving him a hard look.

That look alone is enough to send the guy packing. Getting back into the moment, I close my eyes and begin swaying my hips to the slow rhythm, while running my hands through my hair.

A pair of tatted arms snake around my waist and I get pulled against a hard body with a sexy grunt. My heart instantly pitter-patters when I recognize the ink and smell the sexy scent of Royal. That smell is now burned into my brain and will forever be known as Royal. Forget the actual name of the cologne; it's called Royal now.

"You don't look like the dancing type," I say nervously, almost forgetting how to dance now that our bodies are so close.

He brushes my hair over my shoulder and brushes his lips against my ear. "I'm not," he growls. One of his tatted arms wraps around my neck as he grinds against me, pulling me as close as he can. My breath escapes me for a moment at the thought that this man is even touching me this way. "But what kind of man would I be if I didn't protect my brother's girl from all of these horny assholes by dancing with you?"

The vibration of his voice against my skin and the way his body moves sinfully against mine causes me to clench my thighs and take a deep breath. Maybe I've had a little too much to drink. "It's getting late," I whisper.

Letting out a long breath, Royal releases my neck and spins me around to face him. "I'll take you home."

He whistles over to Blaine and Jax, getting their attention, before pointing down at me, and then grabbing my hand to pull me behind him.

We don't bother speaking until we break free of the bar. Stripping his leather jacket back off, he slips it on me, before once again helping me into his helmet. "You live with my brother?" he questions stiffly.

I shake my head and hop onto the back of his bike after him. "I live with my friend, Madison. It's on Forest Lane. A red house."

He nods his head. "I know it." Then he reaches for my hands again, wrapping them around him. I can feel the rapid beating of his heart and it somehow causes mine to speed up. "Hold on."

I stay on his bike for a few seconds after we arrive in front of my house. Is it weird that I want to spend more time with him? Being around him is so different from being around his brother. It's an exciting and thrilling rush. I want to ask him why they don't talk, but I'm afraid to offend him by getting too personal. I want to ask him a lot of things.

"Thanks," I say, while finally hopping off. "I had a lot of fun, and I honestly needed this."

Royal nods and grabs his helmet from out of my outstretched hands. "Sure. Maybe it will give my asshole brother something to think about."

"I'm sorry about your friend," I blurt out. "Colton is a jerk for the way he reacted. I won't be seeing him again for a while, until he pulls that stick out of his ass."

That makes Royal laugh and I can't deny to myself that the sight is stunning. "Come by the bar next week. Let me put some of my work on your beautiful body."

"I don't know," I say quickly. "Colton kind of has this thing about tattoos and I told him..." I stop and really think about what I'm saying, realizing that I sound like a complete idiot right now. I've been nothing but good to Colton and he's been doing nothing but pissing me off lately. "Actually... I might do that. I'll think about it."

Royal smirks and throws his helmet on. "You do that."

Before I can respond he drives off, glancing back at me for a split second, before disappearing.

"Holy fuck!" I say to myself in a heightened tone as soon as Royal rounds the corner. My breathing is extremely fast now that I have a moment alone. He's sinful and completely stunning and I can't help but want to see more of him. He gives me the rush that I've been craving.

When I look over at the front porch to catch my breath, Madison is standing on it, giving me a funny look. "That was not Colton. Far from it."

"Tell me about it." I walk past her. "It was his brother."

Her face is a mix of shock and exhaustion. "Seriously? This sounds like an awesome ass story that I need to hear." She lets out a breath and gives me a half smile. "I'm still mad at you, but we'll discuss that later. Spill."

After we get inside, I tell Madison a quick version of the story, before disappearing to my room and crashing. I sort of failed to mention that Colton's brother happens to be 'the friend' that was downstairs at the party; the one that I got her kicked out of.

I'll give her time to cool off first. I don't have a death wish...

CHAPTER 4

ROYAL

MY FUCKING BROTHER HAS FINALLY discovered how to use a phone. What do you know? He's been blowing my shit up for the last few hours, worried about his damn girl. Well, maybe if he weren't such an uptight prick, he wouldn't need to be calling me to find out how she is.

Smirking, I answer his call and press the phone to my ear. "What's up, big *brother*? Lose your girl or some shit?"

"Damn you," Colton shouts into the phone. "What the hell is your problem? You were supposed to tell her no, not take her with you."

"And since when the fuck do I follow the rules or what you want?" I lean against the back door of my bar and light up a smoke. "She hopped on my bike, wanting a ride." I take a drag from my cigarette and smile as I blow it out, knowing damn well that this last part is going to piss him off. "So I gave her one."

It sounds like he throws something at the wall and it breaks.

39

"Where is she, Royal? I know she wasn't stupid enough to fuck you, so stop with your shit. Is she with you? Is she home?"

Taking one last drag, I toss the cigarette down at my feet and let myself into the bar. "Calm your balls, brother. The last place I want to sink my dick is where your uptight, overprivileged one has already been. Find her your damn self."

I press the end button and shove my phone into my jacket, before unlocking the door to the shop and preparing the tattoo machine.

Might as well fill what little space I have left on my hands. I need a little something to get my mind back where it belongs, and tattooing takes a lot of fucking concentration.

The last thing I expected was for her to be my brother's fucking girl. Does it make me want to fuck her any less, no, but it gives me a reason not to follow through on my desire to sink between her thighs.

I may have done some fucked up shit in my life, but fucking my brother's girl is not one of them, and I don't plan to start now.

"Fucking shit." I shake my head to clear my thoughts. It doesn't do shit.

Between Riley and now this shit, I feel like a bomb waiting to go off.

Growling out, I throw my tattoo machine across the room, looking up when the door flies open to Blaine standing there, drunk as shit and barely able to stand up without the help of the wall.

"Dude, the next room is overflowing with booze and fucking pussy and you're in here, jerking off or some shit."

I run my tongue over my teeth, while rubbing a hand through my messy hair. He's got a fucking point.

"Or did you already fuck that hot ass chick you left with?" He raises a brow when I don't respond. "Shiiit... I may just need to test her out."

His words cause my anger to build up even more. "Try fucking her and I'll shoot you in your pathetic dick."

Blaine throws his hands up and laughs, while falling across the wall. He grabs his dick. "This shit is royalty, baby. So shut the hell up and get out here."

He disappears around the corner when a few girls walk by, calling for us. For being drunk and barely able to walk, I'm impressed with his ability to move so damn fast when it comes to willing pussy.

Standing up, I turn off the light and spend the rest of my night drowning in cheap whiskey and pussy.

Fuck everything... and fuck her, because I want to. Bad...

CHAPTER 5

AVALON

I'VE SPENT THE LAST THREE days apologizing to Madison every chance that I get. Apparently, Jax hasn't contacted her since that night and she has no idea if she is ever welcome back at his parties. Well hell... I never wanted that. All I wanted was to pee and now my best friend hates me.

I hold up a slice of strawberry cheesecake: her favorite. "Someone looks like they could use some dessert." I wave it in front of her face as she glowers at me. It's a Tuesday night and we are both sitting around like two twenty-two-year-old losers with no work tomorrow morning. "Mmm... extra strawberry sauce just how you like it. A cute guy even handled it before me. He may have even stuck his sexy finger in it a bit. You know you want to eat it."

After a couple of minutes, she finally yanks it out of my hand and practically shoves the whole thing into her mouth before flipping me the bird with both hands. "I ate ou," she mutters with her mouth full.

I lean in closer and place my hand to my ear. "What was

that, babe? I can't hear you. Did you say... yummy, thanks for the cheesecake, you're the best fucking friend in the world?"

She shakes her head but cracks a smile, showing off her cheesecake-filled teeth.

I wait for her to finish chewing before I apologize. Again. "For the twentieth time, I'm sorry. I'm sorry. I'm sorry. I didn't mean to ruin your night and get you kicked out. I mean it. I was about two seconds away from peeing my pants." I hand her a bottle of water to wash down her dessert. "And if it makes you feel any better, I almost peed my pants when I saw his friend, hanging upside down in the dark like some supersized half human bat or some shit."

Madison spits out a mouthful of water as she erupts in laughter. "Holy crap! You poor thing. If you had peed, I would have stopped being your friend. Just saying. I would've had no choice."

I punch her arm playfully. "Shut up. You're horrible."

We both allow for a couple more minutes of just enjoying a good laugh, before she changes the mood and gets all serious. "So tell me." She sits up straight, preparing herself for a story. I knew she would ask sooner or later. "What did this friend look like? Is he some weirdo, like *The Hills Have Eyes* looking dude or what? Did he have bubbles and pus coming out of his neck and shit? Is that why he stayed downstairs, probably jerking off in the dark basement? Spill."

My heart speeds up at just the mention of Royal. The truth is, I haven't gotten that dark look in his eyes out of my head since that first night, and I can't deny the fact that the way he almost made my knees buckle still has me shaken to my core. There's so much I want to ask; to know, but it's such a weird situation that I wouldn't even know where to start. He's my boyfriend's brother for crying out loud. A part of me wants to go to the bar to get that tattoo and the other part is telling me maybe I should just stay away and pretend we never met.

I clear my throat and stand up from the couch. My mouth suddenly feels dry and I can't help my raging heartbeat. She's going to think that I'm either crazy or lying my ass off, but here goes... "He's undeniably gorgeous, Madi. No joke. You think Jax is the sexiest man to walk this earth? Well, Royal blows him right out of the water. And yeah, that's his damn name: Royal. Tell me that isn't sexy. He seriously stunned me speechless and I couldn't take my eyes away. Not even for a second. I still feel like a complete fool for the way I stared at him with my mouth gaping open; not to mention that I got stuck with him the other night."

She jumps up from the couch and stands in front of me, trying to call me out on bullshit. "Whoa, whoa, whoa. Back your ass up a bit. You were with him the other night. I thought you were with Colton's brother?"

I nod my head and swallow. Here it goes again... "I was. Royal is Colton's brother. Strange, I know." I take a deep breath. "I was going to tell you but didn't want you flipping out over Jax. He was there, but I hardly got to talk to him."

She fixes her ponytail and throws it over her shoulder, clearing her throat. She looks as if she wants to call me out again and jump down my throat, but instead, settles on hearing more. "How is anyone more gorgeous than Jax? I mean look at him. He's barely human! He can have any girl he wants with just a flash of his smile, and don't think that I'm not mad that you kept all that from me for three damn days. We'll talk about that later though."

Thank fucking goodness...

"I have looked at Jax and you're right; he's gorgeous. Too gorgeous," I admit. I reach into the fridge for a water and pull the cap off. "But Royal isn't just sexy. He's dark, tempting, and breathtaking. Imagine this: blond hair, shaved at the sides, but long in the middle, falling to one side, and thick, long stubble covering smooth, full lips."

I close my eyes and picture his defined jaw; so perfect and masculine. "His body was like every woman's wet dream: tall, muscular, sweaty, and covered in ink. Don't even get me started on those pale gray eyes. I can't get them out of my head. He's beautiful, Madi. No lie. Stunning even. Colton doesn't even hold a candle to his brother. I don't get how they can be so... different."

We're both just standing there in silence for a moment, taking it in, before Madison's phone goes off, scaring us both. She gives me a quick look before walking over to the kitchen, toward her phone. "I need to see this guy to believe it. It makes no sense that a man *that* sexy would be hiding out. Too bad I'll probably never get invited back. Jax was freaking out that night."

She picks up her phone and her snarl turns to a smirk as she starts typing really fast and hard. "I take that back. Jax just invited us to some bar called, *Savage & Ink*. He said they're doing tattoos all night and we should hang out. I'm so damn happy that I just went from wanting to slap you, to wanting to kiss you." She points her phone at me. "So don't disappoint me again. I'll forgive you... for now." She smiles.

My heart jumps to my throat in a moment of excitement, but then I remember that Royal wanted to tattoo me. I'm not sure I'm ready for this.

"I don't know. It was a long day at the salon and I'm kind of tired." I take another drink of my water and start heading to my room, not interested anymore. I'm still not even talking to Colton. It would be weird to hang out with his brother. "You can go. Just lock the door on the way out please."

Madison grabs my arm, stopping me from walking. "Ah no. I don't think so. You're off till Thursday. You're coming out. Plus, you owe me."

"Why?" I smirk. "So you have more time to play with Jax? And I don't owe you. I had to pee, for the last time. Get over it."

She lifts an eyebrow and fixes her hair. "Maybe, maybe not. Doesn't matter. You want to come and I can see it in your eyes. You can't lie to me, Ava. Don't forget that. Now go and get dressed. I'm good to go." She points at my old jeans and baggy shirt in disgust. "You... not so much."

Twenty minutes later, I find myself in the back of a cab, hating myself for caving in. A different cab, thank goodness; although, I have to say this one smells a little like pee and vomit. Still, I would take a vomit, pee cab over the creepy old guy any day. We could have taken my Jeep, but if it involves alcohol of any kind, we always opt for a cab to be on the safe side.

Madison is dressed up to perfection as usual, in a sexy little outfit, and after a lot of convincing I am squeezed into one of her little black dresses. Sadly, I now plan on buying one of my own. I love it way more than I hoped. I'm one of *them* now.

I can tell by looking at Madison that she's nervous, and I'm surprised. That rarely ever happens when it comes to guys. She keeps fidgeting with her little heart necklace and peering out the window, as we get closer to the bar. She must really have a crush on Jax.

"Stop fidgeting with your necklace. It's making me nervous," I complain. "You look good. There's no need to try to impress Jax. He'll be wanting into your skirt by the end of the night. Trust me."

"I'm not trying to impress anyone," Madison says, trying to sound convincing. "I'm just worried that you'll get our asses kicked out again, so please do me a favor and try not to piss anyone off this time."

"I'll do my best," I mutter as we come to a stop. This time I toss the driver some cash and we both crawl out the one door that actually opens.

The first thing I notice when we get out of the cab is Blaine, standing at the side of the building with a girl on her knees in front of him. His head is leaned back, his eyes closed as he grips the back of her hair and roughly fucks her face.

"Holy shitballs!" Madison screams out, drawing unwanted attention to us. "That's hot."

Blaine opens his eyes and winks at us with a smirk, before thrusting his hips into the girl's face one more time and then pushing her away and pulling up his jeans.

Madison grabs my arm, yanking me to her. "He's sinfully gorgeous and getting head in the damn parking lot, Ava. Call me dirty, but I like this place already."

I shake my head in disbelief as Blaine approaches us all normal like, as if we *didn't* just witness him getting head at the side of the building.

"Damn, ladies. Didn't know you were coming back, beautiful." He throws a tatted arm around Madison's shoulder. "Who's this fine as shit goddess?"

I take a deep breath and roll my eyes, not sure what the hell we've gotten ourselves into tonight. "Madison... my roommate and best friend."

We all look over, as the blonde that was just on her knees walks past us, wiping her mouth off as if she's proud of getting to taste Blaine's man meat.

Madison smiles and looks Blaine up and down, taking in every single inch of hard muscle; his dick included. "Your fly is down, sweets. Not that I'm complaining. Damn, you're packing." She pulls her eyes back up to his face. "Not that you don't already know that."

Getting frustrated, I pull Madison away from Blaine and grab her hand in mine. "Thanks for the show, Blaine, but we're going to the shop. Jax asked us to come."

A sexy smile crosses Blaine's face as he reaches for the door to let us in. "Follow me, ladies."

I nudge Madison in the side as she shamelessly checks out Blaine's ass as we follow close behind him.

"Madi," I snap, quietly. "Close your damn legs. You're almost worse than them."

She elbows me back, but then grabs my arm for protection as some big burly-looking dude in a leather jacket growls at her and then licks his lips.

"And they're pretty bad," I add.

As soon as we step into the hall, all I hear are the sounds of a tattoo machine buzzing. It echoes throughout the small hallway, making me nervous now.

I stop and look through the open door at Royal and my heart literally skips a beat at the sight of him. He's leaned over, concentrating on some middle-aged man's back piece that he's working on. Jax is chilling next to him, watching, them both looking just as sexy as the other night.

Madison stops next to me, raising a brow as she sets sights on Royal as well. "Well, spank my ass and call me Sally," Madison says with a moan. "Sexy, sinful, tattoo heaven... I'm never leaving. Just saying."

Royal glances up with a snarl, but then turns his machine off and sets it down when his eyes land on me, watching me watch him. "We're done for tonight," he says to his client. "Jax will call you a cab."

Looking as if he's not bothered one bit by Royal dismissing him, he stands up, grabs for a stained up white shirt, and walks past us, almost falling into the wall.

Jax stands up and reaches for a bottle of vodka, pouring five shots. "Did Blaine here give you guys a tour of the building on the way in? Zip up your shit, dude."

"Fuck off," Blaine says playfully, snatching up one of the shots while zipping his fly.

I turn my eyes back in Royal's direction, but keep my head still so he doesn't notice me watching him.

He looks conflicted as he starts cleaning his table and chair off. "Didn't think you'd be back," he says stiffly. "You change your mind on that tattoo?"

I grab a shot glass when Jax hands one to Madison first and then myself. "Your friend asked us to come *and* my friend here, forced me to agree." I throw my shot back, emptying the glass, hoping for some kind of liquid courage. "So here I am."

With stiff muscles, Royal stands up straight and grabs the last shot glass, slamming it back, before shoving the empty glass at Jax. "Come here," he demands.

I stand here for a second, not moving, until Madison shoves me forward and calls me a pussy. I look back at her and glower, before stopping in front of Royal.

Grabbing my hand he pulls me to him, and grabs my hips, digging his hands in. "I have the perfect spot for your first tattoo." Reaching for the bottom of my dress, he lifts the front so only he can see, and runs his thumb over my hipbone. "Perfect."

Yanking my dress down, I back away and watch him as he starts preparing his tattoo equipment. "I never said I was going to let you tattoo me."

His jaw clenches as he looks back at me. "You scared that Colton is going to be pissed or some shit?"

I shake my head. "At this point, I couldn't care less about what he thinks. As far as I'm concerned, we're on a break."

"Okay..." He sits down and runs a hand through his messy hair, his eyes studying mine. "You don't want one then?"

"I do," I say quickly, realizing that I do, but I'm just being a pussy, exactly what Madison called me.

"Come on, Ava," Madison says from behind me. "We're already here and from what I can see, Royal is *very* capable of giving great tattoos. I'll let Blaine over there tat me up next."

Royal raises a brow in question, when I turn back to him. "What do you say, babe? Take that damn dress off for me?"

I swallow and look around the room. Having three other sets of eyes on me is making me nervous, extremely nervous.

"Out," Royal suddenly barks out. "Keep the girl close by and make sure Porter stays away from her. He's on some shit tonight."

"Madison can stay," I say firmly, not wanting to send her away. "I don't care if she watches."

Madison looks between Jax and Blaine and bites her bottom lip. It's clear what she wants to do, and that's most likely both of them. "I'll be good with the boys. Plus, I want to check out the party animals in the next room."

I take a deep breath and watch Madison as she follows Jax and Blaine out the door, shutting it behind her with a wink.

I suddenly feel nervous, realizing that I'm alone with Royal. He's so damn intense that I have no idea what to expect from him.

"Lay down."

Swallowing, I sit down on the black, leather chair that is already laid back into a bed. I jump from the coldness on my skin, but then close my eyes and get comfortable, waiting on Royal's next move.

With my eyes still closed, I can see the shadow from him standing above me, before I feel his rough hands brush my upper thighs as he grips my dress and lifts it, stopping just under my breasts.

"Any certain design? I can do it all."

"A feather," I say softly. "Blue with purple highlights; feminine and pretty. Can you do that?"

He lifts an eyebrow while pulling on a pair of black gloves. "I can definitely *do* feminine and pretty. Like I said, I do it all."

I suck in a breath and grip the seat, when I feel his hands brush against my skin as he prepares to mark me for life.

Grabbing my hand, he places it on his thick thigh. My heart speeds up from the feel of his muscular leg beneath my palm.

"If it hurts, dig into my leg and take it out on me. It will help you feel better."

I hear the buzzing of the machine and instantly grip his thigh, feeling anxious. When I open an eye to peek up at him, he's smirking.

"Ready?"

I nod my head. "Mmm hmm..."

I feel my fingers dig deep into the denim of his thigh as the needle hits my sensitive flesh. My stomach instantly sinks and I flinch, more unprepared than I thought.

I do my best to keep my eyes closed through most of it, but then open my eyes closer to the end, when my skin starts to feel numb. It's a bit of a relief.

Royal's face is stern, set in a line of concentration. I notice that he even bites his bottom lip once in a while when he really gets into a good spot. I find myself watching him, my legs slightly opening, as I get lost in my own little world. He's delicious to watch. There is absolutely no denying that.

Royal's hand gripping my thigh wakes me from the moment, snapping my eyes up to his.

He pushes my legs together. "Keep those things closed, unless you want me between them," he growls.

I squeeze my legs together, slightly moaning as the thought of him between my legs causes my body to clench and jerk.

"Is it almost done?" I ask, hoping to come back to reality... the one where he'll *never* be between my legs.

"Almost..."

Getting lost in the way that his jaw muscles tighten as he adds the finishing touches, my legs relax and slightly open again.

Tossing his tattoo machine aside, Royal stands up and growls, gripping my hips and pulling me down to the end of the chair, until his jean-covered erection is pressed against my pussy. A shock of pleasure runs through my core as he presses against it.

His right hand digs into my hip as the left one tightens around my neck. His eyes meet mine for a brief moment, before his right hand slides down my thigh and he releases my neck, stepping back.

"Keep flashing that smooth little pussy at me... Fuck, Avalon." His jaw tics as he looks between my thighs one last time. "Those little underwear don't cover much."

"Sorry," I say in aggravation. "I got comfortable a couple times and wasn't thinking. I didn't expect you to get a fucking hard-on over it and freak out."

Letting out a long breath, Royal sits back down, grabs my hand, and places it back on his thigh. Except this time, I can almost feel the shape of his hard dick above my fingers. I suck in a breath at the near contact.

"This last part might hurt; especially now that we've taken an unwanted break. Hold still."

I jump when the needle touches my skin. He was right. It's sensitive as shit now and I just want it to be done.

With one hand, Royal lowers my panties a little more to get to the bottom part of the feather.

I grip his thigh and groan out from the pain. That's when I feel his dick now hard against my hand. He's got an all-out boner right now and seems as if he couldn't care less about hiding it.

"Sorry," I say as I pull my hand away. I blush at the thought that I've just touched his dick, when I didn't mean to. "Didn't know that was going to happen."

Royal raises a brow and glances over to meet my eyes. "My cock has a mind of its own, Darlin'. It's a real fucking beast when it wants to be." He sets the machine down and checks out his work. "I hope that's *pretty and feminine* enough for ya. Looks real fucking good on you."

Reaching behind him, he grabs for a handheld mirror, handing it to me, before reaching for some kind of tattoo goop to rub over the finished tattoo.

I hold the mirror in front of my hip and look into it. My breath catches in my throat and I can't help but to smile. "It's so damn pretty. Wow..." I look up at him and then back down at my very first tattoo. It's only been minutes since I've had it and I already want more. I've heard this was going to happen. "How much?"

"Nothing," he says, while cleaning his equipment up and getting something to cover my new art up with.

Right after he covers up my feather and pulls my dress down, the sound of glass breaking from somewhere in the bar causes him to punch the wall and yell. "Fucking Blaine!"

He cracks his knuckles and then takes off out the door as if he's about to hand someone their ass.

"What the..."

Grabbing my purse, I take off after him to see what is going on and hope to God that Madison is all right.

Being around Royal and his friends, never falls short of crazy and chaotic...

CHAPTER 6

ROYAL

WHEN I WALK INTO THE bar, Blaine has Porter by the back of the head and is pounding his face into the *now* broken window, breaking what's left of it.

Lifting Porter up straight, Blaine slams his face into the brick wall next to the window, before yelling in his face. "Your dick ain't fucking hard now, motherfucker. Does that feel good? Do you fucking like it?" he yells.

Blood is dripping down Porter's face, but he's laughing like a fucking maniac, fucked up as shit on whatever he took before he got here. He may be in pain, but he doesn't feel it... at least not yet, but he'll definitely be feeling it once his high wears off.

Surprisingly, this isn't the first time that damn window has been broken. It seems to be Blaine's stress reliever. I guess we all have one, but fuck, his sucks.

"Fucking shit..." My eyes meet Jax's from across the room and he just shrugs and brings his lit cigarette to his lips. He's too used to Blaine's breakdowns to try stopping them anymore, apparently. "Don't worry, asshole. Just stay there; I got it."

Shaking my head, I walk up behind Blaine and grab him by the back of his neck, breaking him free from Porter. "That's enough." I tense my jaw and yank the unlit cigarette out of his hand, flicking it at the side of his head. "You're paying for that shit."

"Fuck." Blaine runs a bloodied hand through his hair, before knocking all the drinks off of the table next to him and throwing an unbroken bottle at Porter. "I know, dammit. Don't I always?"

My attention gets drawn back to Porter's fucked up ass, when he turns around and wipes his arm across his bloodied face. That's when I notice that his dick is out.

"What the shit..."

I take a step toward Porter, but he throws his arms up and takes a stumble back. "I'm going." He points at Madison. "Bitch should have kept her mouth shut. She asked for it." He mumbles some more shit, before swiping his phone from one of the tables and storming out the front door, while reaching to put his dick away.

I turn to Jax to scold him for not pulling Blaine away, and stop dead in my tracks when I see Avalon has now joined them and is looking at the broken window with her hand over her mouth. This is the exact reason why Jax shouldn't have invited them here tonight in the first place. There are only certain nights that it's tame enough here to mix the crowds and Jax should have known that.

"What the fuck happened?" I light a cigarette and take a long, deep drag, holding the smoke in for as long as I can, before releasing it. "Don't everyone jump all at once to fucking talk," I snap. "Why am I looking at a broken window and why the fuck did Porter have his dick out?"

Jax and Blaine look at each other and smirk. Jax is the first to speak. "Porter doesn't know what the word *no* means." He nods to Blaine. "So he showed his ass what it looks like. He got to him first. It could have been a lot worse. Trust me."

Blaine reaches for the nearest glass of beer and pours it over his head, before shaking his wet hair out and popping his neck. "He was all up Madison's ass, trying to dance up on her and get under her skirt. Madison told him to fuck off and that he can't handle a woman like her, so that motherfucker pulled his dick out and bent her over the bar. I grabbed him up before he could touch her and threw his head through the window. I should have *killed* his big ass."

Taking a deep breath, Blaine steps in front of Madison and grabs her face to check her out. "I'm sorry that he even fucking touched you. You alright, babe? I told you to stay next to Jax."

Madison nods her head and begins telling Avalon that she's fine and not to worry, when Avalon pulls her away and starts questioning her away from us.

Blaine is exactly like me when it comes to women. He is rough, unfiltered, and likes to fuck... a lot, but touching a lady when she doesn't want to be touched is how a man can lose his fucking dick in my bar; that or his fucking life.

"I'll get the window fixed," I say as I exhale. I'm not making him pay for it now. Not after knowing why he did it. I would have killed the fucker. He got off easy. I'd rather have a broken window any day over a woman getting sexually abused in my presence. "Good shit, Blaine. You're lucky you have a good reason this time." I turn to Jax. "Get Avalon and Madison home safely. They don't belong here."

I allow a quick glance in Avalon's direction, to see her worried expression, before disappearing into my office and breaking the first thing that my hands can touch. This is the last thing I wanted her to be here to witness and the last thing that I needed to have on my mind right now. It brings up too many damn memories.

I sit here in the dark and let my past consume me... killing me from the inside out.

Life is a bitch... and she has me by the fucking throat.

CHAPTER 7

AVALON

LOOKING COLTON STRAIGHT IN THE face, I say it. The one thing I came here to say. It's been eating at me since his party, and partially even before that to be honest.

"We need a break, Colton. I'm not happy anymore, with us, and I think you can feel it too."

Rolling his eyes, he runs his hands over his face in frustration, and then takes a seat on the top of the picnic table. I stare at his overly expensive watch as he exhales deeply and prepares to talk me out of it. I've been preparing for this moment for days now, already knowing that he'll either try talking me out of it or think I'm joking. "Babe, don't do this. Nothing good *ever* comes of a break and you know it. It would be stupid of me to allow it. You belong with me. I don't want a break."

I purse my lips and watch him as he pulls out his phone and begins to reply to a message, as if it's the most important thing in the world and can't afford to wait five damn minutes. "This is my point."

Standing up, I look down at his fast typing fingers and

shake my head in annoyance. "The only thing you seem to care about is your work. There's no room for me in your busy life and I'm honestly getting worn out just waiting for the right time to make my appearance. If we can't even sit down and have a ten-minute conversation about our relationship without you pulling out your phone and getting lost in your own little world, then we have a problem. A huge problem, Colton."

I suck in a deep breath and exhale when he stops typing to look up at me. "You've changed, and I hate to admit this, but it's not for the good. We either take this break or we end it for good; your choice, because I'm not going to sit around and watch you act like a prick anymore. A break is the best option we have at the time. What will it be?"

Colton stands up and grabs my arm, attempting to pull me into his lap, but I stop him. It's not going to work on me. I'm too fed up at the moment.

"Babe..." He sets his phone down. "I know I've been sort of a dick lately, but my job can be very stressful. You can't blame me."

"Yeah," I say stiffly. "And so can a shitty relationship. You can't blame me."

Closing his eyes, he grips the picnic table and lets the reality of our situation sink in. It takes him a few minutes before he actually turns back to look at me. "Fine. I can handle it for a few weeks, but no more than that, Marie."

"Avalon," I spit out. "Damn, you're good at pissing me off. Come talk to me when you fall off your damn high horse. Hopefully it knocks some sense into you, or at least hits you in the damn balls." I take a deep breath. "I need to go. I have *work* to do. Important clients waiting to be seen." I take off in a hurry, making my way to my jeep.

"Yeah, you do that... but do me a favor."

I stop walking to turn around. "What is that?"

"Stay away from my maniac brother and his friends. You're too good for those assholes."

I let out an annoyed laugh. "You really are a lot different from what I remember six months ago. I hope you can see that before it's too late. Goodbye..."

With that, I jump into my jeep and drive off, wanting nothing more than to get away before my chest explodes.

I LOOK BESIDE ME AT Madison and shake my head at her last question. She never ceases to amaze me. "No he didn't get on his knees and cry like a pussy."

Madison gives me a brief look of disappointment. "Oh damn." She pouts. "I was hoping he would cry, or at least wet his khakis." She waves her comb at me. "He didn't do either, huh?"

I laugh and turn back to my client, Kaci, to start on cutting the next layer of hair. "Sorry for the disappointment, Madi, but *no*."

I see her shrug from the corner of my eye. "I wouldn't have been there to see it anyway. There's always another time." She smiles and reaches for the blow dryer to dry Susan's hair, her regular client.

Focusing on the task at hand, I spend the next fifteen minutes or so giving Kaci her newly layered look, before walking her to the counter to take her payment and say goodbye.

It's close to closing time, so I start cleaning up my station while Madison finishes up with Susan and sees her out.

We both plop down into our chairs when done, and start chatting as the other girls finish cleaning their stations.

"How's that tattoo?" Madison reaches for my shirt and lifts it up. I lean back and let her examine it. "It looks really fucking good." She replaces my shirt. "You getting another one soon? I think you should. You would look badass tatted up. You're just the kind of chick that can pull it off."

I pull my bottom lip into my mouth in thought. After the other night I'm not sure that we're welcome back to the shop, and after having Royal's work on me I don't think I'd let anyone else tattoo me.

"We'll see." I stand up and pump her chair up as high as it will go. She's super short; tiny but lethal for sure.

"Is this your way of distracting me, woman?" She slaps my hands away as I start playing with her hair. "Not going to work." She points over to my chair. "Thanks for the lift, but take a damn seat."

"Madison, I'm tired." I close my eyes and yawn; not just for show either. I'm actually pretty exhausted, and ready to get the hell out of here, but we still have about fifteen minutes before close. "I don't really know if I'll be getting another tattoo, and I don't feel like thinking about it right now either."

"I think you should. Just saying." Madison's eyes widen and she sits up high to look out the window when the sound of motorcycle engines come into close range. She stands on the bottom part of her chair. "Is that... Holy shit. I think Blaine and Royal just pulled up."

My heart involuntarily starts going wild in my chest as I look out the glass to see the two guys, now pulling their helmets off. I get ready to say something, but then stop when I realize that I have no idea what to say.

I never thought I'd see two badass, tatted up guys in ripped clothing pull up outside of a pretty little feminine salon like *Stylin'* on motorcycles.

Apparently neither did Ellie and Anne, because they're watching with wide eyes and flirtatious grins as the guys walk past the glass and reach for the door.

Suddenly feeling nervous, I turn away from the door and start organizing my station as the door dings.

"Boys," Madison says cheerfully. "Miss us already?"

I look up into the mirror to see Royal watching me with curious eyes. He lifts a brow when our eyes meet.

Next thing I know he's taking a seat in my chair and lowering it.

From the corner of my eye I see Ellie and Anne whispering to each other and watching the boys' every movement.

"Do me," he says huskily.

"Excuse me?" I shake my head and pull it out of the gutter when I realize he's not *actually* demanding me to *do him*. "You want me to cut your hair?"

I smile in amusement as Royal reaches for the stylist apron and snaps it around his neck, before pulling his hair toward his face. I swallow hard as a thick strand falls over his eye and he peers up at me. It's that sexy, lethal look again that makes my legs quiver with both fear and excitement. "A number two."

When I look beside me Blaine is sitting in Madison's chair, but facing her. He grabs her by the thighs and pulls his bottom lip into his mouth, giving her a sexy look.

She laughs and reaches for her apron.

"Alright." I turn back to Royal and grab his shoulder, yanking him back to sit straight up. "Hold still or I might shave that gorgeous hair off."

He smirks at me through the mirror as if my sassiness entertains him. Oddly... that makes me smile to myself.

Shaving his hair is somewhat nerve-racking. I've been cutting hair for five years now, since I first turned seventeen, but the thought of shaving off any of his pretty hair by accident has me almost sweating.

He notices me getting nervous when I get to the top of his hair, so he places his hand on mine and yanks it up, just under the long part. "There you go, babe. Loosen up a little."

Our eyes meet in the mirror, before I move his hand off mine. "I'm not tense." I take a deep breath. "I'm just tired. It's been a long day."

He reaches up and grabs the clippers from my hand after I shut them off, then watches me through the mirror as I reach for his apron to undo it.

Setting the clippers on the desk in front of him, Royal spins around in the chair and places both of his hands on my hips. Looking up at me, he begins sliding my shirt up.

As hard as I fight it, a small moan escapes my lips at the feel of his hands running up my sides. "You been taking care of that tattoo?"

I close my eyes and nod my head as his thumb lightly brushes the skin, just under the feather. My stomach fills with butterflies from the contact, but I do nothing to push his hands away. I don't remember the last time I've gotten that feeling.

"Yeah. Jax sent the aftercare instructions to Madison and she sent them to me," I breathe.

He lowers my shirt and our eyes meet. "Good. It looks good. What about my brother? Did he flip his shit?"

I shake my head and watch his hands as he runs them over the sides of his head. "We're on a break. He hasn't seen it."

He lifts a brow, but then looks up and winks at Ellie and Anne when they walk over to my station, smiling at him.

Both of their faces are completely fucking red; especially after that little wink and from the look on Royal's face. I know he's aware of the effect he has on women with little effort at all.

Anne clears her throat and then speaks. "We're out of here. You girls need anything else done before we leave?"

"We don't mind sticking around for a bit," Ellie adds, while looking between the boys.

Don't ask me why, but this annoys me. They both know damn well that they're only offering because of the tatted up eye candy. They've been bitching all day about how they have better shit to do tonight and how we should close early.

"No thanks." I motion for Royal to get out of my chair. "We're walking out in just a few minutes anyway. We've got it."

"Sure thing," Ellie says, while grabbing Anne's arm. "We'll see you in the morning." She turns to Royal and pulls a business card out of her bra, handing it to him. "In case you ever come back."

With that, the girls walk out the door, looking back to get one more glance at Royal and Blaine, before jumping into Anne's Range Rover.

Blaine jumps to his feet and starts checking his fresh haircut out in the mirror. "Damn, I'm looking dope as shit."

I laugh under my breath at him. "Thanks for stopping in boys, but you've got to get out. We closed ten minutes ago. Claudette will have my ass for letting you guys stay inside after close."

I reach for the broom and start to sweep, but glance up at my desk when Royal tosses a fifty down. "What's that for? I don't want any cash for the cut." I pick it up to hand it to back to him.

"We'll be outside." Royal looks down at my hand, and then walks toward the door with Blaine following behind him.

"Seriously," Madison says with a grin. "They're gorgeous and tip well?" She shoves a fifty into her bra that Blaine left on her chair, and starts sweeping up her station. "Remember the lousy ass tip that Colton left you the day y'all met?" She bursts out laughing. "About as pathetic as his dick. I told you not to fall for him."

Shaking my head, I hold back my laughter and continue cleaning up so we can get the hell out of here.

We're walking out the door about twenty minutes later. Royal and Blaine are sitting on the sidewalk, but stand up when they notice us come outside.

I lock the door, my heart racing in anticipation of what's to come next. "You guys didn't have to wait for us. I'm sure you have shit to do."

"We did," Royal says stiffly. "Fucking creeps come out at night. You can't trust anyone; no matter where the fuck your business is located."

I offer Royal and Blaine a smile as I walk over to the passenger side of Madison's car. I look down to reach for the handle and let out a sigh. "Again, Madi? I thought you took that tire to get replaced."

"Hell no. I've been busy. It's called Fix-A-Flat. I've been using it for weeks and it's a quick fix."

"Yeah, and a temporary one too," I point out.

"Hop on," Royal says while holding out his helmet for me. "I ain't got shit to do until tomorrow."

I shake my head and start digging through my purse for my phone. "That's okay, I'll just call —"

"Who? My fucking brother?" I shake my head, realizing that I had no idea who I was even going to call, but definitely not Colton though. "Then get on."

Blaine grabs Madison by the hand and starts pulling her away from the car. "I'll take care of your car. Let's go." He hands her his helmet and watches her put it on, while pushing down on the crotch of his jeans. "Dayum, girl. Want to ride on the front of my bike?"

It almost looks as if Madison is considering at first, but then she walks around to the back of his bike, sporting a huge grin, and hops on.

"You coming or what?" Royal asks, making me pull my eyes away from Blaine and Madison.

"I don't think I have much of a choice."

Royal stands up, while holding his bike up, to put my helmet on. Then he sits back down and grips the handle as I climb on behind him.

Wrapping my arms around him, I notice how my heart goes crazy in my chest. I've been on the back of his bike three times now, and being this close to him still makes me nervous.

We ride for about ten minutes before we pull up in front of a little white house. Royal kills the engine and helps me climb off his bike.

"Who lives here?" I keep my eyes on the house, looking for any lights that might be on, while handing my helmet to Royal. "It looks like no one is home."

"They aren't," he says without hesitation. "Come on."

Royal grabs my hand and pulls me behind him when I don't make an effort to move. I almost think he's going to break into this person's house until I see him pull out a set of keys.

Relief washes over me as I watch him unlock the door and flip on the lights, not trying to hide the fact that we're here.

With my hand still in Royal's, I follow him through the small living room and into the even smaller kitchen.

I stand back and watch as Royal opens the cabinet and pulls out a stack of plates. Popping his neck, he lets out a breath and then throws one across the room, breaking it against the wall.

I jump and cover my mouth in surprise. "What the hell are you doing?"

He flexes his jaw, looks at me, and then throws another one at the wall, breaking it. "Blowing off steam."

"By breaking someone else's shit?" I instinctively jump when another one breaks against the wall.

"Blaine's shit," he corrects me. "He breaks my window... I get to come to his house and break some of his shit. That's how it works with us."

Backing me against the counter, he grabs me by the hips and picks me up, setting me down with a smirk. "You need to blow off some steam, and since I can't *fuck* it out of you..." He hands me a plate. "Here."

I swallow hard from his words and look down at the plate in

my hands. Is it possible to choke on air... because I think he just made that happen? I swallow again. "I'm not going to break Blaine's dishes. I don't feel right. I hardly even know him."

"The fucker just cost me close to two grand from throwing some dick's head through my bar window." He runs a hand through my hair and tugs it. "Break it."

He's got a point. These dishes will cost him less than a hundred bucks to replace. Blaine does sort of deserve it. He could've slammed that guy's head into the wall or took him outside or something.

"Fine." Holding the plate like a Frisbee, I toss it across the room, slightly jumping when it crashes into the wall.

I find myself smiling after a few seconds. "Hand me another one," I say excitedly. "This does feel nice."

Smiling, he hands me a stack of smaller plates and chills against the fridge, crossing his arms across his chest to watch me. "Damn," he says as I toss another one. "Watching you break Blaine's shit is making my cock hard. Keep going."

I look over at him and can't help but to smile when he does. He doesn't smile often, but when he does, it's extremely contagious. "Stop watching me like that," I say with a small laugh.

I toss another one and watch as he opens the window next to him and lights a cigarette. My chest quickly rises and falls at the way his lips look as he slowly blows out the smoke.

I've never found smoking to be attractive, but watching Royal and the way he moves his mouth is oddly making me hot for him.

Pulling my eyes away, I clear my throat and toss the last plate. This is the weirdest activity I have ever done with anyone, but oddly freeing. "That's it. That's the last one."

Taking one last long drag, Royal puts his cigarette out in Blaine's sink and starts walking over to me. "Good girl." Grabbing me by the hips, he sets me back down to the ground and grabs my chin, pulling it up to look at him. "Feel better?"

I nod my head. "Surprisingly I do." I almost feel like breaking more shit. I've never done anything like this before.

"Good." He sucks in a deep breath. "At least one of us does."

"Ah fuuuck!"

I look away from Royal, who is smiling, and over to Blaine who is now standing in the doorway.

"I should have hidden the fucking dishes."

Royal grins and tosses a shot glass at Blaine. Blaine attempts to catch it but misses, with it landing and breaking at his boot. "Or just learn to buy paper plates, asshole."

Blaine scrunches his forehead and reaches for a cigarette. "Fuck that. Then you'll find other shit in my house to break."

"Where's Madison?" I ask, when I realize that she's not in the house with us. "Is her car already fixed?"

Blaine pulls the cigarette from his lips and nods his head. "Yeah, I'm fast as shit with cars. Been working on them since I was ten."

"Good," I say softly. "Thanks for helping her. She's been putting it off forever."

He nods his head. "Sure thing." He lifts a brow at me. "Thanks for helping this dickhead break my shit."

"Sure thing," I reply back, fighting to keep my cool and not show my nerves.

Blaine and Royal both smile at my response.

"Have fun cleaning this shit up." Royal grabs my hand and pulls me close to his side. "I'm dropping her off and then heading to the bar to take care of some shit."

"Fuck... okay." Blaine runs a hand through his hair while checking out the mess in his kitchen. "See your ass tomorrow." He turns to me. "Later, babe."

I smile when he winks and blows out smoke. "Later, Blaine."

We pull up outside of my house and I quickly hop off this time, handing him his helmet. "Thanks for the ride. Later."

I attempt to walk away, but Royal grabs my arm, stopping me. He pulls me back, turning me around to face him.

He looks at me for a few seconds, as if he's not sure he should say anything, before finally speaking. "Come by my place on Friday night. We need to celebrate you handing Colton his ass by adding another tattoo to that beautiful body."

I pull my arm out of his reach and smile, while backing away. I almost can't stand to listen to him talk, because everything he says has a crazy effect on my body. He does something to me that I'm not familiar with. "Maybe. I'll think about it."

Without saying a word, he growls when I turn to walk away.

By the time I reach the porch and turn back around, he's pulling away, speeding off on his bike.

I find myself smiling as I let myself inside and close the door behind me.

There's no way in hell that he came to the salon tonight just for a damn haircut. Guys like *that* don't need a fancy hairstylist to cut their hair. They do it themselves in their bathrooms, kitchens, or at a friend's house.

That somehow leaves me happy, knowing that he most likely came just to see me. Colton has *never* shown up at the salon to get an unneeded haircut. In fact, the day I met him was the only time he set foot in there.

Royal may be a little rough around the edges, but there's something hiding deep inside, wanting to come out; possibly a bigger heart than his brother's got.

The question is, should I hang around to find out?

CHAPTER 8

ROYAL

"WHAT THE FUCK, JAX," I snap, when he pushes my door open, interrupting me for the third time in the last twenty minutes. "Can I finish this shit so I can get home to Olivia already? I'm tired of looking at you dickheads tonight."

His face turns hard. "Nah, man. James is here again looking for Brian and he is fucking heated. He said he's going to break everything in this fucking bar if you don't come out and see him. Doesn't look like he's leaving."

"Fuck!" Slamming the pile of twenties down, I stand up and point at the drawers of cash. "Watch this shit. Don't walk away from it for nothing. I'll be back. I'm going to kill that Brian fucker myself if he ever sets foot in here again. I've had enough of this shit."

I walk out, slamming the door behind me. I look around the dark bar until I spot James and two of his guys going through my liquor stash.

70

"What the fuck can I do for you fuckers?"

James and his guys walk around the bar to meet up with me, one of his guys still holding a bottle of my whiskey. I watch him carefully as he tilts the bottle back and takes a swig of it, trying to intimidate me and show me he has balls. Fucker's lucky it's almost empty or he'd lose them.

"I need my fucking money; all twenty grand of it," James barks out. "And since I can't fucking find Brian, I'm getting it from the fucktard that allowed his dirty ass to fuck me over in his bar. That's you my friend. Now where's my fucking dough?" He grabs the bottle of whiskey from his friend and tosses it at the wall, breaking it.

Out of instinct, I grab him by the neck and slam him against the wall behind him. I squeeze, digging into his neck as I lean in close. "Get. The. Fuck. Out. Of. My. Bar." I squeeze tighter, knowing that this prick's life is in my hands right now. One wrong move and I'll take it. "I didn't allow that fuck up to do shit in my bar," I spit out. "Don't expect shit from me. Got it, bitch!"

I feel the barrel of a gun press against my temple, before I hear the hammer being pulled back. For a split second, I worry for my life, knowing what I have at home waiting for me, but still I test the water, hoping that they aren't stupid enough to shoot me right now.

Growling out, I squeeze his neck until he's fighting for air and pulling at my fingers with both hands.

"Go ahead... shoot me. I fucking dare you to. As soon as you do, you're dead."

James stops fighting me and lifts his hand up to his friend. I feel the gun disappear from my head and I release his neck a few seconds after.

He instantly starts coughing and fighting for air, bent over, grabbing at his neck.

"Fuck you," James coughs out. "Crazy dick."

Turning to the bigger guy that had the gun to my head, I lift up the bottom of my shirt, showing him that I too am packing. This isn't some little kid shit that they're dealing with. They're not just going to walk into *my* bar and intimidate me. "Get the fuck out. If that fucker ever comes back..." I grab James by the shoulder and pull up, until he's looking at me. "I'll tell him you bitches stopped by."

Turning around, I walk toward the front door and hold it open. "I said, get the fuck out."

Grinding his jaw, James keeps his eyes on me while whistling for his guys to follow him to the door. Once his guys are outside, he stops and turns to me. "This shit ain't over. Enjoy your fucking night." A sickening smirk crosses his face that makes me feel sick to my fucking stomach.

An unsettling feeling sets in as he backs away with me watching his every damn move. His eyes stay locked with mine, unwavering until he laughs and finally turns around.

As soon as they're through the parking lot and to their bikes, I slam the door closed, before punching it as hard as I can. I feel like a cannon ready to explode.

"Fuuuck!" I start pacing, while nervously running my hands through my hair. "That shit was not cool."

Jax appears in the bar and looks at the dent in the door. "I had my shit ready if those fuckers tried making a bad move. Fuck, I'm happy I didn't have to kill someone tonight."

I let out a hard breath and grip my hair tighter, while stopping to look at him. "Me too." I take off walking back to my office, in a hurry to get out of here now. "I'll be finishing this shit up. You can go."

"Nah." Jax takes a seat at the bar and reaches for his half empty glass of vodka. He lifts it up. "I'm good for a while. I'm not going anywhere in case those dicks come back."

I nod my head, thankful for Jax. "Thanks, man."

My mind is so fucked up after James and his minions left

that it takes my ass another thirty minutes to finish with my closing shit. All I've been able to think about this whole time is how I want to kill those fuckers, and it was pretty close to coming down to that. I've never wanted to kill anyone in my damn life.

Locking up all the cash and downing the rest of my whiskey, I walk out and lock my office behind me.

Jax stands up and slips on his leather jacket. "You good, man?"

My nostrils flare in anger as I pull out a cigarette and light it. "I'm good. Let's just get the fuck out of here."

I know some shit is off as soon as I turn down my street to see three Harleys parked at the nearby park. My heart instantly stops and I know that I'm fucked, because I'm most likely going to be taking a few lives tonight after all.

PRESENT

"FUCK!" I SIT UP IN bed and run both of my hands over my flushed, sweaty face. I can never fucking sleep. This shit happens every damn night, and I find myself drowning in a bottle of whiskey until I'm close to waking up in a hospital with a fucking IV in my arm.

Taking a few deep breaths, I reach beside me for the bottle I keep close by and toss the cap across the room. It's the only way I'll be able to close my eyes without feeling as if I'm dying from the memories; the fucking images in my head that haunt me until I can't breathe, almost making it easy for me to lay down and just let it fucking take me.

I'm doing my best to fight it, but someday I need to realize that my best isn't good enough. That shit will never go away.

Throwing my feet over the edge of the bed, I stand up and

strip out of my boxer briefs, before grabbing the bottle of whiskey and heading for the shower.

With the door open, I keep the light off and turn on the shower, hopping in. With one hand pressed against the shower wall, I let the frigid water pour over my heated flesh, while holding the bottle to my lips and taking a desperate swig.

My body is freezing, but my insides are fucking burning, feeling raw from the warm whiskey. It's a fucked up combination, but at least I'm feeling something.

Anything at all...

AVALON

I'M JUST WALKING OUT OF the salon when I get a text from Colton. Today's only a half-day for me, so it's nearly three o'clock. It's not very often that I have the pleasure of getting off early.

Seeing his name flash across the screen causes my body to flood with anxiety and lose that small bit of freedom that getting off early brought me.

Exhaling, I open up his text and read it, hoping that it's not about his family dinner tonight.

COLTON

Tonight is dinner at my parents' as usual. You'll be there, right?

AVALON

We're on a break, Colton. Remember?

COLTON

Yeah... but my parents don't know that and I don't want a reason to alarm them if we're only on a break. Please come.

AVALON

Idk...

COLTON

Please. It's not that big of a deal. It's only dinner and you don't even have to sit next to me. They're expecting you and will be disappointed. I'm only asking this and then I'll give you your space.

Feeling guilty, I know that I'm going to end up agreeing to go. It's not that I feel bad for Colton, but his parents have been nothing but good to me. They're going to be expecting me, and it would be rude to stand them up.

Shit! Shit! Shit!

AVALON

I'll be there... for them, Colton. Nothing is changing between us so please don't push it and make me uncomfortable.

COLTON

You have my word, Marie.

Shit!

I meant Avalon.

AVALON

See you around 5:30.

Shaking my head, I get ready to shove my phone into my purse when it vibrates again.

"Dammit, Colton."

I unlock the screen, expecting it to be Colton, but it's from a number that I don't have saved in my phone.

UNKNOWN

Avalon... come to my house tonight. I'll be set up and ready by 6.

AVALON

Umm... who is this and why am I going to your house tonight?

My heart jumps to my throat when the next message comes through.

UNKNOWN

Royal... that tattoo.

AVALON

Did you ask for my number? And I can't.

ROYAL

Yes... And why not?

AVALON

Well... your damn brother guilt-tripped me into going to your parents' house for dinner tonight.

ROYAL

Even your text messages are tense. Didn't my brother ever fucking relieve your tension? And just fucking tell him no. You don't owe him.

AVALON

Hah! I'm not even going to answer that. And I know I don't owe him. It's out of respect for June and Ken.

ROYAL

I knew that stiff asshole wouldn't know shit about pleasuring a woman. I'll see you later.

AVALON

I can't come...

A wait a few minutes for a response from Royal, before

putting my phone away and heading home to get ready for this awkward dinner that I really don't want to go to.

All I really wanted to do when walking out that door was to go home, eat junk food, and watch reality TV.

Now... all I really want to do is take Royal up on his offer for that tattoo. He just has this weird way of making me want to drop everything and have this crazy little adventure that being around him always seems to bring.

Instead, I'll be spending the night feeling awkward at a family dinner that I really don't want to be at, and pretending that everything is normal when it's anything but.

COLTON IS SITTING ON THE front porch when I arrive at his parents' house. He immediately stands up and puts his phone away.

"Hey, baby. Thanks for coming."

I nod and turn my head to the side when he leans in to give me a kiss. "Hey... Sorry I'm a bit late."

He clears his throat and loosens his stiff collar. He *never* wears a damn shirt without a collar and it drives me nuts. "No worries. Mother is just setting the table and I was finishing up some business." He pauses for a second and stares at me, taking in my yellow dress. "How have you been? We haven't talked in days. It's weird."

I smile small and answer him honestly. "Good. I've been pretty happy." And I have. I'm happier than I have been in a while now.

His jaw tics in anger, before he turns away and opens the screen door. "Good to hear," he says flatly. "Let's get this over with."

Walking into the kitchen, I'm greeted by Ken, who is

already seated at the table. Just like his son, he's dressed in a blue, collared, button-down shirt.

"How are you, Marie? It's a pleasure seeing you, as always." He stands up, flashing a stiff smile. "Please, take a seat."

Waiting to see which side Colton's going to sit on first, I take a seat opposite of him after he sits down. "Good to see you too, Ken." I glance at Colton from across the table. "I'm doing well. Just keeping busy at the salon."

Ken nods his head and looks at Colton, but doesn't offer a response.

A few awkward minutes later, June walks in carrying two huge bowls of pasta and sauce. "Hey, kids. Hope you're hungry." She smiles at me and then over to Colton, looking confused to see us across the table from each other. "Alright, this is different. Let's eat before it gets cold. There's plenty, so dig in."

I wait for June to take a seat, before saying my usual thanks; the one I give them every week at dinner. "Thanks for having me for dinner again. I appreciate your hospitality and the food looks delicious."

"Oh, honey. We're always glad to have you." She peers over at her husband. "Right, Ken?"

Ken nods in agreement and places his napkin over his lap. "Of course."

We all start digging into our food, eating in this awkward silence that we've all grown accustomed to, until the front door opens, surprising us all.

We all look over at the doorway, at the same time, as Royal walks in dressed in a white V-neck shirt, showing off all of his glorious tattoos and a pair of ratty old jeans.

My heart begins to palpitate, practically leaping out of my chest when his eyes meet mine and he runs his tongue over his lips.

Without saying a word, he walks into the kitchen and then returns with a plate and silverware, taking a seat next to me and digging into the food while everyone at the table watches him uncomfortably.

Ken clears his throat a few times, trying to get his attention, but Royal just ignores him and starts eating.

"Royal," Ken says tensely. "What are you doing here? A little notice would have been nice. What if we had not made enough dinner? We have a guest."

Royal looks up from his plate and shoves a bite of spaghetti in his mouth.

"Your father is right, Royal. We weren't expecting you. It's rude to just drop in unannounced." She makes a disgusted face at his long hair falling to the side of his face. "And it would've been nice if you had at least pulled your hair out of your face. We don't want it getting in the food. It's unsanitary."

Tilting his head, Royal gives his mother a dark look, before brushing a hand through his hair and slicking it back. "Ken is not my fucking father."

Feeling uncomfortable for Royal, I turn to him and smile. I've never seen a family treat their son as if he's unwelcome, and it makes me sick to my stomach to witness Royal in his position. "Nice to see you, Royal."

He smiles back and then looks across the table at Colton, cocking a brow. "How's it going, brother?"

Staring daggers at Royal, Colton slams his fork into his plate, stabbing at his food. "It's funny how you decide to show up for a family dinner for the first time in two years. Don't you have better shit to do, like break up a bar fight or drown in whatever poison it is that you drink at that dirty bar?"

Royal lifts a brow, but just shrugs off Colton's words as if his opinion doesn't matter. I don't blame him. Who is Colton to judge, just because his brother doesn't live the same lifestyle as him?

"Marie, honey," June says. "Why don't you move across the table by Colton? Sorry for the interruption."

I sit up straight and look around the table, making sure they all see my disgusted face at their behavior. "I'm good. I'd rather sit here, thank you." I turn to Royal. "Would you like more noodles? Here." Without waiting for a response, I fill his plate back up with noodles, showing everyone that I'm in no hurry to get rid of Royal.

Assholes...

Royal's hand grips my thigh from under the table as he slowly pulls me closer to him. I don't think anyone else seems to notice, except for maybe Colton, who growls under his breath while watching his brother's every move.

Ken looks up from his plate a few times to watch Royal as he eats his spaghetti. His eyes widen as Royal smiles at me and then reaches over to my plate to take a bite of one of my meatballs. "You should move across the table, Marie. Royal here doesn't have any manners."

"Her fucking name is Avalon," Royal corrects him.

Picking up the meatball that Royal bit off of, I place it in my mouth and chew slowly. "It's fine. I don't have a problem with sharing. I have too many meatballs anyway."

I jump and grip the edge of the table when I feel Royal's hand glide up my leg, pulling my skirt up along the way.

A shaky breath escapes me when I feel him spread my legs open with his pinky and thumb and cup my mound in his rough hand.

"You okay?" Colton questions, looking as if he's about to stand up.

"I'm fine, Colton." I hold up my glass of ice water. "I just spilled a few drops of water on my legs. It was an unexpected sensation. That's all." *That's no lie.*

Royal growls next to my ear and quickly slips two fingers inside of me, causing me to moan against my fork and almost drop it.

I feel as if I'm about to come if he makes any movement. A

part of me wants him to stop, while the other part has needed release for a while.

Looking across the table at Colton, Royal starts pumping his fingers in and out, going harder each time Colton gives him a dirty look and grinds his jaw. Being quiet has never been so hard.

Within minutes, I'm clenching around his thick fingers, my intense orgasm sending a surge of heat shooting through my body and a tingling sensation begins in my feet.

"Royal, your plate is empty. I'm sure you have business to take care of," June says, while looking between the two of us with suspicious eyes.

Taking a few quick breaths, I look the other way and try to catch my breath, hoping that his parents didn't catch on to what just happened under the table. It was so quick that I'm hoping it went unnoticed.

"I think that means you can fucking leave now," Colton spits out, while locking eyes with Royal. "You haven't been welcome here for years, so say goodbye to my girl and leave."

Royal pushes his fingers in me as deep as he can and smirks, before pulling out of my throbbing pussy. Then he stands up and sucks his fingers into his mouth; the ones that were nowhere close to the food... but maybe no one noticed. "Fucking delicious. Thanks for dinner."

Ken and June watch hard as Royal pushes his chair under the table, locks eyes with me, and then turns and walks away.

I sit here with my heart pounding and my pussy shame-lessly throbbing as he disappears out the front door.

Making a quick decision, I stand up and push my chair in. "Thanks for dinner, but I have to run."

Colton stands up fast as hell and rushes over to stop me, with his parents watching us in confusion. "Don't fucking leave. He wasn't even invited. Stay."

I let out a small laugh of disbelief. "I can see what a great family you all have here. Thanks for having me, but unfortunately I don't think I fit in here. We're just *different* people. I think I'll leave with my friend. Have a nice night."

With that, I rush out the door to find Royal leaning against a huge black truck. He lifts a brow and bites his bottom lip as his eyes roam over my heated body. "Follow me."

Pulling his eyes away, he hops into his truck, watching me from his rearview mirror as I jump into my jeep and prepare to follow him home.

I have no idea what the hell just happened in there, but I think I liked it... Shit!

ROYAL

PARKING MY TRUCK IN FRONT of the lake, I turn off the engine and wait for Avalon to make her way down the winding dirt path.

I wasn't planning on bringing company here tonight—or ever really—but after what happened at dinner, I couldn't just leave her and pretend that what she did for me didn't have some kind of an effect on me.

Going to my family's house is never easy. That's why I stay the fuck away, but after watching Riley being lowered into the ground earlier today, my heart ached to see something beautiful, so I went where I knew *she* would be.

My plan was to keep to myself, but when she opened that beautiful, sassy mouth of hers, I fucking reached under the table and allowed myself to show my appreciation.

Taking a deep breath, I jump out of my truck and lean against it, as Avalon parks her jeep and kills the engine.

Not bothering to look at me, she grips onto her steering wheel and leans over it with her eyes squeezed shut. She looks as if she's struggling with something and I have a feeling I know what that is: *me.*

Hell... I struggle with my damn self.

A few minutes later, Avalon jumps out of her jeep and slams the door shut behind her, walking at me fast. "What the fuck was that, Royal?" She shoves my chest, completely out of breath. "Did you seriously just finger fuck me in front of your family to piss your brother off? Huh?"

I lift a brow and watch her plump breasts as her chest quickly rises and falls with each heavy breath she fights. With one hand, I reach out and grip her hip to keep her from backing away when I sense she's going to run. "That's not the only reason. Fuck, Avalon."

She brushes her hair out of her face and takes a deep breath. "Seriously!" she yells. "Please do tell me."

I look her dead in the eyes and speak the fucking truth. She may not like it, but... "I've been thinking about *finger fucking* you for days and hearing you stick up for me turned me the fuck on."

Her nostrils flare, as she looks me up and down. I prepare myself for another shove, but instead she just removes my hand from her hip and takes a step back. She looks a bit surprised by my answer and her demeanor calms a bit.

Swallowing, I reach into the back of my truck and pull out a twelve-pack of beer, before walking over to the water and taking a seat on the huge rock.

I stare out at the murky water and tilt back a bottle of beer, knowing exactly how I'm going to feel as soon as the emotions of being here take over. It's been exactly one year since I have been here. I had been coming here for eight years and up until two years ago; I always had the company of Olivia. Now I come here alone in hopes to get away and remember the good moments, but they always seem to hurt me more by the time I leave.

Taking me in with soft, understanding eyes, Avalon takes a seat beside me and reaches her hand out. "Can I have one of those?"

Looking straight ahead, I reach beside me and grab a bottle, twisting the top off and handing it to her.

We sit here in silence, both of us enjoying a few beers, before Avalon finally speaks, breaking the comfortable silence.

"Do you come here often?"

I shake my head. "Not anymore."

"Oh..." She takes a sip of her beer and shivers from the coldness of the drink and the wind blowing over her bare shoulders.

I stand up, take off my jacket, and drape it over her for warmth. "You're shivering."

She watches me as I take my seat next to her again. "Thank you."

Seeing her beside me, draped in my leather jacket, makes my cock hard, just thinking about her wearing that and nothing else. She looks so badass in it that it really makes me fucking curious about her and Colton.

"How long have you known Dickhead?" I question in between drinks.

She lets out a long sigh. "For a little over six months. Not too long." She empties her beer and hands it to me. "He came into the salon one day and was really charming; not so much anymore."

I can't help but to laugh at someone even considering Colton as a charmer. "That fucker... charming? Nah. I may be far from Prince Fucking Charming, but I know how to take care of a woman a hell of a lot better than that selfish prick."

She erupts in laughter and covers her face with both of her hands. "He's such a dick, Royal." Her words come out a little slurred now that she's on her fourth beer, but seeing her smile is a small relief to the pain I've been feeling all day. "I can't believe that I even went for him in the first place. He was just so different from the other jerks I dated. I actually thought I hit the jackpot with Colton, but then I realized that he's more of an expired lottery ticket that I never cashed in on."

I'm not sure if she really knows what she's saying at this point, but it's kind of fucking cute to see her babbling on about my idiotic brother.

"So..." She stands up and spills her bottle down the side of her leg as she starts talking and swinging her bottle at the same time. "The more I think about being with him, the more suffocated and nauseated that I feel. That's not how being with someone should feel. You should be dying inside to see that person and be willing to give your last breath just to touch them and hold them near. I can't breathe when I'm around him, but it's not because he takes my breath away. It's because I'm dying inside to run away."

Her face scrunches up as if she's just figured it all out. "So then tell him to fuck off and go out and find that shit."

She lets out a saddened laugh. "Yeah..." She quickly runs her hand over her face and flares her nostrils as if she's fighting back tears. "Maybe someday. I don't see that happening anytime soon."

I stand up beside her and grab her almost empty bottle out of her hand. "Leaving my brother?"

She looks down at my hand and then up to meet my eyes. "Finding someone that falls in love with me for who I truly am, and me loving them back so much that it fucking hurts. The one man I thought I truly loved only wanted me for my fucking tits and ass. That jerk."

She shakes her head as if waking up and realizing that she's talked too much. "Never mind that. I'm just babbling now from the damn beer."

I close my eyes for a second and feel the overwhelming

sensation as her words hit me like a fucking freight train. I found that once, but it was fucking ripped from me.

Pulling Avalon to me by the front, bottom part of my jacket, I reach into the inner pocket and pull the single white calla lily out and walk over to the water.

My chest fucking aches so bad that I can't even breathe as I close my eyes and listen to the water.

"What's that for?" Avalon asks softly from beside me.

My heart stops. "For my fiancée Olivia. It's her birthday."

I can hear Avalon's breathing pick up as she prepares to ask the question that I know is coming next. "Where is she?"

I drop the Lily into the water and turn around, looking her in the eyes. "Dead."

I catch the sight of Avalon's mouth dropping before I brush past her and hurry back over to my truck. I get ready to jump inside and drive off, but stop when I look back over to see her face buried in her hands.

I may not know much about Avalon, but I know for a fact that she's buzzing and a bit overly emotional at the moment. I can't fucking just leave her here. The thought makes me feel guilty, which is an odd feeling for me these days.

"Get in my truck."

She looks up from her hands and covers her mouth as if fighting off what she truly wants to say or ask. "What about my jeep?"

"I'll bring you back to it. No one will mess with it here."

She's hesitant at first, but then slowly walks over to the passenger side of my truck and hops inside as I open the door for her.

Once we're back on the road, I can feel her eyes watching me. I glance over and witness the hurt and sympathy in them. It's the first time that I've gotten that look since Olivia's death. Everyone else looks at me with something different in their eyes: Fear. I've gotten used to it and have learned to live with it.

It's part of who I am now, and as soon as she finds out the truth of that night she'll be looking at me in the same way they do.

Avalon doesn't speak the whole car ride back to my house. Instead, she asks for a beer as soon as we walk inside.

Knowing that we both just want to get lost and forget, I walk to the kitchen and pull out a handful of beers, motioning for her to follow me out back.

Getting a comfortable chair for her to sit down and relax, I grab for a beer, twist the top and take a seat next to her, just enjoying the night sky.

"I'm telling Colton that it's over in the morning. I should have just done that in the first place," she admits.

"Yeah..." I take a sip of my beer and close my eyes. "Good."

"Colton was the good guy. The clean-cut one without a record that my uncle always said I should go for. Back when I lived with him and my aunt..." She pauses to finish the last bit of her beer and sets it down by her feet. "I was always getting in trouble and letting them down. Running the streets late at night, and not coming home for days. Dating guys in and out of juvie. My mom couldn't handle it, so that's why she made me move in with her brother: my uncle. Believe it or not, I even landed in the back of a police car a few times." She lets out a sigh and stops talking.

It's quiet for a while.

By the time I look over again, Avalon is fast asleep, curled up into my big jacket.

"Thanks for the chat," I whisper to myself. "I guess I know why the fuck you gave that douche a shot now."

Closing my eyes again, I allow myself to just enjoy the peace and quiet of the night, hoping that this odd fucking calming feeling of having her near drowns out the rest of the noise in my head for a while.

Maybe I'm just an idiot for having any hope...

CHAPTER 11

AVALON

I WAKE UP IN A panic, looking around a cold, dark room. It takes a few minutes for my eyes to adjust enough to see that the room is unfamiliar.

Fear sets in until I look over to the right to see Royal sitting in a chair with his face buried in his hands. His long, messy hair is hanging over his inked hands, his shoulders slumped in defeat: a beautiful, but heartbreaking sight to take in. It makes my chest hurt at the realization of what he told me earlier at the lake, and I have a feeling that he's still lost in his thoughts over his loss. Seeing him in pain almost physically hurts me.

"I'm sorry," I say softly, while sitting up. "I didn't mean to fall asleep and intrude. I should go. I'll go find Jax and ask for a ride."

Royal looks up from his hands and rubs his hand down his mouth. He clears his throat and reaches beside him for a bottle of whiskey. "Go back to sleep. You're fine."

Getting comfortable against the headboard, I watch him as he tilts the bottle back and takes a long swig. "I'm not really tired anymore. I can go upstairs and watch TV so you can have your bed back at least."

I get ready to get out of his bed, but his command stops me, making my heart jump from the firmness of his voice. "Stay."

Keeping his eyes on me, he slowly stands up and strips out of his shirt, tossing it aside. My heart begins racing with unwanted desire as my eyes gradually trail over his firm body, bit by bit, taking it all in; every inch of pure inked muscle. This man is undeniably beautiful, and I could spend hours just admiring the art of his body and tattoos and never grow tired.

My eyes follow his hands as they lower down his body to undo his jeans, before pushing them down his tattooed legs. Watching him take them off sends a surge of excitement through me and I find myself wanting to just reach out and touch this man. The feeling makes my chest ache with need.

I can't pull my eyes away as he walks over to the opposite side of the bed and crawls in beside me. That's when I notice the scars on his right thigh, just below his black boxer briefs.

My heart drops as I take in the three, long, jagged lines. Without thinking, I reach out and run my fingers across them. "How did you get these?"

Grabbing my wrist, he pulls it away and squeezes it. "A knife."

My eyes widen at his confession, and I get this strong urge to just reach out and comfort him and let him know just how beautiful every inch of his body truly is; the scars included. I have to fight with everything in me not to ask him why or how. I want to know everything about this man and why he is the way he is: dark and demanding.

Feeling a small bit of confidence, I crawl in between his legs and grip his thighs, watching his reaction as I run my hand over his scars again. Feeling his legs flex under my touch has my stomach doing somersaults and my breathing uneven.

His eyes leisurely close and a deep growl escapes him as I move my hand higher up his thigh to the top of the first scar.

"Watch yourself, Avalon." I squeeze his thighs, just wanting to feel him. Right now, I couldn't care less about the consequences. This man gets my heart pumping unlike anything or anyone else. "Dammit, you're fucking pushing it."

For some odd reason, a part of me wants to know what he'll do if I continue to push it. Taking a deep breath and holding it, I slowly move both of my hands up his strong thighs, stopping just below his thick erection. I allow my fingers to trace the outline.

"Fuck!" he yells.

Next thing I know, his hands are on me and I'm somehow below him on the mattress, with our faces only inches apart.

Gripping my thigh with one hand, he opens my legs wide and presses his body between them, squeezing my thigh so hard that it hurts.

I feel his lips next to my ear as he captures both of my wrists in one hand and holds them above my head with force. "If I fuck you... I will hurt you. Every fucking inch of this beautiful body will crave to be touched by me... devoured by me, and I can't promise you more than one night, so stop."

"Oh yeah?" I challenge, feeling my heart pumping with adrenaline. "What makes you so sure of that? Maybe all I want is one taste." I tangle my hands into his hair and tug on it, pulling his neck to the side. "Maybe you're just afraid that you'll want it more than once, or maybe you don't fuck as good as you look."

I almost regret that last part and can't believe that I actually had the balls to say it. I don't apologize though. Instead, I search his eyes, demanding a response.

His eyes stay on mine for a heated moment, burning me from the inside out and making my whole body flush, before he bites my bottom lip and sucks it into his mouth. The feeling of his beard rubbing my lips surprisingly turns me on, mixed with the pain of his mouth and I find my body already lashing out, wanting more, so I bite him back when he tries pulling away.

Releasing my hands, he yanks my dress over my head with force and tosses it aside. Lifting me up, he flips us, leaving me to straddle his lap, then tangles his hands into the back of my hair and thrusts his hips into me, hard. So hard that I bounce out of his lap and fall back down, my breath getting knocked out of me.

I let out a loud moan, just imagining the way it would feel to actually have him inside of me. He's so thick and long that a part of me is almost afraid it will hurt. Pushing me down against him as roughly as he can, he thrusts his hips a few times, grinding his erection against my now aching pussy. His rhythm has me almost dying above him, and I can tell by the satisfied look in his eyes and his devilish grin that he knows he has me right where he wants me: hot and ready to lose myself to him.

His grip on my hair tightens as he yanks my head back and bites my neck, thrusting against me again, his erection driving between my wet lips. That's all it takes for me to lose it, my pussy clenching hard as my whole body shakes in his arms and I scream out his name.

He waits until my orgasm is done, before tossing me down beside him. "Now go to sleep. I've been drinking all fucking night so don't test me."

Swallowing hard and rubbing my hands over my face, I turn around and face the wall, surprised at how easily and hard he just made me come that I can still feel myself throbbing and aching for more. I'm not ready to go to sleep yet.

"What about you?" I ask softly.

Grabbing my shoulder, he turns me around. "What about me?"

I swallow and look down at his painfully hard erection. "Don't you need release?"

Letting out a long breath, he pushes down on his cock. "If you touch me, I will end up fucking you. My head is too fucked up right now to keep any restraint. It's best if we both just go to sleep."

I swallow back my nerves and meet his eyes. "No one said that *I* have to touch you."

Growling out, he sits up on his knees and grips my neck, rubbing his thumb over it. He lightly squeezes it, while reaching behind me with his other hand and undoing my bra, letting it fall down to reveal my bare breasts.

His eyes devour my tits as he runs a hand through his hair in frustration. "Fuck, Avalon. Are you still drunk? What the fuck are you doing to me right now?"

I arch my back to give him easier access to my body as he pulls his bottom lip into his mouth and admires my bare flesh. "Maybe just a little, but not enough to not know what I'm doing."

My heart is pounding so fast right now that I wouldn't be surprised if Royal could see it with each beat or even feel it from his closeness. I've never been this bold before, but he has a way of making me want to do things that I never have before.

"Fucking shit..." He releases my neck and backs away from me to get a better look. "Fucking perfection."

Grabbing my panties with both hands, he rips them open at the side and yanks them from my body, causing me to grip onto the blanket in surprise as I slide down it.

His teeth dig into his bottom lip and he moans as he spreads my legs open, baring my slick, wet pussy to him. "So fucking beautiful."

Having his dark eyes on me makes me feel an instant rush throughout my body. I can feel myself starting to sweat as I wait for his next move. I want him to touch me so damn bad, almost as much as I want to touch him.

Lowering the front of his tight briefs, he pulls his thick erection out and wraps his strong hand around it, stroking it. I swear I about die just from the sight of it. "Touch yourself," he growls out.

With my whole body heated by the sight of him touching himself, I lower my hand between my legs and follow his command. The faster I move and the louder I moan, the faster and harder he seems to stroke himself.

Holy hell... What a dangerously beautiful sight.

I lick my lips and moan out as a drop of his pre-cum slides down the tip of his dick, coating his head as he continues to stroke it so damn good that I find myself on the brink of another orgasm.

It's not from my own pleasure or the way I'm touching myself. Honestly, I've always had a hard time finding any kind of orgasm. It's the way that he touches himself and knows how to pleasure so well that has me clenching and screaming out.

"Oh my God... Yes, Royal..." I pant. I close my eyes and shake as my orgasm rolls through me. I don't open my eyes again until I hear him growl out in pleasure and feel his warm cum hit my breasts.

"Fucking shit." Taking a deep breath, Royal reaches his free hand behind my neck and pulls me closer to him with force, stroking out every last drop of his release.

Releasing his still hard cock, he runs both his hands through his hair, while breathing heavily.

I can't help but to keep my eyes on him in wonder as he gets off the bed and reaches for his shirt to clean me up. Our eyes meet, but neither one of us speaks.

After cleaning me off, he stands up and starts cleaning himself off.

Seeing him standing there, breathing hard, with his dick in

his hand and his eyes closed is so damn beautiful. I get an ache in my chest because I can't just reach out and touch him. I want to so badly, but don't want to push him anymore tonight.

"Now we can go to sleep," I say shakily.

Clenching his jaw, he walks out of his room still naked.

I lay here for twenty minutes, before realizing that there's rock music softly coming from the room next door. I'm assuming he's in the same room that I walked in on him that first night: his workout room. He's most likely working out his frustrations and a part of me feels bad that I may have just caused him more.

I really don't know what came over me tonight, and I'm hoping that I wake up tomorrow with a clear head and realize that it was just the alcohol and lack of orgasm speaking.

Taking a long breath, I close my eyes and lay here restless for what feels like forever, until I finally end up dozing off, feeling a bit ashamed, yet completely turned on by him at the same time.

CHAPTER 12

AVALON

HE COMES AT ME SLOWLY, yet it's so powerful and intoxicating that the air gets sucked straight from my lungs. Every muscle in his body is tense, his tattooed flesh moist with sweat as he stares down at me with an intensity that has me gripping the sheets around me. He's breathing heavily, his lips slightly parted as his powerful eyes meet mine and capture them. I'm lost in his darkness, wanting to be right there with him.

He doesn't say a word as he crawls above me, and in one swift movement he bites onto my neck as he rips my shirt open, baring my breasts to him.

I moan out in desire, just wanting to touch him, to feel my hands on him in any way I can, but when I reach for him... I can't move my arms.

I struggle against the leather restraints but they're too tight. I can't move. His mouth hovers above mine so dangerously close that I can almost taste him. His sweet breath caresses my lips, but I can't reach them. I can only breathe in his scent and it's driving me completely mad.

My desire to touch him is too strong, fueling me to lash out. I want to feel him, I need to, but I'm afraid I'll never get the chance, so I scream so painfully loud that my throat feels raw.

I need this man...

I wake up gripping the sheets so tightly that my fingers hurt. I feel a bead of sweat trickle down my heated neck and look around me as I fight to catch my breath.

It takes me a few seconds to realize that I'm in Royal's empty bed. He never came back last night. I'm not sure that I expected him to, but a part of me hoped that he would.

I've never had such an intense dream in my life; that I have to admit. I'm a bit freaked out by the way it's left me feeling. It felt so damn real; too real.

Taking a few deep breaths, I close my eyes and everything from last night hits me all at once, making me feel like a damn fool for the way I acted.

Yanking the covers off of me, I look down to see that I'm still completely naked. My temperature rises from embarrassment.

"Shit! Shit! Shit! I can't believe this."

Jumping to my feet, I quickly look around to be sure that I'm alone while reaching for what's left of my clothes to quickly get dressed.

It's amazing what liquid courage can do for you. I can't believe that I seriously suggested that Royal pleasure himself for me last night, and I can't believe that he actually did. That insanely hot image will forever be in my head, making it hard for anything else to *ever* compare. That thought is sort of scary.

Breathing heavily and feeling a bit insane, I look up at the doorway to see Royal standing there, watching me. He looks a mess, as if he hadn't slept at all last night. I have to admit that a mess looks sinfully sexy on him, and that alone makes me realize that I need to go before I do anything else stupid.

"Let's go." He grips the doorframe and takes a few seconds to look me up and down, before turning and walking away.

I walk outside a few minutes later, expecting him to be in his truck waiting, but instead he pulls up next to me on his motorcycle, looking damn sexy and dangerous; a lethal combination that I can barely handle right now.

After my dream of him this morning, just the thought of touching him sends me over the edge. This man seriously has no idea of the effect he physically has on me. I don't even get it.

"Shit," I whisper. "Don't think about last night."

"Hop on," he yells over the sound of the bike, while pulling me to him and sliding the helmet on me. His eyes meet mine, but he quickly clenches his jaw and turns away, leaving my heart sinking.

Feeling anxious from his cold shoulder, I jump on behind him, but grab onto the bike instead of him.

"Arms around me," he demands. "And hold on tight."

He leans his head back and stiffens a bit when my arms wrap around his waist, before finally taking off in a hurry.

When we reach my car, I quickly jump off and hand him his helmet. I really just want to get away from him right now. He's so damn hard to read and hard to deal with this early in the morning. "Thanks for letting me crash in your bed, Royal."

He nods his head and slides his helmet on, looking me over. "Better my bed than Colton's," he says stiffly.

I'm not really sure what to say to that, so I just pull out my keys and walk over to my car, trying my best not to glance back at him as I hop inside and start the engine. He waits for me to pull out and take off before I notice him following behind me.

He's behind me for a few minutes, following closely, before he finally turns off in the direction of the bar, allowing me to breathe for what feels like the first time since dinner last night.

"Holy shit," I breathe out. He's so damn intense. I've never met a man so powerful and heart-stopping in my life.

I grip the steering wheel and take a deep breath when I pull up at a stoplight. I'm supposed to work in less than two hours and I have a feeling that it's going to be extremely hard to concentrate now.

There's so much running through my head right now that it's giving me a headache. The thing eating at me the most is that I need to meet up with Colton and break things off completely. If I don't do it as soon as possible, it's only going to get harder, and then I'm going to explode with anxiety.

My plan was to go home, but instead, I find myself parked outside of Colton's home. The first thing I notice is the red BMW in the driveway that isn't his.

This is supposed to be when I feel some kind of jealousy or anger or something, right? That feeling that you would get if you were in love with someone... but all I feel is relief. I knew when he introduced me to his *business partner* that there had to be more there. The problem was I just didn't care to question him on it.

I want to do this, but I want to do it right and say it to his face. I know that's most likely not going to happen before work, so I send him a quick text, ignoring the handful of ones that he sent me last night.

AVALON

> We need to talk in person. Are you available to meet up?

Setting my phone in the passenger seat, I drive back home and park, before checking for his response.

COLTON

> I can't. I'm already at the office. We need to talk about yesterday, Marie. I am not happy with you or the little stunt that my brother pulled. Meet me for dinner tomorrow?

AVALON

> Yes, we do need to talk about yesterday. Dinner tomorrow will work.

Good... I miss you. I miss us...

I know he's probably waiting for me to respond with *I miss you too*, but that's not happening. I just can't lie and pretend anymore. The truth is, I stopped missing him months ago.

I WATCH FROM THE CORNER of my eye as Claudette walks around examining each of our stations. She always does this when she stops in for her three-hour inspection every Thursday and it drives us all crazy.

Madison bumps my shoulder, stopping me from sweeping. "Where were you last night? Please tell me you weren't with Colton."

I flash a fake smile when Claudette looks my way. "No," I whisper. "I'll tell you when Claudette leaves."

"You suck," she hisses.

"Madison," Claudette calls out. "Now would be a nice time to clean your station. Is it not?"

Madison huffs in my ear and backs away to her station. "On it."

The salon is pretty much uneventful for the next hour; everyone working like good little robots until Claudette finally walks out the door for the day.

"Oh thank God!" Madison screams, while plopping down in her chair. "I haven't had a client in thirty minutes and she expects me to just stand here like a damn stiff with a smile plastered on my face. How does her husband deal with her? She must give some damn good head."

A few of the other girls laugh and a couple of clients actually join in on the chuckling as well. It's no secret that no one here can stand Claudette. Even the regulars seem to steer clear when they know she'll be dropping in for her weekly inspection. I don't blame them, because I wish I could too, but unfortunately, being the manager doesn't allow me that pleasure.

Of course, as soon as I finish with my three o'clock appointment Madison jumps into my chair, waiting to hear my story about not coming home last night.

"I was at Royal's," I admit. "We had a few too many beers and I fell asleep outside by the pool. There. Happy?"

"I thought you went to Colton's parents' house for dinner last night? How the hell did you end up with Royal?"

I find myself smiling at the reminder; just thinking back to the way my heart skipped a beat when he walked through that door. "He showed up there and I left with him."

Madison's eyes widen in excitement. "Are you serious? That's hot." She rubs her hands together. "You showed up there with one brother and left with the other. The hotter brother might I add. My old Avalon is coming out to play."

I let out a frustrated breath and push her out of my chair. "Yeah, well maybe she never left. Maybe she was just trying her best to be good."

I'm so lost in talking to Madison that I don't even notice my uncle until Madison is undressing him with her eyes.

"Hey, Uncle Mark."

Leaning in, he kisses me on the side of the head, before taking a seat in my chair.

"Hope you have time for a quick cut. I've got a good five minutes or so before I get a call." He smiles at me, and then turns to Madison as she growls at him. "Nice to see you too, Madi."

"It's always a pleasure, Mr. Knight. You sure you don't want to take a seat in my chair?"

Rolling my eyes, I reach for the comb. "Stop flirting with my damn uncle. Didn't Claudette ask you to clean the merchandise before your shift ends?"

"And I will. The end of my shift isn't coming anytime soon, sweets."

Used to Madison ogling him, my uncle just laughs it off and looks at me through the mirror. "You staying out of trouble, Ava?" he asks as I start trimming the ends of his longish, brown hair.

"Yes. I'm a little too busy to rebel against the law these days, or have any kind of fun, actually."

"You sure about that, Ava?" Madison asks with a smirk. "You're definitely not too busy to ride on the back of that sexy man's motorcycle or fall asleep at his house."

My uncle looks up at me through the mirror with a surprised look. "No shit," he says with a crooked smile. "You and Colton break up?"

I glare over at Madison and point the scissors at her. "You... shut up. I'm not afraid to use these." I look at my uncle through the mirror. "And yes. Well, sort of. We're on a break, but I'm telling his ass tomorrow at dinner, and yes, I'm fine with it. It's been coming for a while."

I get ready to talk again, but Madison's big mouth interrupts me. "You're looking exceptionally well in that uniform today, Officer. Have you been working out in the nude or anything? I promise not to picture it." She winks.

He chuckles. "I'm guessing *you're* not staying out of trouble," he says to her. "Not that mouth of yours at least."

She leans over my desk. "Never, Officer."

"Seriously, Madison," I say irritated now. "He's my damn uncle. That's just weird, and creepy as shit."

"He's your young and very attractive uncle," she corrects. "How old are you now, Officer Knight?"

He pulls out his wallet and starts digging through it. "Thirty-three." He tosses me a few bills. "Here... You ladies buy some good dinner on me. Anything to keep you girls busy and out of trouble."

"No, thanks." I shove his money back at him as he stands up, but he just gives it to Madison instead, knowing that she'll take it with no problem.

Holding his hand up, Mark pulls out his phone and quickly answers it in a professional tone. "What's up, Liam? I'm just about to leave my niece's salon." He pauses and listens for a second. "Shit. Yeah, I'll be on my way there. No, I will handle it alone."

"Is everything alright?" I ask as he puts his phone away and steals a quick glance in the mirror to check out his hair.

"Yeah..." He lets out a frustrated breath. "Just some bar fight that I need to go deal with. Nothing new. I get this call at least once a week."

My heart sinks and the first thing I can think of is Royal's bar and wonder if something happened there. "And they're sending you there alone? Is it bad?"

He lifts a brow and starts backing away toward the door with a grin. "Someone's got to do it. I can handle it. That's why I'm the cool uncle. You girls be good."

With that, he turns and rushes out the door, jogging over to his car. Madison leans over her chair and shamelessly watches as he climbs inside and pulls out in a hurry.

She spins around in her chair to face me. "Damn... please tell me how your uncle gets hotter each time I see him? Did he get a new tattoo too?"

I nod my head. "Yeah, he did. Now stop thinking about fucking my uncle. Not happening."

She shrugs her shoulders. "Well your aunt isn't around anymore. I'm sure he gets lonely."

"I'm sure he doesn't," I admit. "He's a young—and from what you say—attractive officer. I'm sure he does fine."

"A girl can dream," she sighs.

I try to focus on cleaning up my station, but all I can seem to think about is Royal, and that has me wondering if my uncle is headed to *Savage & Ink.*

"Hey."

"Yeah.

"Do you think the fight my uncle is going to break up is at Royal's bar?"

Madison bites her lip and smiles. "Damn, I hope not. I'd like to be there when all that sexiness went down. Just saying…"

A part of me wants to text Royal and find out, but I decide against it after his distant attitude this morning. Maybe it's best if I just forget about him altogether.

Good fucking luck, Avalon. Looks like you're going to need it…

CHAPTER 13

ROYAL

KICKING MY FOOT BEHIND ME, I rest it on the side of the brick building, fighting off thoughts of last night.

Olivia's birthday is always the hardest for me. It kills me every single time that I have to go to our spot alone, but the thing that scared me more than anything was the fact that having Avalon with me eased just a small bit of that pain that was crushing my damn heart.

She has a way of getting to me unlike anyone else, and the more I'm around her the more I see it. Then she had to go and test me last night. I wanted nothing more than to fuck her into oblivion and bury myself so deep inside her pussy that she'd never be satisfied with another man touching her.

There's two reasons why that's the last thing that I should fucking do. One: my asshole brother has already been there. Two: I can't give her more than one night and the thought of only having her once is not enough.

I stick my cigarette between my lips, releasing it with my hand and take a long needed drag. I'm on edge today, and if I don't relax soon I'm going to lose my shit on the next fucker that even breathes in my direction.

Blaine rounds the corner and pulls a smoke out of his pocket, taking a spot next to me against the building. "I just heard some shit, man. You're not going to like this."

I grab my cigarette and pull it away from my lips, exhaling. "Then don't fucking tell me," I say stiffly. "I can't handle shit right now, man."

"It's about that dipshit Brian."

My ears instantly perk up at the sound of that fucker's name. "I'm listening."

Huffing, he shakes his head and stomps out his smoke. "I was tatting the back of Gage's big ass dome when Pete started running his fucking mouth, saying that fucktard was coming back to town next week. His ass stopped talking as soon as he saw me listening. Fuck! I walked away so I wouldn't scare his ass off before you got to him."

My heart starts racing as adrenaline pumps through my body, my blood boiling. I'm fucking heated. There's nothing I want more right now than to rip that fucker's heart out and feed it to him.

Tossing my cigarette down, I crack my neck and breathe in deeply, preparing for the explosion that I know is coming. "Yeah. Well, this motherfucker better be ready to talk, 'cause his ass ain't going nowhere until he does."

Brushing past Blaine I rush inside the bar, stopping at the door to look around for Pete's dirty ass.

"Fuck," he mutters and stands up from the bar when our eyes meet. He points at me. "Blaine is a little bitch. He has no idea what he heard. He's been smoking reefer all fucking morning."

"Is that fucking right?" Anger overtakes any rational thought that I have left and before I know it, I'm rushing at

Pete, flipping over the table in front of me, sending beer and shot glasses flying everywhere.

One of the guys from his MC tries stepping in front of me, but I pull out my knife, flipping it around and holding the blade to his throbbing neck.

His fists clench at his sides, but he steps away, keeping his eyes on me the whole time.

"Put that shit away, because I'm not telling you shit about my cousin." Pete stands up straight, tensing his jaw as I slide my knife away. I don't plan on using the shit unless I have to. I won't hesitate to kill a motherfucker for the lives I've lost.

Stopping in front of him, I swing my elbow out hard, connecting it with his jaw. Then I grab the back of his head, slamming it into the side of the bar.

I rotate my shoulders in anger as I look down at him, waiting for him to get up. "You're not going to tell me shit, huh, Pete?"

Standing up, he looks down at the blood on his leather vest, before wiping his thumb under his nose. "Fuck you. You really want to do this?"

He swings out, his fist connecting with my nose. With all the adrenaline pumping through me, I don't feel shit.

I wipe my nose off and tilt my head, tensing my jaw at him. I no longer give a shit about anything. That's not a good thing for him. I don't give a shit who he rides with.

Grabbing him by the jacket, I throw him across the top of the pool table, before wrapping my arm around his neck and squeezing as hard as I can without killing the fucker.

He grabs at my arm, fighting me off, before reaching for a ball and attempting to swing it at the side of my head. I dodge it and swing my right elbow into his nose twice, before releasing him.

"I called the cops," a woman yells out from the door, holding her phone up for us to see.

I nod my head at Blaine. "Get her the fuck out of here."

Blaine shakes his head at the woman and backs her out of the door, shutting it behind her. Then he leans against it. "Proceed, brother."

Running my hand through my bloody hair, I reach for the nearest beer and slam it back, before tossing it across the room.

"We're not done, Pete."

"Fuck off, crazy motherfucker."

I let out a slightly crazy laugh, while reaching for my knife and rubbing it across my palm, before running my thumb across the blade as he walks away. Maybe the fucker is right. I'm a crazy son of a bitch and I stopped caring a long time ago.

I nod at Blaine to move and wait until Pete is right in front of the door, before throwing the knife as hard as I can and watching as it sticks through the door, grazing his fucking ear.

He grabs his ear and quickly dodges out of the way, cussing as he looks up at the knife. "Fuck! You've lost your shit."

I start walking at him fast, eyeing down his guys on the way to him. Kane, the biggest one, stands up straight and flashes his gun at me. "I'd be careful, Royal. Don't make me fucking use this. You know I got that asshole's back no matter what kind of shit he gets in."

Blaine pushes away from the wall and opens his jacket, flashing two guns, before grabbing his dick. "I'm packing everywhere, motherfucker. Don't test me."

Our attention gets drawn away as police sirens blast right outside the door as a warning.

"Fuck!" Blaine yells out. "Everyone, be cool."

Knowing that I'm fucked on getting any info from Pete at the moment, I walk behind the bar and pour a shot of Jack, before slamming it back right as Officer Knight walks through the door.

He turns around and looks at my knife sticking out of the door, before turning to me. "Did you lose something?"

Flexing my jaw, I watch him with distant eyes as I pour another shot and bring it to my lips, just wanting a way to escape.

Mark pulls his eyes away from me and looks around, stopping on Pete when he sees the blood covering his face. "Get the fuck out of here before I have to arrest someone. Shit."

Pete points at me, while wiping his hand over his face. "Another time." Then him and his guys gather up their shit and exit the bar, leaving me with a bad taste in my mouth and not just from the blood. I have a feeling they're going to get in my fucking way when it counts.

Mark examines the messy bar; looking around quietly at the broken glasses and splattered blood, not stopping until we hear Pete and his bitches pull off on their motorcycles.

He just shakes his head in disbelief and walks over to the bar, taking a seat across from me. "Are you shitting me? It's not even five yet and you're already throwing knives?"

I slam my empty shot glass down and grip the edge of the bar to keep my shit in check. I want nothing more than to storm out that door and get the info I seek. "What can I say, Officer Knight. I've had a shitty fucking day. I wanted to play and have a little fun."

He leans over the bar to talk quietly, even though the only people that remain are Blaine, two older regulars, and myself; none of which couldn't care less about the drama that just went down. They see that shit and worse, every other week.

"One day it's not going to be me that they send. It's going to be some *asshole* cop trying to be brave and prove a point that puts you in cuffs. Remember that shit before you end up in a cell."

I release my grip on the bar and stand up straight, rubbing my middle finger over my left eyebrow. "I'm in hell no matter where I'm at," I say stiffly.

Mark gives me a somewhat sympathetic look and stands up

to leave. "Just don't make me come back here again today. I'm going to get my ass handed to me if I don't take someone with me next time. Got it?"

I lift a brow at him. "You know it, Officer."

He turns to walk away.

"Hey."

He stops walking and turns around.

"How's the new ink?"

Smiling, he lifts his arm, showing off the eagle I put there last week. "It's as good as it was when you put it there."

I nod my head. "Alright. See you in a few weeks for the next one?"

He laughs. "No one's better than you. That's why you better keep your ass on the outside world. I can't finish this sleeve with you behind bars, taking out every asshole that looks in your direction."

I give him a half-ass smile. It's about all I can manage right now. "Good. Now get the fuck out of my bar."

"On it. I've got other shit to do anyway. Real criminals to deal with."

Blaine pats him on the back and nods at him as he walks past him and out the door.

He waits a few seconds before turning to me and pulling out a cigarette. "What the fuck you going to do about Brian?"

I walk out from behind the bar and take a seat on top of one of the tables, bringing a bottle with me. "What I have to do." I tilt back the bottle of whiskey and then hold it between my legs, clenching it as tightly as I can. "As soon as I find the fucker... he's dead."

CHAPTER 14

AVALON

I LOOK UP FROM MY uncle Mark's huge TV when I finally notice him leaning over the couch above me, repeating my name.

"Huh? Were you saying something?" I look up with wide eyes and shake my head as I take in his amused expression. "What?" I ask again.

He laughs and walks around to plop down on the couch next to me, nudging me with his elbow. "It's your day off, kid. Why in the world are you here on my couch, eating my chips?"

I smile back at him and try to pretend to act normal. "Oh... no reason. It's just been a while since we've hung out. That's all. I figured you could use the company."

"Seriously? More like I could use some sleep. I feel like I haven't seen my pillow in days." He grabs the bowl of chips out of my hand and starts digging in, eyeing me over curiously. "Have you heard from your mom? She said she was going to call you when she got back from California."

Annoyed, I shake my head. I don't even know why he bothered with that question when we both already know the answer. "Does she ever *really* call? Come on. She's too busy dealing with her perfect little life and current fuck to worry about her only daughter." I roll my eyes and grab a handful of chips, eating out of the palm of my hand. "I could be dead in a gutter for all she knows."

"I would never allow that to happen. She knows that." Mark gives me a look of sympathy. "She's always been selfish, Avalon. It's nothing personal toward you. Trust me. I dealt with her for fourteen years, until the day she moved out of your grandparents' house. She wasn't easy having as an older sister." He stands up and hands the bowl back to me. "Why do you think she can't keep a guy around for longer than a few months? The woman is annoying as shit."

We both smile.

"And because she sucks at communicating," I say matter-of-factly. "Very much."

"Exactly." He pulls out his phone when it goes off in his pocket. "Shit. I should take this. I'll be back."

"Alright." I turn back to the TV and try to get back into my show when Mark disappears into the hallway to take his call.

The real reason I'm here is because Madison is at work and I didn't want to be alone in my thoughts all day. I tried for a few hours this morning and *all* I could think about was picking up my phone and messaging Royal to ask him why he was such a dick. Yes, things got a little sexual between us. We were both drinking and vulnerable. That's it. There's nothing to be mad about.

I haven't spoken to him since he dropped me off at my car the other day and for some reason, that bothers me. I've gone days without talking to Colton before and have *never* felt this way.

I figured if I spend most of the day at my uncle's that he could at least keep me busy so I won't give into this silly temptation to make a fool of myself. I don't even want Royal to know that he's crossed my mind since the other day.

Mark appears back in the living room about ten minutes later, looking more exhausted than he did when he walked away. He looks down at me on the couch and rubs his hands over his face, clearly tired. "I need sleep. Lots of it. You're welcome to stay here until your dinner with Colton tonight, but if you bother me I'll cuff your ass and shove you in the back of my police car until I wake back up."

A small smile appears on his tired face and I can't help but to smile back.

This man is who I take after. He's the one that I've grown up with since I was fifteen, and he's more family to me than my mother ever will be. I love him for that and am lucky to have him around. I don't know where I'd be without him.

"Just go to sleep, Mark. I know you need it." I look up at the clock on the wall and grunt when I notice the time. As much as I don't want to see Colton, it has to be done, and I'm the lucky lady to do it. "I have to meet Colton in less than an hour anyway. I'll clean my mess and lock up on the way out."

"Good luck. Just do me a favor."

I stand up and wipe my hands off on my jeans. "Yeah?"

"Make sure you get it on video if he cries. The guys at the station would get a kick out of that."

"Seriously!"

He nods his head. "Dead serious."

"Why does everyone think he'll cry? Does he really come off as that much of a pussy, Mark?" He nods again. "That's it. I'm done with pretty boys. No more."

"I'm surprised you dealt with that one for as long as you have. I just hope this guy on the Harley that Madison was talking about isn't bad news. You've been so good for the last couple of years and I'd hate to see you mess up because of some guy. I'm up for you having fun and dating a tough guy instead of that pussy, but if he hurts you, I'll have to kill him. Arresting him might not be enough."

My heart instantly flutters at the mention of Royal. He's definitely bad news; every single inch of his beautifully tattooed flesh, and I want nothing more than to run my tongue across it.

I clear my throat and close my eyes, mad that I'm letting my thoughts go there. "There's nothing going on with Harley dude, so there's nothing to worry about. Ignore Madison. She's crazy and we both know it." I wave my arms at him to move him along to his room. I suddenly don't need his company anymore and can't wait to escape him. "Now, get your beauty rest. You look a hot mess. I'll be fine."

"Better be," he says while crinkling his forehead. "Don't forget to lock the door. I'm passing the hell out while I have the chance."

"Got it," I mutter. "I'll call you tomorrow and let you know what happened."

I wait until my uncle disappears into his bedroom, before cleaning up my mess and locking the door on my way out.

Jumping into my car, I toss my purse into the passenger seat and look over at it. Then I start my jeep and look back over at it again, losing my willpower.

"Ah... screw it."

I reach into my purse and grab my phone out, typing out a quick message to Royal.

AVALON

Your cold attitude wasn't necessary yesterday. No worries... I plan to keep my distance.

Letting out a long breath, my shoulders relax a bit as I look down at the message being sent. As soon as it goes through, I toss my phone back over to the passenger seat and head home.

I don't check my phone again until after I take a quick

shower and throw on my favorite pair of holey jeans and a thin, black top that hangs off my right shoulder. I don't have to impress Colton anymore and it feels so good showing him that.

When I unlock my phone, my stomach does flips at the sight of Royal's name along with three missed texts.

ROYAL

It was more necessary than you know, Avalon…

I almost lost my shit with you and I'm not sure you can handle it.

Where are you at right now?

Swallowing, I hit the box to his last message and stare at my phone, going crazy inside, as I try to come up with a response. Just the thought of replying has my heart racing so hard that I can feel it pulsing in my fingertips.

I let out a small breath when my phone starts vibrating in my hand to a call from Colton. That's when I realize the time. Colton has never been a patient man.

"I'm on my way," I say quickly into the phone. "Walking out the door now."

"I'll be waiting," he responds. "I'm already seated at a table so try to hurry so I don't look like a lonely idiot, please."

"I'll try my best," I mumble. "Gotta go so I can drive." I hang up before he can respond.

Feeling anxious, I decide now is not the best time to reply to Royal's messages, so I lock the screen and quickly shove my phone in my purse.

Plus, I still have no idea how to respond, but his words definitely have my heart going crazy with curiosity. Everything he does and says does.

THE LAST TWENTY MINUTES HAS been nothing short of awkward, as we've sat here making small talk. I decided to wait until after we order our food, so I can at least get some delicious food inside my stomach before ruining our little dinner date. We just got done placing our orders about five minutes ago.

"So..." Colton says over the top of his water glass. "Did it feel good to have my brother's fingers inside of you at my parents' dinner?"

Slamming my glass of soda down, I look him in the eyes. "Yes," I admit. "Did it feel good to fuck your partner the other night and probably many other nights before that?"

His body stiffens and he anxiously fixes the collar of his black shirt. "There is nothing going on with Misty." He tries to sound convincing, but completely fails. His guilty blue eyes give him away.

"Let's not sit here and pretend that we have a chance of us working out, Colton."

We both smile up at the waitress as she drops our food off and asks us if we need anything else. She walks away when we both shake our heads.

"And why is that?" He watches me with hard eyes as I dig into my chicken alfredo. "Because you're fucking my filthy brother and probably getting gangbanged by his tatted up, biker friends? Is that the kind of shit you like now?"

Taking Royal's approach, I do my best to stay calm. That seemed to really work Colton up at dinner a few nights ago, and pissing him off as much as I possibly can has just become my fucking goal now. I *was* going to play it as nice as I could. "Not yet." I look up and flash him a smile, before taking another bite of my food. "I'm waiting until I can get Royal, Jax, and Blaine at the same time. The other boys were busy the other night."

Leaning over the table, he slams his fist down. "Dammit..."

He looks around to be sure no one's watching, before continuing. "I'm sorry. I know you're not sleeping with Royal. You're smarter than that. I'm just upset because I want you back with me. This break is not working for me. I'm completely stressed without you."

"Am I too smart for that though?" I question, ignoring everything he has just said. "What is your deal with Royal that you think you're so much better than him?"

He lets out a dickish laugh, as if the answer to that is obvious. "Look at him, Avalon. Open your pretty little eyes and look. He's dangerous, twisted in the head, and doesn't care about anything around him. He will hurt anyone that gets in his way. You have no idea of the shit he's done in the past; shit so fucking dark that I don't even want to bring it up."

"That's the past," I point out. "He's not going to hurt me. In fact..." I stand up and lean over the table. "He's done nothing but try to keep me safe. When I'm with him, he gives me his full attention. He doesn't let me out of his sight, which is the total opposite of you. All you've tried to do for the last four months is keep me at a distance and pretend like I'm not even in the same room."

"That's not fair," he complains. "You know damn well that my job keeps me busy." He reaches across the table and grabs my hands. "Stay away from my brother and come to my place. You can stay there every night if you want to. Hell, you can even move in."

A feeling of discomfort takes over as he rubs his thumbs across the tops of my hands. His touch is making me feel sick to my stomach. "Colton." I pull my hands away and sit back down to get away from him. "I don't want that. We're done."

"No," he says while jumping to his feet and rushing over to my side of the table. "Don't do this to us. You're going to regret it."

He desperately reaches for my hands and attempts to pull

me to my feet. "Don't touch me, Colton." I keep trying to sit back down, but he keeps pulling at me to stand up, his grip on my wrists tightening. "Let go, asshole!"

Out of instinct, I lift my knee and connect it to his balls. He instantly releases my wrists and doubles over, holding his precious jewels. "Shiiit!"

"Fuck you, asshole." I reach for my purse and lean in close to his ear. "Don't ever put your hands on me again. You never did know how to touch me right."

I look around me and take a deep breath when I notice everyone watching us. "I'm leaving. Just eat your damn food," I say harshly.

Shaking, I rush out the door and jump into my jeep, slamming the door behind me.

I'm so pissed off right now that all I want to do is choke Colton and scream at the top of my lungs.

Right now, I feel stupid for ever dating someone like him in the first place. Him and that Misty bitch belong together. I never belonged in his world. I just wished I saw that earlier.

Not giving two shits about anything at the moment, I pull out my phone and start typing.

AVALON

I need to see you. I'm on my way to your house.

A small wave of relief washes over me at the thought of seeing Royal. I have no idea what's to come of it, but it's the only thing I want to do right now and there's no way I can fight it.

I need to see this man's beautiful, broken face, and I don't care at what cost...

CHAPTER 15

ROYAL

PUSHING MY BLACK HOOD BACK, I run a hand through my sweaty hair and pull my last cigarette out of the pack, before tossing the empty package in the backseat.

With tired eyes, I scope out the dump in front of me, while bringing the cigarette to my lips and lighting it, in hopes of calming my nerves a bit. I'm getting anxious, really fucking anxious, and my patience is running low.

I've been sitting across the street from Pete's house, chilling in my truck for the last thirty minutes, and counting down the minutes until he arrives. I know that stupid fuck will be here soon, and I plan on surprising him with a little visit before he can disappear and hide out.

He gets off work at seven o'clock on the dot and arrives home a quarter after. I've done my research. His club might protect him when they're in his presence, because they have no other choice, but that doesn't do shit for him when he's alone and in my hands.

Taking another long drag, I watch as Pete's broken down Dodge Neon pulls into the driveway.

My heart instantly comes alive with adrenaline and my blood starts pumping as I watch him jump out of the brown shitbox and slam the rusty door shut. For being a mechanic he sure as shit doesn't put any of his skills into fixing his own car...

I wait until he's pulling out his keys to unlock the house door before I step out of my truck and crack my neck, tossing my cigarette across the yard.

Walking fast, I rush up the steps in three long strides and place my foot in the door, right as he's attempting to close it.

"Ah fuck!" Pete pushes against the door to close it when he notices it's me, but quickly realizes that he's fucked and I'm not going anywhere. "Crazy, dark motherfucker."

Lifting a brow, I stand up straight and kick his door open, sending him flying back to land on the floor. "I'm crazy as hell." I cock a brow as I look down at him. "The devil is in my veins and he's about to come out and play."

Slamming the door shut, I lock it behind me and grab his neck, pulling him up to his feet. I swing out my fist, connecting it to his mouth, then swing again before he can even recover.

Cussing, he grabs his jaw and stumbles back, attempting to back away from me. "Are you fucking serious? In my own damn house."

"Dead fucking serious," I say tightly. "I suggest you tell me what the fuck I need to know." I pull out my knife and rub my thumb across the blade. "Or you'll be riding that piece of shit bike one handed for a while."

He picks up an empty beer bottle and tosses it at my head, missing. "Shit!" He jumps over his couch and quickly falls to the floor to reach underneath it.

I wasn't born yesterday. I know he's packing and most likely keeps an extra there for quick access.

I spin my knife around and kneel down, stabbing it through his hand before he can pull his gun out.

He screams out in pain and grabs at the knife with his good hand. "Fuck me! Shit! Shit! Take it out!"

Pinning his free hand under my boot, I grab the knife handle and slightly twist it, leaning close to his greasy face. "Tell me when the fuck Brian is coming, you stupid piece of shit!"

He doesn't say anything, so I push down on the knife, making him scream out again as blood gushes from his shaking hand. "Okay!" he screams. "Okay. Okay." He closes his eyes and takes a few small breaths. "All I know is that he's coming to town either next week or the week after. He'll be around for a few days visiting some old friends."

I suck in a deep breath and slowly release it. My whole body is screaming to cut his fucking heart out. "That's all you know, Petey?" I grab the handle tighter and pretend to twist it again.

He instantly cries out and starts squirming below me. "Yes! I swear. That's all he said."

Leaning my head back, I growl out, before ripping the knife out of his hand and standing up.

Pete rolls over and cradles his fucked up hand in his slightly less fucked up hand. "He'll be contacting me once he gets to town. I know he'll stop by at some point to visit. Fuck this shit. Brian can fuck off now." He grabs his hand tighter and crawls to his knees in pain. "Fuck!"

"I'll be watching. Thanks for the info, asshole." I wipe my blade off on his dirty brown couch, before letting myself out and shutting the door behind me.

I jump back inside my truck and look around for a cigarette, punching the steering wheel when I remember that I'm out.

"Shit!"

I run both of my hands through my hair and look over

toward the passenger seat when I notice the light on my phone blinking.

I'm surprised as shit to see who the message is from. I almost don't open it, but realize that I can't stop my fingers from moving.

> I need to see you. I'm on my way to your house.

I read her message a few times, taking in her use of words. She *needs* to see me... I get a small ache in my chest at the thought of her needing me.

My heart sinks when I look at the time, noticing that it's been almost an hour since she sent the message.

Without taking the time to reply, I drop my phone into my lap and grip the steering wheel to get my thoughts in check.

My plan was to stay far away from her so there's no chance of pulling her into my hell, but the thought of her waiting for me has me pulling off and heading toward my house like an idiot, hoping that she's still there.

Fuck. If you're smart... you'll be gone.

CHAPTER 16

AVALON

I STARE UP AT THE night sky while taking a bite of my Snickers bar and replaying tonight's dinner in my head. I'm still so heated over our conversation and the way he handled me.

The thought of me *ever* seeing something in Colton makes me angry with myself. It's embarrassing that I dealt with him for as long as I did and makes me feel like an idiot.

He was full of himself and always did well at making me feel as if I wasn't good enough. I just looked past it for too long.

Well I'm done now...

I look down at my phone when it buzzes in my hand. Yes, I've been holding it, waiting for a response from Royal. My heart does a little happy dance, but then drops to my stomach when I see that it's Madison and not Royal like I was hoping it'd be.

Holding the candy bar with my mouth to free both hands, I open her text and read it.

MADISON

Please tell me you didn't change your mind
and you're still with that douche face. Please!

AVALON

Colton is long gone... I'm sitting outside of
Royal's house, waiting for him to get home. If
he's not back soon, then I'm coming home.
You there?

MADISON

Oh damn! If you're outside of Royal's house...
I better not see your ass for a long time. That
man is... I don't even need to say it. You're not
blind. Not anymore at least. If you leave before
he gets home I will dropkick you.

AVALON

Ha! Ha! Funny... I would love to see you try,
short ass. BUT you're right. I had to have been
blind to deal with Colton's shit for as long as
I did.

MADISON

Fuck yes! And STUPID... so tell me... Did he
pee his pants or at least cry this time?
crosses fingers

AVALON

Unfortunately... no. But yours truly did knee
him in the balls. So... you're WELCOME!

MADISON

YES! My life is complete now.

Smiling from Madison's last message, I look up from my
phone when I hear a truck coming down the long driveway. My
heart begins racing.

"Please be Royal. Please be Royal," I chant softly, while
standing up to get a better look.

My heart about leaps out of my chest with excitement when

I see that it's Royal's black truck, but then quickly sinks at the realization that he may not even want me here.

I sent him a message over an hour ago and he never responded. He may not even be expecting me to be here.

Grabbing my candy bar from my mouth, I wrap it back up the best I can and watch as he exits his truck, slamming the door behind him.

He stands on the other side of the truck for a few minutes, before his feet start moving.

The first thing that I notice as he steps around his truck is that he's wearing a black hoodie and his hands are stained in what looks like dried blood. The second thing I notice as the blue lighting hits his face is that the area underneath both of his eyes is bruised and slightly swollen.

I toss my Snickers aside and rush down the porch in a panic, my whole body screaming to take care of him and pull him into my arms in comfort.

Instead, I stop in front of him and gently run my fingers over his beautiful face as he stands there breathing heavily.

"Holy shit, Royal. What happened to you? Are you okay?"

He looks at me, his eyes tearing into my soul, paralyzing me. All I feel in this moment is his pain and suffering, and it feels like my heart is being ripped from my chest. Only Royal has the power to make me feel so damn much from one single look.

"My hell is what happened. Nothing that you should be concerned with."

Swallowing, I pull my hands away from his face and drop them to my sides. I'm afraid to know this next part, but ask it anyway. "Did you hurt someone?"

My heart beats wildly against my rib cage, waiting for an answer. "Not as much as he deserved."

Seeing the pain in his eyes is enough for me to understand,

and I find my words coming out without me thinking. "You shouldn't have stopped then."

His eyes widen a bit as if he wasn't expecting my response, and he slowly starts walking at me. Unable to pull my eyes away from his, I walk backwards, stepping back every time he steps forward, until I'm pressed against the door.

He brings his bloodied hands up to press against the door, pinning me in. Then he leans in until his lips are hovering above mine, only a small breath away. His voice is thick with emotion as he stares into my eyes and speaks. "You think I should have kept going?"

I nod my head and grab both of his arms, squeezing them through the thick fabric. "If he hurt you, then yes."

He breathes against my lips, causing me to tilt my head and brush my lips against his, wanting to taste him.

"What did you need me for? Did someone hurt you?" he questions in a tensed voice.

I shake my head. "I just had dinner with Colton and broke it off for good. The only thing I could think of as I was rushing out of there was coming here."

He moves his body closer to mine, bringing his arms against the side of my head. His smell is so damn hypnotic, bringing me to close my eyes. "Yeah... and how did he take it?"

Doesn't he realize how hard it is to talk with him this close? He looks and smells too good to be true.

"He wasn't happy," I admit. "He wanted me to stay with him, but when I refused he grabbed my wrists and kept trying to force me against him."

Royal's jaw tenses and his gray eyes darken as he scans my face. "So he did fucking hurt you?"

I smile small to show him that I'm okay. "When he wouldn't let go I kneed him in the balls. The fucker got my message loud and clear. He was holding his junk and whining when I left."

Royal's lips turn up into a half smile, making my insides melt from the beauty. "Good."

He finally backs away from me and digs in his pocket, pulling out a set of keys. After he unlocks the door, he turns to me. "You ready for that other tattoo?" He motions for me to walk inside first. "I could use the distraction."

"Me too. I'm more than ready." I walk inside first, stopping and waiting for him to shut the door behind him and lead the way.

"Go downstairs. Wait for me in my room." He yanks his hoodie over his head, pulling it off, and looks down at his dirty hands. "I need to shower first and wash this shit away."

I look at his firm chest, pressing against his black tee, and swallow. It fits him so damn well, and looks extremely sexy, showing off his sculpted, inked arms. "Take your time," I breathe softly.

Pulling his eyes away, he turns and walks away, pulling his shirt over his head, before jogging up the stairs to the top floor.

I wait until he disappears before walking down the hall and into the kitchen in search of some water or something to drink. My mouth suddenly feels extremely dry.

"Whoa!" I cover my face with my hand and back into the wall when I see Jax's firm ass, flexing as he fucks some leggy chick on the kitchen table. "Shit! I'm sorry."

Jax laughs and keeps going about his business as if he couldn't care less. "What you looking for, babe?"

I peek around my hand to see Jax roll his hips and then thrust forward hard as shit, making the redhead scream out and grip the table. "I was just thirsty. I'll go."

"There's shit in the fridge. You're not bothering us," he says with a slight growl as he pounds into her again and turns away from me.

"I'm good." I back out of the kitchen and rush down the hall, feeling embarrassed that I just witnessed Jax fucking.

"Oh. My. Goodness."

It was hot; extremely hot, I admit, and definitely not something that I've ever walked in on before. Well, I did walk in on Madison once, but they were both under the covers.... Thank God, but Jax... hot damn.

Catching my breath, I walk down the stairs to the cool basement and let myself into Royal's bedroom. I look around in curiosity as I take in his oversized bed that I slept in not too long ago.

The memory of that night causes my heart to beat wildly in my chest. My body is still aching for him to touch me since he refused to that night, but I quickly shake off the thought and plop down in the middle of his bed to wait for him.

Everything in his room is either black or gray. There's a black chair that sits next to his bed, and across from his bed is a black, leather couch with gray pillows.

Grabbing the remote off the nightstand, I turn on the huge TV that's hanging on the wall above the couch and turn it on to keep me distracted.

When I go to place the remote back, I notice a black knife. Letting my hands wander, I pick it up and look at it, trying to imagine what Royal uses it for. Oddly, it sends a surge of excitement through me.

About twenty minutes later, Royal walks into his room, shirtless with a pair of sweats hanging low on his narrow hips. I can't turn my eyes away as he stands there just looking at me.

His body and hair are still wet, as if he just jumped out of the shower and got dressed without even bothering to dry off first. It's a glorious sight to take in, and all I want to do is run my tongue over his slick body and lick the water off. Screw the bottle of water I was searching for when I walked in on Jax. This looks much more fulfilling.

"You comfortable in my bed, Darlin'?" he asks while walking closer to me. His eyes land on the knife in my hand, but he doesn't say another word as he watches me play with it.

I swallow and nod my head. "Yeah. It's really soft. I like it. Oh and by the way, I would probably wash the kitchen table before you decide to eat a meal from it."

"Yeah, Jax will take care of it." He looks me over as if he was expecting me to be gone by the time he got out of the shower. "You're not scared to be in here alone with me?"

I sit up straight and meet his eyes. "I'm not afraid of you, Royal. I couldn't care less about anything your brother has said. You're not twisted... you're just hurting."

With purposeful steps he walks over to the bed and grabs my legs, pulling me to him, and positioning himself between my legs. "Yeah..." He brushes his lips over mine and tangles his hand in my hair, causing me to moan. "What if I told you that I stabbed a knife through a man's hand tonight and didn't feel one bit of remorse as he screamed out in pain? Would you still say I'm not twisted? I'm a slave to darkness, Avalon, and all I feel is pain. Nothing more."

I shake my head and wrap my arms around his neck—still holding the knife—afraid that he'll pull away from me. "There's a darkness inside your eyes that tells me you're fighting demons, that you're driven by the pain and not willing to give up until you feel the peace you're seeking. It's part of being human. Fighting is the only thing you *can* do. Pain is part of who we all are."

He closes his eyes and pulls me closer to him, wrapping my legs around his waist. "You don't know the demons that drag me down. They're darker than you think."

I lean in and kiss his closed eyes, before wrapping my hand in his hair and whispering, "Not dark enough to make me want to leave." It's the honest truth too. The last thing I want to do is leave.

This man truly has no idea how drawn I am to him. The rush he makes me feel keeps me wanting more of him.

With raw need in his eyes, he crawls onto the bed, pulling me below him. After he's positioned between my legs, he sits up straight and brings the knife in my hand to his chest, slowly moving the blade down his body, slightly cutting himself.

His eyes close and he tilts his head back when I pull the knife away and my free hand wipes away the drop of blood before tracing every hard muscle, leading down to the V that disappears into his low hanging sweats.

"It feels so fucking good when you touch me." He opens his eyes and tilts his head down to look at me. With dark eyes, he brings my hand up to run the knife across his neck, before pulling it out of my hand. "So touch me."

He releases my hands and growls out as I slowly tug on his sweats, but stop before pulling them down. I've never been so nervous in my life.

"I need you to feel me," he says tensely. "Every part of me, and none of me is good."

"I don't believe that," I admit.

Locking eyes with me, he balls his fists into my hair and slams his lips against mine, kissing me so damn hard that the air gets knocked right out of me.

He bites my bottom lip, pulling on it with his teeth, before he runs his tongue over it and then sucks it into his mouth.

His kiss is so intense; almost hungry as his lips devour mine, and I haven't been able to catch my breath yet. I don't need to. All I need is to feel his mouth on me.

Pulling away from the kiss, he roughly grabs the top of my shirt, cutting it open with his knife.

Admiring my breasts, he wraps his free hand around my throat and squeezes, before gently running the tip of the blade between my breasts and cutting my bra off. I suck in a breath and hold it as he gently runs the blade over my bare flesh, my nipples instantly hardening as it grazes against the sensitive skin.

My legs tremble with need as he slowly lowers the knife down my body, cutting the button off my jeans. My whole body is craving for this rough, dark man to take me. A knife has never turned me on so much.

Tossing the knife aside, he yanks my jeans down my legs roughly, and then my panties, before flipping me over and slapping my ass, hard.

His fingers wrap into the back of my hair and pull as his other hand reaches around to grip my throat again. His heavy breathing caresses my ear as he presses his lips against it. "Fuck! You'll never understand the darkness in me until I show you. You want to feel it? No part of me is gentle. I can promise you that. You really want to be hurt by me?"

I suck in a deep breath and close my eyes as his hand releases my throat. "Physically, yes. In this bed right now, yes. I want nothing more right now."

He growls and pushes my head down into the mattress, before slapping my ass and then biting it. He bites it so damn hard, making me scream and bite down on the blanket.

An aching pleasure runs throughout my body, causing me to tremble as he inches his way down my body and then up my inner thigh, biting down close to my pussy. This man's mouth does things to me. "Royal," I say breathlessly. "I want your mouth on me. I want to feel you."

I moan out as his tongue slides up my pussy, slowly and teasingly, before he stops and pulls away. "You're going to get my mouth and so much more," he moans. "I've warned you."

Fuck... that moan is so sexy; so deep, rough, and raw.

His tongue works slowly at first, causing me to moan out, wanting more of his perfect fucking mouth. His rhythm is precise and in control, as if he knows the exact way to work me up and pleasure me. I've never felt something so good in my life, and the thought of him stopping makes me want to scream.

I need this man touching me, every single inch of me, before I explode. I want all of him. His darkness included.

I arch my back and moan out loudly as he slides his tongue down further and shoves it into my pussy as deep as it will go. He's fucking me with his tongue and the feel and the thought is enough to almost bring me to climax.

Slipping his tongue out, he slides it down and over my clit before sucking it into his mouth. It feels so good that I grip onto the blankets and scream out as my orgasm rocks through me in intense waves. "Oh shit... I can't..." I pant.

I feel him moving behind me, working on pulling his sweats off, before I hear the nightstand open as he pulls out a condom.

Next thing I know, he reaches around and grips my throat, hard, pulling me up flat against his chest. His hold on my throat tightens right before I feel the coolness of his blade graze across my sensitive skin. "Are you sure you can handle all of me?"

I nod my head. "Yes..."

He presses the blade a little harder against my throat, but not hard enough to cut me. "The darkness included?"

"Yes," I whisper.

I swallow and he removes the knife. "Fuck, Avalon. You asked for it."

Closing my eyes, I hold my breath to prepare for his entrance. I know it's going to hurt, but I don't want him to think that I want him to stop if I scream.

I feel the tip of his dick slide across my entrance, before he bites my neck and slams into me hard; so fucking hard that I bite my bottom lip, drawing blood.

His tongue works my neck, easing the pain from his bite, as he pulls out and thrusts back into me, even harder. "You feel better than I imagined," he growls. "So fucking good. Come here."

Tilting my neck back further, he runs his tongue over my mouth, before sucking my bloody lip into his mouth as he rolls his hips, making me moan into his mouth.

He pulls away from the kiss and licks his lips, no doubt tasting my blood. As weird as it is, it turns me on more. He's so rough and unfiltered and I love it. It's a complete turn on and so different from anything I've experienced.

Both of his arms wrap around my body, him pulling me as closely as possible as he thrusts into me repeatedly.

Pounding into me hard, he grabs my throat and pulls my neck back. He's holding it so tightly that I can barely breathe for a minute, until his grip loosens and he growls out in frustration at the realization of him almost choking me.

I scream out in a mixture of pleasure and pain, only causing him to go faster and harder. I don't want him to stop being rough. I want to feel what's inside this man.

"Fuuuck!" he yells out, while picking me up and carrying me out of bed and over to the wall.

I grab his hair and moan out as he slams me against the wall and buries himself deep between my legs. "Deeper," I growl against his lips.

He pushes in deep and stops. His heavy breathing caresses my mouth as he looks me in the eyes and wraps his hand around my throat again. "Like this?"

I lean my head against the wall and scream. "Yes!"

"Grab my hair and hold on," he demands.

I tangle my right hand into his glorious hair again and hold on as he pounds into me fast and hard. So fucking hard.

"I'm about to come..." I yank his hair, causing him to shove in as deep as he can go. "Royal!" I scream out as my body shakes in his strong arms, as another orgasm shakes me to my core.

He waits until I'm done, before placing his forehead to

mine. He keeps it there, while slowly pulling out of me and then slowly thrusting back in. "Fuck! I can't hold back."

Placing his hand at the back of my neck, he presses his lips against mine, before rolling his hips and then fucking me as fast and hard as he can.

His teeth dig into my bottom lip, causing me to scream out as he releases himself inside of me. His roughness is such a turn on that the pain is the least of my worries.

Breathing heavily, he runs his tongue over my lips, before pulling me away from the wall and laying me back down on the bed.

His eyes look into mine for a few moments of silence, before he slowly pulls out of me and turns around, baring his beautiful ass to me.

"Why don't you take a shower and clean the sweat off of you." He runs a hand through his hair and lets out a long breath. "Then meet me in the room across the hall for that tattoo."

My heart sinks as he walks out of his room, leaving me alone. My whole body is aching for him to come back even though deep inside I know it probably won't end well for me.

"Holy shit..." I pant. "What the hell just happened?"

I run my hand over my face and then look up at the doorway to see him standing there, watching me. "Grab some clean clothes out of my dresser. You're staying here tonight."

He disappears again, leaving me alone in my mixed-up thoughts.

This man is going to ruin me, but I have a feeling that after tonight, nothing will be able to keep me away...

CHAPTER 17

ROYAL

SHIT! WHAT THE FUCK...

My heart is racing. My body is full of sweat, and all I can smell is her sweet fucking scent, intoxicating me. She's not even in the same room with me, yet she's fucking surrounding me, making it hard to breathe.

I knew without a doubt that if she was still here by the time I got back, waiting at my door, that I'd give in and *fucking* take her. There's too much shit running through my head, locking me inside my fucked up mind, and a release was far past needed. I was just hoping it wouldn't have to be *her*.

But her words... They had to go and fuck with me and give me a reason to have to bury myself so deep inside her that it hurt. I wanted her to feel me. She needed to see the darkness in me, yet she's still fucking here.

Anyone else would've been scared and ran off after I told them what I did tonight. Not her though. She thinks I should have kept going, and fuck, I wanted to.

Running a hand through my wet hair, I grab the bar above

my head and do pull ups, fast and hard, until every muscle in my arms ache and my chest feels as if it's going to burst from my racing heartbeat.

Dropping from the bar, I shake my sweaty hair out and walk over to my stash of liquor, tilting back the first bottle that I can grab. I close my eyes as it burns my throat, giving me the pain that I need.

Standing with my bottle, I wait until I hear the shower water turn off before I walk back into my room to find a pair of jeans and an old shirt to throw on.

Leaning forward, I grip the dresser until my knuckles turn white. I have the urge to rip this motherfucker apart and destroy it. My thoughts are messing with me again, knowing that I have less than two weeks before I get to hopefully find some kind of peace. I know I won't find much, but killing that son of a bitch has to bring some. It's the best I can hope for.

I just better hope that Avalon is far gone from my system by then. There's no way I'm dragging her into this shit with me, or allowing any harm to come her way. That would be my sure death, because protecting her feels like a part of my life now.

I look up from the dresser, toward the door at the sound of Avalon's voice. "I'm ready. You good to do this tonight?"

My eyes scan over her beautiful, tan body as she stands there in a pair of my boxer briefs and a gray shirt, her skin glistening with moisture. It takes everything in me not to throw her onto my bed and fuck her hard again.

"Yeah." I push away from the dresser and walk past her, slipping an arm around her waist to spin her around to follow me.

Flipping on the lights, I point to the black, leather chair and tell her to sit, while I gather my shit.

"Do I need to take any clothes off for this spot?" she questions. "I have no idea what your plans are. I'm just going to let you take control and trust your talent."

I turn to her, my eyes slowly trailing her body to find the perfect spot to place her next tattoo. There are many options, because any place on her body is beyond fucking perfection, but there's one spot that I would die to see covered in ink by me. "Take my boxers off."

Without hesitation she slips my briefs off, setting them beside her in the chair. I have to grit my teeth and grab the chair in restraint, when I see that she's not wearing any panties beneath them. "Just my briefs, huh?" I ask stiffly. "No fucking panties..."

She nods her head and pulls her hair over her shoulder to get comfortable. "I didn't expect to have to take them off. Is this going to be too much of a distraction for you?"

Walking over to her, I grab her waist and roughly flip her over on her side to get a better angle of her lower hip. That whole section of her magnificent body is going to be branded with my art.

My cock instantly hardens at the sight of her perfectly round ass and thoughts of me marking her again. "It might be more of a distraction for you," I say, while running my hand over her full ass and then walking back over to set up the supplies. I need to keep my shit together; at least long enough to finish this.

"How is that?" She sits up slightly to look at me, looking so damn beautiful with her big curious eyes on me. "I'm not the one tattooing a panty-less woman and standing there with a hard-on."

Raising a brow, I push down on my rock hard dick and take a seat in my chair, before I end up pulling my cock out and slipping it between her perfect ass. Her mouth is making it even harder to fight. "Exactly," I say firmly. "Now lay down and be still, before I lose my shit and bend you over every surface in this room."

I glance over and see her close her eyes as she takes a long, shaky breath. Her body is shaking as if she's imagining just that. "Hurry, before I get nervous and change my fucking mind."

Grinning at her sassy ass mouth, I scoot my chair over to her backside and slap her ass, hard.

She yells and grips the chair. "Fuck, Royal!"

I grab her hip and position her where I want her. "You sound so fucking good screaming my name, babe. Do it again and I'll give you a real reason to."

She quiets down and takes another long breath to calm her nerves. "Okay... I'm ready. Let's do this before it's too late."

I take a few seconds to finish preparing my machine, before I start free handing a large phoenix.

About four hours through it, I notice her gripping the chair and tensing up in pain.

"Can you handle it or do you need a break?"

She shakes her head and bites her bottom lip. "No break. Keep going."

"We're almost done," I say. "Just hang on for about another hour."

She looks over her shoulder at me, and smiles bravely, while giving me a thumbs up. "I can do it... I can..."

When I'm done, I look down at her body and just admire how damn beautiful her body makes my art look. She's the perfect fucking canvas.

"Are we done?" she asks eagerly.

"Yup." I scoot the chair over to the table to get rid of my machine and gloves, before standing up and helping her to her feet. "Check it out."

I guide her to the full mirror and watch her mouth as it drops open in shock and admiration. "Holy hell... this is absolutely beautiful. I'm completely in love with your beautiful hands. So much talent and heart."

Her words cause my heart to beat slightly faster as I watch her taking in her new ink.

She turns in different angles, checking out the phoenix with the biggest smile I've seen on her, before throwing her arms around my neck and kissing me hard on the mouth, surprising me.

She tries pulling away after a few seconds, but I bite her lip pulling her back to me. Her mouth tastes so fucking good that I'm not ready to stop yet.

Both of my hands tangle into the back of her hair as she moans into my mouth. "Sorry," she says breathlessly. "I didn't mean to kiss you."

I yank back on her hair and suck her bottom lip into my mouth, before releasing it. "And I didn't mean to kiss you back."

Clenching my jaw, I release her hair and walk away. "Let's get your tattoo cleaned up so you can get some rest."

"Yeah," she says softly. "Sounds like a good idea. I need to go home before work so I can shower and change my clothes. It's already really late."

I swallow hard, while cleaning her off and bandaging her up for the night, before sending her to my bed to get some sleep.

I keep myself busy for a while, cleaning up the rest of the stuff and organizing the inside of my desk.

I need to keep my distance right now, because the way I'm feeling from that unexpected kiss is not fucking good. It felt too damn good for me to be okay with it.

Flipping off the lights, I close the door and walk down the hall to my release room. I usually go in there to work out and release some stress... but not tonight. Guilt inside of my chest has me opening the desk in the back of the room and pulling out *the* box. I haven't looked inside of it in months.

With my breath held, I open the box and pull out the letters and photographs from Olivia that I kept after she passed.

My heart aches so fucking bad as I take in her smiling face. She was always so happy and full of life, and it's because of me that her life was stolen from her.

Her piercing green eyes stare back at me, making me feel so much guilt that I can't breathe. Looking at these pictures makes me feel like I'm suffocating, but there's one that I can't close the box without looking at.

With shaky hands, I find the picture that I'm looking for and my heart fucking stops in my chest. I'm broken and dead inside, missing the biggest part of me that I'll never be able to hold, and there's nothing that can bring me back from this.

I'm completely fucking lost...

CHAPTER 18

ROYAL

TWENTY MONTHS AGO...

"SHIT! NOT HERE. NOT HERE... fuck, I'll kill you assholes."

I make it halfway up the driveway, with my heart going crazy in my chest, before slowing my bike and jumping off in a hurry. I don't want these fuckers to know that I'm here yet and give them the upper hand. I'll do everything in my power to show these fuckers that they've messed with the wrong family.

Walking fast, I pull out my gun, squeezing it in my hand while fighting to catch my breath. The thought of them hurting her is making it hard for me to breathe and is scaring the shit out of me. I've never been so damn scared in my life. Losing her is the only thing that terrifies me. I can't let that happen.

Protecting her is my job. She's my fucking life and these assholes are fucking with my world by being here right now. That makes me want to rip their throats out.

Running up the steps, I hurriedly reach for the handle and turn. My whole body runs cold at the fact that it's fucking locked. Olivia always leaves the door open for me, making it easier for when I get home. I've never given her a reason to have to lock it before, which means James and his guys have a reason to keep me out.

"Fucking shit!"

In a panic, I start searching through my leather jacket for the keys. I feel like I'm running out of time and it's making me want to scream and kick this damn door down, but that gives them the chance to hear me coming and outgun me. I need to keep my cool.

Gripping the key, I shove it in the lock and turn it, leaving it hanging in the door as I open it and step inside.

The house is dark. Olivia hates the dark.

"Fuck!" I say under my breath, while walking through the house in search of Olivia. "I'm coming for you, baby. I'm here."

The living room and the kitchen are empty, making me even more anxious to just get to her.

It's not until I hear her scream of pain come from down the hall that I know exactly where she's at: the family room. That sound is enough to make my world stop.

With my heart racing out of my chest, I take off running through the house, not caring anymore if they hear me. I need to get to her.

When I reach the end of the hall, I look over to the right to see one of James' men walking out of the room, buckling up his jeans.

He looks up with wide eyes and mutters, "fuck," while reaching for his gun.

Without hesitation, I aim my gun at his head and shoot, taking his fucking life, before rushing past his body and into the room.

Rage surges through me at the sight in front of me and no matter how many fucking breaths I take, I still can't breathe.

James has Olivia against the wall with one hand on her

neck and the other one covering her mouth as he pulls out of her and peers over his shoulder at me.

Olivia's head is dangling to the side, lifeless, as if he went too far, and blood is dripping down her legs, but he's too worked up at seeing me to realize that she's no longer fighting him.

James' other guy is standing beside him, struggling to pull his jeans up and reach for his gun.

James yells at his guy to shoot me, while trying to fix his own jeans and hold Olivia up at the same time. "Shoot him, Lou! Hurry the fuck up!"

My heart is in failure, seeing her like that. *What have I done?*

The second I really realize what they've done to her, I lose it, seeing red, and all I can think about is getting to Olivia and helping her. I don't care the price; I'll pay it.

"You're dead, motherfuckers! Enjoy your last fucking breath."

I aim my gun at Lou, firing two bullets into his dick and one into his skull, before aiming at James' leg and catching Olivia as he releases her and falls to the ground in pain, screaming.

"Ah... shit!" He grabs at his leg, while slapping the ground in agony.

Well, fuck him! His pain will never compare to mine.

My heart stops and a cry of pain roars through me, as I cradle her body in my arms and fall down to the floor with her. I can't feel her breathing and it hurts so fucking much. "Olivia," I cry. "Baby, wake up. Open your fucking eyes. I'm here. I'm here."

With my gun aimed at James, I grab Olivia's face and squeeze it, shaking it in an attempt to wake her up. I lean my face next to her mouth to check for her breathing, but feel nothing. "Fucking breathe! Wake up! Please, baby! Please! Breathe, dammit. Breathe!"

A scream roars through me as I maneuver to my knees and

attempt to give Olivia mouth to mouth. I hold her as closely as possible and press my mouth to hers, willing to give her all of my air. I'd give her my very last breath if it kept her from feeling any of this pain and kept her alive.

That's when I hear James grunt and feel a knife stab into my thigh, cutting me three times as he fights to push it in deeper.

"Fuuuck!"

I pull away from Olivia and fight the knife out of James' hand, stabbing it into his shoulder and twisting. "Does that feel good, motherfucker!" I scream out. "Show me how much it fucking hurts!"

I push the knife in as far as it will go, making him scream out and grab at his knife. The further I push, the louder he screams.

This motherfucker needs to pay for taking Olivia from me. He needs to feel her pain.

Pulling the knife out of his arm, I lay Olivia down as gently as I can and kiss her lips for the last time. Feeling them cold against mine drives me into a rage.

I lean over James and press my gun to his dick. "You sick son of a bitch. Are you ready to fucking die?"

He shakes his head back and forth and starts backing away from me. "Fuck! Don't do it. Don't do it. We didn't mean to kill her. I swear." He grips his wounded arm and snot starts dripping down his face as he cries and pleads with me. "We only meant to send a message, but she screamed so fucking loud. It was an accident. I didn't know I broke her neck. It wasn't meant to happen."

I swing the gun, hitting him in the dick and then grab the back of his neck to scream in his face. "And you think that makes it any better? Huh?" I hit him in the dick again, but harder this time.

He shakes his head, while grabbing his dick in pain. "No! Fuck!"

"Yeah... you're definitely fucked."

Looking him straight in the eyes, I shoot him in the dick and then in the neck, watching his life and blood slowly drain out of him as he struggles to breathe.

I never thought watching a man die would feel so fucking good, but I'm elated as I watch him take his last breath before me.

Kneeling down in a puddle of blood, I hold Olivia with one arm, while pulling out my phone and calling 9-1-1.

"9-1-1. What's your emergency?"

I look down into Olivia's glossy eyes and clench my jaw in pain. I can barely speak. "Three men broke into my home and raped and killed my fiancée." I run my fingers over her eyes, closing them. "And then I killed them."

Pulling the phone away, I throw it against the wall as hard as I can, breaking it.

I feel numb; so fucking numb.

Holding Olivia in my shaking arms, I close my eyes and cry into her neck, for what seems like forever. Then I lay her down and press both of my hands to her swollen belly and kiss it.

More rage surges through me as I see that the blood is still dripping down her legs, letting me know that our child is not okay. There's so much blood; so fucking much.

Our baby girl; she was due in seven weeks. Seven fucking weeks left and now she'll never get the chance to live.

"Fuuuuck!" I cry.

Standing up, I grab everything in my sight and break it, while screaming out in pain. Nothing else matters to me but them, and now I've lost them both. I can't do it without them. I can't have a life without them in it.

After everything I can get my hands on is broken, and my hands are bloodied and bruised, I walk over to the window, light a cigarette, and take a drag, while looking out.

The only thing I long for is to fucking fade away and

pretend as if I'm not standing here, covered in blood; crimson fucking red from head to toe with my heart pounding so viciously that my chest feels as if it's going to burst the fuck open.

My lungs burn as I inhale another long drag from the cigarette I've been holding. The smoke fills my lungs, expanding them and sending a cooling sensation throughout my shaking body. I long for some kind of relief, but it fucking brings none. I take another drag anyway, waiting for what's to come next.

Red and blue flashing lights.

I stand frozen in the window, numbly watching as they grow near, the sounds of sirens getting louder with each passing second.

Taking one last drag, I toss the cigarette at the glass and turn away. I couldn't care less if this motherfucker burns down. There's nothing left here for me. Not anymore.

My body starts moving, mentally checked out and lost somewhere in this never-ending nightmare of my world at its end. I feel the hatred starting to build, and the animosity of the night overwhelming me.

I bring my blood-covered hands up to rub my face as I growl out, releasing some of my pent up anger. I growl out until my throat feels raw, but just like the cigarette it does shit to relieve this pain that is slowly killing me.

I walk slowly, in a daze, passing three breathless bodies, before I stop in front of... her. Blood covers her blonde hair and her once pink, plump lips are now ice fucking blue. I reach over to pull her into my arms, feeling my heart die a little more with each breath that she doesn't take.

That's when the door flies open and I hear them piling in. Heavy footsteps take over until that's all I can hear, besides the erratic beating of my dead fucking heart.

A buzzing fills my ears. My heartbeat speeds up at an

uncontrollable rate and all I see is red as I'm yanked to my feet, two officers fighting to restrain me. I don't care if they fucking take me away. I will rot in fucking hell for her, but I'm not done saying goodbye yet.

I feel the cuffs snap around my wrists, hard. Too fucking hard. My hands may not be free, but that won't stop me. Rotating my shoulders, I swing my head back as hard as I can, slamming it into a nose that I hear crack. That shit is broken. I know that for sure, and so does he by the way he curses and steps away to hold his bleeding nose.

Another set of hands attempts to grab me from behind as I make my way down to the floor, on my knees, burying my face into her lifeless neck. I kiss it gently, for the last time, before my head is yanked backward and I'm torn away from her, and then pushed down to my face before a knee digs into my neck.

PRESENT

I RUN MY FINGERS OVER the last ultrasound taken and swallow back the pain at the reminder that I never got to hold my baby girl.

The pain and guilt eats at me every fucking day. I not only lost one life that night... but two.

I only allow myself to look at it for a few more seconds, before gently putting it back into the box and closing it.

Then I put the box away, before going to my bedroom and crawling into bed.

Avalon is already fast asleep.

I stare at the ceiling until finally falling asleep, letting the darkness of the night consume me.

CHAPTER 19

ROYAL

STANDING IN THE DOORWAY WITH a bottle of beer in hand, I stand back and watch Blaine as he concentrates on tattooing some chick's left ass cheek.

He looks up at me once in a while, lifting a brow in curiosity as he watches me tilt back my beer and grip the doorframe. "What's good, fucker? You've been standing there without moving for like twenty damn minutes. Did some shit happen that I should know about?"

"Nah. I was just thinking of going out for a bit." I finish off the last bit of my beer and toss it in the trash across the room. "You good here?"

Blaine gives me a look, meaning, *are you shitting me*, and leans back in his chair as if he's the coolest fucker to walk the earth. "When am I ever not good? Come on, bro. I got this shit. If you got something to do then go."

I run my hand over my face and look over at the clock. It's just a little past noon, making me anxious to get out of here.

"Alright." I slick my hair back and lock eyes with Blaine. I really can't deal with his shit today. "If I come back and my window is broken, I'll shoot your fucking dick off. I'm not in the mood today."

"Dude... seriously? Why do you always threaten my manhood? It's my best fucking feature."

"Because your dick pisses me off even more than you do. You're always fucking touching it and shit," I say with a scowl. "Keep shit under control until I get back and don't text me if it's important: call."

"Yup. Got it." He pulls his machine away and backs the chair up a bit to admire the chick's ass. "Damn... that is one fine piece of work?" He smirks and adjusts his cock with his free hand.

The girl leans up on her elbows and looks back, then smiles at him, while watching his hand. "It better be if it's covering my beautiful ass."

"Damn straight," Blaine says in agreement, while watching her lift her ass up closer to his face. He tilts his head at me. "Go, fucker. Jerk your shit if you need to. You're bumming me out here and putting my dick in a bad mood."

I let out a frustrated breath, not even bothering to respond to his dumb ass, and walk out the door while reaching for my phone.

I have no fucking idea why I'm about to do this right now, but after waking up early this morning to an empty bed, I haven't been able to stop thinking about Avalon and how she left without saying bye.

There's no way in hell she needed to be up and out of my bed for work by five in the fucking morning. She left because something was bothering her and keeping her awake. That doesn't sit well with me, and I can't help but to wonder what the fuck was running through her head when she left in the middle of the night without someone to make sure she made it home safe. It was fucking with me.

I sat up in bed for a good hour, unable to fall back to sleep, before hopping on my bike in hopes to clear my head. Before I knew it, I was sitting outside her damn house, contemplating on whether or not to go up to the front door and knock.

It only took me a few seconds to realize that I was acting like a fool, so I turned my bike around instead, and rode the mostly empty streets for a while, until it was time to meet Blaine at *Savage & Ink*.

It's now been seven hours since she left my bed and it's still bugging the shit out of me. The only thing keeping my nerves somewhat under control is knowing that she at least made it home safe.

ROYAL

You on lunch?

I walk out the back door and light a cigarette while waiting for her response. My phone vibrates about five minutes later to her name lighting up the screen.

AVALON

Not until 12:30. I swear time is going by extremely slow today. You at work?

ROYAL

Not anymore... Where you going for lunch?

AVALON

Nowhere. I only get thirty minutes today because I have a client coming in at 1. I won't have time to leave and pick up lunch. I could so use a steak sandwich to make it through the day. SUCKS! Shit... gotta go. My 12 o'clock finally just walked in.

I slide my phone into my pocket and toss my cigarette aside, before wiping sweat out of my eyes. It's really fucking hot today for some reason and it's really not helping my shitty mood any.

"Shit! I'm really going to do this."

VICTORIA ASHLEY

Pulling my hair back into a bun, I yank my shirt off and shove a small part of it into my back pocket, before mounting my bike.

I rev the engine a few times, smirking as a police officer at the light watches me. His eyes look me over, sizing me up as I pull up next to him.

Keeping my eyes on him, I lift a brow as he revs his engine at me and looks back and forth between the light and my bike, as if he wants to race.

He keeps his eyes on me for a few seconds longer, before turning away and laughing, as if he's just intimidated me.

Fuck that. If he wants to race, we can race. I'm all about keeping the law around here entertained.

The light turns green, making my heart pump with adrenaline.

I smirk at the mustached douche behind the wheel when he looks over at me, and motion with my head for him to go. "After you," I yell.

He takes off fast, me taking off a few seconds behind him to give his pathetic ass a fair chance.

Within seconds I pass his ass up, watching as the front of his police car trails my ass as he tries to pass me, but fails for the next three miles, until we're caught at a red light.

Stopping, I look over to the left and wait for him to pull up next to me. "Was it as good for you as it was for me, Officer?" I ask with a wicked grin, just to piss him off more. "I'm down for round two."

Revving my engine, I cock a brow at him, causing him to slam his fist into the steering wheel and cuss under his breath.

I wait for him to say something, try to pull my ass over, anything, but he just grits his jaw at me and drives away as the light turns green again.

As short of a ride as it was, I have to admit that it felt

fucking good and relieved some of my tension, and I desperately needed that right now.

Taking off, I glance over at the car next to me when a girl whistles out the window, getting my attention.

"That was hot!" The brunette in the passenger seat shouts, before giving me the thumbs up and gripping the door as her boyfriend turns down the next street to get away.

That fucker didn't look happy one bit, but I don't blame him. He looked stiff and stuck up just like Colton. I wouldn't be surprised if she's just as bored as Avalon was with my brother.

She might just crave that boredom once she gets a glimpse of my fucked up world...

CHAPTER 20

AVALON

I HAVE TO ADMIT THAT hearing from Royal was completely unexpected and surprised the hell out of me. I expected it to be Colton again, since he has already texted me twice today to tell me how much he misses me.

So when I saw Royal's name flash across the screen, my heart jumped with excitement.

I'm dying inside to pick up my phone and continue talking to him, but I can't until I'm done with my client and it's making me shaky with anticipation.

Last night after he tattooed me, I went to his bed alone and tried my hardest to fall asleep, but all I could think about was the way it felt to have him inside of me, holding and kissing me. I've never felt something so pleasurable and intense in my life. It was absolute torture trying to fall asleep alone in his bed when all I wanted to do was feel him inside of me again.

My emotions were all over the place after that, and when I woke up in the middle of the night to see him lying there, all I wanted to do was look at how beautiful and peaceful he looked when he didn't have to be awake and hurting. He's a beautiful, tortured soul, and seeing him in peace made my heart melt.

I had to stop myself over and over again from reaching over and touching his beautiful, soft lips. Having them so close caused an ache inside of me, craving to lean over and taste him again.

Knowing that I wouldn't be able to fall back to sleep with all of the emotions he brings out of me, I left and went home to sleep in my own bed.

Now that he's texted me, I'm left with wondering what he's thinking. Since he asked me if I was on lunch, I'm guessing he wants to talk about what happened last night.

It has my nerves completely working overtime right now and I'm hoping I can get my client out of here without a lopsided haircut.

"Can you take a little more off the right side?" my client asks. She turns her head from side to side, checking it out in the mirror. "Yeah, just a tad bit more. It's not really even with the left side."

I force a smile. "Of course. Let me take a quick look." Checking out her hair, I turn the chair to the side to face me, to get a better look.

Then I carefully trim the right side to match the left. "Looks good to me. Take a look and let me know if you want me to fix anything else."

I turn her chair back around and step back as she checks out her hair in the mirror.

My heart almost stops when I hear a motorcycle pull up outside of the salon.

Swallowing, I look over to see Royal hop off his bike, shirt-less, with his hair pulled up into a bun. It instantly gives me naughty thoughts, bringing me back to last night. He's so rough and fucking dirty.

Ellie must notice him at the same time as I do, because

before I know it, she's staring at the door and fixing her red hair. "Holy…"

She hits Anne's arm, causing her to look over as well. "That man must be my lunch. Damn… I'd eat him right up."

Ignoring them, I turn back to my client in hopes to get her the hell out of here before I freak out. "How does it look? Everything good?" I ask in a hurry.

She runs her fingers through her graying hair and lets out a small breath. "Looks even enough…" She stares into the mirror for a few more seconds, before turning around to face me right as the bell on the door dings.

Her eyes widen as she looks over at the door to see Royal walk in shirtless. Then she quickly reaches into her purse and pulls out a twenty, acting like she's in a hurry to get the hell out of here. "Here. Keep the change. I'll just call and make my next appointment."

Keeping her distance from Royal, she squeezes past him and rushes to her car, most likely locking the doors once inside.

I can't help but smile at Royal as he lifts a brow and then turns to watch the lady speed off. "What can I say… She just can't handle sexy very well. Her poor heart probably can't handle it."

"That's most likely it," he says stiffly. "Good thing I decided at the last minute to wear pants."

"You can take them off," Anne says quickly.

"We don't mind," Ellie adds in. "Not one bit."

My stomach knots up at the thought of Anne and Ellie getting a chance to see what's under Royal's jeans. It makes me sick with unwanted jealousy.

Royal must notice my discomfort, because before I know it, his arm is around my waist pulling me to him.

Wrapping his hand into the back of my hair, he slams his lips against mine, roughly sucking my bottom lip into his mouth as he pulls away. "You left last night," he says tightly.

"Don't fucking do that shit again without me knowing that you're safe. Got it?"

The intense look in his eyes has me nodding my head in agreement. "Yes."

"Good." His eyes search mine as if he's trying to tell if I mean it or not. "Come on." He grabs my hand and pulls me outside, leaving everyone watching us through the window.

He notices me watching them, so he places his hand on my chin, bringing my attention back to him. "Why did you leave in the middle of the night?"

I close my eyes as he rubs his thumb over my bottom lip. "I couldn't sleep," I admit. "So I left to sleep in my own bed."

"Why couldn't you sleep? And no bullshit, Avalon."

I swallow as I watch him watching his thumb as it slides across my lip again. "Because I wanted to touch you," I admit. "But I didn't know if you wanted me to."

He inhales deeply and slowly releases it, looking taken aback with my response. "You still hungry?" he asks, changing the subject.

I nod my head, glad for the change of topic. "Yes. I'm starving."

He releases my chin and grabs for a brown paper bag that is sitting on the seat of his bike. "It's the biggest, juiciest steak sandwich that I could get. It should help you get through the day."

Opening the bag, I place my nose in the top and sniff. "Oh my God..." I take another quick whiff, feeling my stomach rumble in anticipation. "It smells like heaven. Thank you!"

Feeling thankful that he came here just to bring me lunch, I grab him by the back of the neck and pull him to me, kissing him.

My heart goes crazy as he kisses me back, his lips tasting me just about as desperately as I need to taste him.

Without breaking the kiss, he grips my thighs, pulling me up to wrap my legs around his waist.

I feel him growl into my mouth, before he bites my bottom lip and roughly grips my ass, as if he wants nothing more than to fuck me roughly right here.

"Come over tonight," he demands, against my lips.

Every part of me wishes that I could say yes. This is such a shitty feeling.

"I can't," I breathe. "I told Madison that I'd go out with her tonight."

"Where?" His jaw clenches as he pulls me closer against him, slightly grinding his hips into me.

"Oh fuck," I whisper, barely able to keep my control. "*Hooligans*. She needs a night out of dancing and doesn't want to go alone."

He grabs the back of my neck and meets my eyes. "You two are going alone?"

"Yes. We usually do."

He closes his eyes and takes a deep breath, slowly releasing it against my lips. "Call me if you need me."

"Alright," I agree.

"Okay," he says, setting me back down to my feet and looking me over in my jeans and white tank top. "Eat your lunch before your time is up. I need to go before I take up all of your time."

I stand here with my lunch in hand, watching as he walks over to his bike and straddles it. "Thanks for lunch. I'll let you know how it tastes."

He nods his head and starts his bike, before quickly taking off, leaving me standing here with a racing heart and a sore lip from his bite.

I've never craved to be bitten so badly in my damn life. This man makes me want to be tied up to a bed and have every inch of my body bitten by his glorious fucking mouth.

That's the power he has over me, and I couldn't care less what anyone thinks about him.

I've never felt so alive in my entire life...

CHAPTER 21

AVALON

WE'VE BEEN AT *HOOLIGANS* FOR less than twenty minutes and I'm already in the mood to just go home, strip out of this stupid dress that Madison talked me into wearing, and text Royal.

I've never really been comfortable in dance clubs to begin with, so having Royal on my mind is making me ten times more anxious to push all of these sweaty, hip thrusting horn balls away from my private space and leave.

I swear if one more asshole "accidentally" grinds their limp dick against my ass, I'm going to take off my heel and stab their precious manhood with it.

"Loosen up, chick!" Madison screams over the music, while pulling me closer into her dancing space, nearly spilling her drink all over me. "There are so many hot guys here. Look around you and choose one, before I choose one for you. I swear you need to get laid."

I look around me and tilt back my beer, scoping out the room of wild, drunken men. None of them appeal to me...

because none of them are Royal. I want tattoos, long hair, leather jackets, and a sexy beard covering an even sexier mouth: a dirty one. I want to feel a rush, just by being in his presence.

Looking around this room just has me bored out of my mind.

"I'm good, Madi. I don't need some douche rubbing his dick all over my ass and trying to grope my tits to get off. I'm here for you." I force a smile and hold my beer up. "Plus, I already got laid." I tilt my beer back and walk away to the bar, before she can bombard me with questions.

I hold up my empty beer to the bartender, when she notices me standing there. "Another, please."

Madison appears next to me, grabbing my arm to spin me around. "You slept with Royal?" Her eyes widen when I slightly smile. "God, you're a lucky bitch. I bet he was damn good too. I've heard shit about men with beards. I know they're orgasm donors and you definitely needed a donation."

"Well, thanks, jerk. You make me sound pathetic." I grab my beer and pay the bartender, before grabbing her arm and pulling her through the crowd with me. "You heard right though. He was definitely good. The fucking best," I say truthfully. "Now let's dance so you can get it out of your system and we can go. I'm not liking it here and I'm getting grouchy from all of these jerkoffs grinding on me."

"Ugh! You're no fun sometimes," she complains, while lacing her fingers through my free hand and swaying her hips to the slow rhythm. "Two hours and then we can leave. No sooner, dammit."

Forty minutes later... and unfortunately she's not bored with forcing me to dance with her yet. Every time I try to step away she pulls me back to her and captures me in her ninja grip.

Sweaty and out of breath, I finally escape and reach for my

phone when I feel it vibrate in my purse. *THANK YOU!* "Give me a sec," I say breathless. "My phone is going off."

Pulling it out to look at it, my heart drops when I see Colton's name flash across the screen. It's not the name that I was hoping to see and disappointment quickly sinks in.

COLTON

> Are you having fun dancing? You look sexy in that dress.

Huffing, I look around the room in search of the jerk. He knows damn well that Madison likes to drag me here every couple of weeks, so I'm really not surprised that he's here.

It takes me a few seconds to spot him across the bar, watching me from one of the small tables. He's dressed all slick in a black shirt and dress pants, fitting in perfectly with the rest of the guys here.

AVALON

> Trying to, Colton. Please don't come over here and start anything. We're leaving soon.

COLTON

> I just want to dance with you. Nothing more. Stay...

I look up from my phone and shake my head in annoyance. I really don't want to deal with him tonight. Every time I think about him, it angers me.

"What's wrong?" Madison questions over some guy's shoulder that she randomly started dancing with when I escaped her grip. "Who is it?"

"Colton," I say stiffly. "He's here."

"Great!" Madison scoffs. "He's such a pain in the ass. He better not come over here."

AVALON

That's not a good idea... No.

By the time I hit send and look back up from my phone, Colton is standing in front of me, giving me a creepy ass smile.

"Crap, Colton." I shove my phone into my purse and take a step back when he gets too close for my liking. "I really don't think it's a good idea for us to dance and I honestly don't want to."

"Why?" he questions, while fixing his watch and rolling up his sleeves. "We dated for six months and you can't let me have one fucking dance?"

"Take a hike, asshole." Madison eyes him up and down as if she's a vicious junkyard dog, ready to bite his balls off. "She said she doesn't want to dance. Don't you have some pants to go piss or something," she says with hope.

Colton ignores Madison and turns back to face me. "We're both already here... might as well try to be civil and enjoy the night. We used to have fun, remember?"

I release a small breath as Colton reaches out and grabs my hip, rubbing his thumb over my side. "Used to," I remind him, while pushing his hand away. "As in we don't anymore and I don't want to. Please," I say in aggravation. "Just drop it and go back to the other side of the bar. I don't want to fucking dance."

"Avalon."

I freeze at the sound of my name and slowly look up to see Royal pushing his way past a dancing couple with Blaine following at his heels, looking intense.

My heart stops in my chest at the sight of him looking so damn sexy and lethal in his beat-up leather jacket. His eyes are so fierce as he looks Colton over that it even makes me nervous at what he might do.

"Back the fuck off." Facing Colton, he pushes in between us

and protectively guides me behind him with his arm. "She's with me, and she'll only be dancing with me, motherfucker."

Royal and Colton stare each other down for a few seconds, before Colton finally speaks. "No way she's with a fuck up like you." He motions around the room. "You don't belong here. Look around, asshole. Go back to your own shithole of a bar and let me work things out with *my* woman. You had your fun at dinner, but it's done now."

"I'm not your woman," I seethe. "And as far as I see it, you're the one that fucked up. We're done."

Royal tilts his head from the sound of my voice and then turns around to face me.

I swallow from my nerves as his eyes search mine with an intensity that makes my heart skip a few beats. His power makes me want to break down at his feet and beg for him to take me: any and every part of me.

"Come here," he demands.

My breath hitches in my throat as he grabs the back of my neck and pulls me to him, not waiting for me to obey.

His lips lightly brush mine, making me release a small breath of desire, before possessively claiming them as if to tell the whole fucking room that I'm here with him and to back the fuck off.

It feels *so* good, and is something I wasn't used to with Colton. I was always lucky if he even acknowledged we were in the same damn room.

Kissing me hard and deep, he moves both hands up to grab my hair, tugging gently as he deepens the kiss. While breathing hard against my lips, he finally pulls away, roughly biting my bottom lip to leave his mark.

"You're here with me now," he says firmly. "No one fucks with you. Not even my brother."

"Are you shitting me, Marie? You're going to let him kiss you like that? Get over here with me. Now."

Releasing my hair, Royal turns to face Colton again, but gets up close and personal in his face this time. "Do I need to *fuck* her in front of you for you to get the fucking hint, brother? Leave. Her. The. Fuck. Alone. Touch her again and I'll slit your fucking throat. Don't test me."

"Fuck you both. You're a crazy lunatic and she'll figure it out soon enough." Colton pulls out his phone and grins as he looks away from it as if he's just won something. "I have better pussy waiting for me anyway. You remember Misty, right? Not that dried up shit..."

Before Colton can finish, Royal swings out hard, punching him right in the mouth. Colton falls back into some guy that pushes him back to his feet and complains about him spilling his beer.

"Watch what the fuck you say," Royal growls. "Better show her some fucking respect."

Grabbing his mouth, Colton looks at me as if I should feel sympathy for his ass. "That's really the kind of guy you want? He just fucking punched me in the middle of a nightclub. He's crazy as hell."

Closing my mouth from the initial shock of Royal swinging at him, I smile with confidence and run my hand over Royal's dick, before moving it up his body to stop on his stiff abs. He needs to see just how much better Royal is than him. I'm sick of his shit.

"Yes, because unlike you... your brother knows how to work his *big* cock and keep my pussy wet." I try to pull my hand away from Royal's body, but he grabs my wrist, stopping me. "So fuck you, Colton," I continue. "I'm here with Royal."

"Fine. Whatever. I'm out of here." Colton turns around and bumps into Blaine, flinching when Blaine playfully flexes at him.

Blaine lifts a brow and smirks in amusement as Colton backs away and walks around him.

"Fuck, I've always hated that walking douche," Blaine says with an amused laugh, while watching Colton shove the door open and leave.

"Me too," Madison agrees. "I've been telling this girl over here that for months." She shakes her head at me and rolls her eyes. "Thank God, she finally dumped his pussy ass. Her vagina was aching for some real action."

"Seriously!" I give Madison a hard look, but then look over at Royal as he slips his arm around my waist and pulls me against him.

God... I love it when he touches me. Probably a lot more than I should.

"How long have you been here?" I ask, while looking him over, suddenly curious as to how long he's been hanging around.

"Long enough to make sure no assholes bother you while dancing." He presses his lips to mine again, before pulling away and licking his bottom lip off. "Let's get out of here. You girls follow us to *Savage & Ink.*"

Blaine steps up to Madison and picks her up, throwing her over his shoulder with a cocky smirk. "You're mine tonight, babe. You got a problem with that?"

Madison squeals and grabs onto the back of Blaine's jacket as he turns a bit to look at the guy Madison was previously dancing with before the show went down. "Definitely not, as long as you'll be handling me like this. Fuck dancing. Let's get out of here, Ava." She glances over to the somewhat scared looking guy. "Sorry, guy. Thanks for the dance."

Blaine takes off walking toward the door in a hurry and Royal reaches out and grabs my hand, pulling me through the crowd behind them.

By the time we make it outside, Blaine has Madison backed up against her car, leaning in close to her neck. They're talking, but I can't make out anything that they're saying.

"You riding with your friend or me?" Royal questions, grabbing my attention.

I turn back to Madison and watch, as she pulls out her keys, ready to unlock her door. "I'll ride with Madison since she's not leaving her car here." I run my hand through my tangled hair, fixing it a bit. "We'll meet you there."

Smiling, I back away and walk over to Madison, pulling her away from Blaine's sexy, dirty ass. "We'll meet you guys there, playboy. Just keep it in your damn pants a little longer. Zip it back up."

"I'll try my best," he says while checking out Madison's ass and then walking over to join Royal by the bikes.

"I guess you got what you wanted. Thanks to those sexy men. You better be sure to thank Royal later." Madison smiles at me over the top of her car and then opens the door, jumping inside.

"I want to," I say to myself, while watching Royal watch me. "So damn bad."

They wait until we're both in the car safely, before starting their bikes and taking off for us to follow them.

CHAPTER 22

A VALON

ONCE WE PULL INTO THE back of *Savage & Ink*, Madison turns off her car and starts checking herself over in the mirror. "I'm so damn sweaty and my hair looks like ass."

She runs her hands through her hair a few times and then turns to me. "Better?"

"Do you really think Blaine cares what your hair looks like? I'm pretty sure he plans to mess it up later."

She perks up and watches Royal and Blaine through the window as they park their bikes and start walking our way. "Damn, I hope so. Everything about that boy is ultra-sexy."

I laugh and reach for my purse, joining her in watching the boys talking while slowly making their way over. "What about Jax?"

"I'm willing to take them both."

My heart slightly jumps as Royal pulls the door open and reaches for my hand, pulling me out to my feet.

"Thanks." I give Royal a thankful smile and look over to see

Blaine on the other side of the car as Royal shuts the door for me.

"Oh damn," Madison says, while eyeing Blaine up and down in his leather jacket and ripped jeans, as he guides her out of the car and to the back door. "Sexy as hell, tough as nails, and knows how to open doors for ladies. God, I've been missing out on so much for the last twenty-two years."

"I can make up for it," Blaine says playfully, while slapping her ass, making her yelp. "Damn you have one fine ass, girl. Stay close to me when we get inside."

Royal shakes his head at his friend and possessively grabs for my hand, pulling me against him. "Tonight should be pretty calm, but if someone makes you feel uncomfortable, let me know and they're out. No fucking exceptions. You're here with me and I take care of you."

With my heart pounding from his words, I nod my head and walk in front of him as he holds the door open for me to walk in first.

I notice right away that it's a lot quieter than the last time we were here and I'm hoping that's a good sign, and that nothing crazy like the last time we were here will go down.

I've already seen Royal knock a grown man on his ass tonight and I can't deny that it oddly turned me on. Something about his demanding and powerful tone sets my whole body ablaze with a need that is impossible for me to snuff out.

With his hand still in mine, Royal walks straight up to the bar and pulls out a stool for me to sit on.

As soon as my ass hits the stool, he places both of his hands around my face and looks me in the eyes. "Stay here while I grab us some drinks."

He turns to Blaine who has Madison sitting one stool over from me, standing between her legs. "Don't let anyone even breathe on her. Got it?"

Blaine smirks. "I can handle both girls. No need to worry."

VICTORIA ASHLEY

"Fuck you." With that, Royal walks away and joins Jax behind the bar.

I see them both talking, but can't make out anything over the rock music playing softly in the background.

A few minutes later, Royal walks back around to my side of the bar and places two beers down for us, as Jax places a beer down in front of Blaine and a mixed drink for Madison.

Jax smiles at me and runs a hand over his firm chest. "Hey, babe. Sorry about the show the other night."

I smile back, trying to block out the memory of his firm ass flexing over the table as he pounded roughly into that girl. "Hey, Jax." I take a sip of my beer, watching him over the top. Yeah, I can't block it out, so I quickly pull my eyes away. "It was quite a show."

Royal gives Jax a hard look and pulls my stool closer to him. "Thanks for fucking up my table, asshole. I set some shit on it earlier and one of the legs gave out."

"Really?" Jax questions with cockiness. He turns to Madison, looking her over as Blaine wraps her legs around his waist. "I like to play hard. Shit gets broken sometimes."

Madison's eyes widen and Blaine watches her with a grin as if he's enjoying her reaction.

"When the fuck did Matthew get here?" Jax suddenly grinds out. "He's with his boy again."

Royal turns behind him, setting his sights on some rough, dirty guy that is here with some boy that looks to be in his teens. He looks like he's been drinking since the ass crack of dawn, and is pushing the teenage boy around, yelling at him as they play pool.

"That fucking piece of shit!" Royal suddenly shoots straight up to his feet. "Stay here." He punches Blaine's shoulder to get his attention. "Let's go."

Blaine finally looks over to see what Royal is so pissed

about. "Well, he fucked up now. Damn idiot." He pushes away from Madison and follows Royal over to the pool table.

Looking harder to see what's going on, I notice that the kid has a black eye and what looks to be some bruises on his arm, so I quickly jump to my feet, ignoring Royal's demand to stay seated. "What the hell."

Royal shoves the father into the wall, before grabbing the boy's face and looking him over.

His eyes go so fucking dark that my heart stops beating. I've never seen Royal look so pissed before and I know that something is about to go down.

"Blaine... take the kid for a minute."

I quickly rush over and grab the boy's hand. "I got him."

Royal's nostrils flare in anger as he looks me over, realizing that I disobeyed him, but he quickly turns his anger to the drunken guy as I hurriedly pull the kid away and start walking back over to the bar where Jax is.

Turning the stool away from the scene, I help the kid take a seat and ask Jax to get him a soda. "How old are you, kid?" I ask with a slight smile to comfort him.

The kid refuses to look me in the eye as he answers. "Fourteen."

"Is he okay?" Madison questions over my shoulder.

I glance up when I hear a loud noise, to see that Royal has the guy across the top of the pool table and is repeatedly punching him, while screaming threats in his face.

The kid tries looking, but I grab his chin like Royal always does to me to stop him.

"Is he hurting my dad?"

I swallow, not knowing how to answer that.

"He deserves it," the kid says. "I don't like it when he hurts me, but I'm not big enough to stop him."

My hearts aches from the sadness in his voice, and suddenly I want to hurt his father myself.

"What's your name, kid?" I question softly.

"Ian Bradley," he answers. "Is that guy going to make him stop hurting me?"

"Yes," I answer without thinking. I have a feeling that after Royal is done with him, that fucker will be too sore to do anything for a while. "He'll do everything he can to make sure it doesn't happen again." I run my thumb over his bruised eye. "Stay here."

Storming my way over to the pool table, I stop dead in my tracks when Royal pulls out a gun and shoves it in the guy's mouth.

The guy starts mumbling and trying to pull away, but Blaine grabs the back of his head and holds it still.

"You like the way my gun fucking tastes, you piece of shit?"

The guy shakes his head in a panic.

"No! No, motherfucker!" Royal shoves the gun deeper into his mouth and pulls back the hammer, making him squirm and drool as he struggles to get away. "Touch your kid again, and next time you'll be tasting my fucking bullet."

Blaine slaps the back of the guy's head as he starts mumbling something over and over again. "I can't fucking hear you," he says in his ear. "Gonna have to talk louder."

"I'm sorry," he mumbles louder so we can all hear this time. "I'm sorry. I'm sorry."

"Remember that shit," Royal barks. "Be expecting visits from me for a while."

He pulls his gun out of the guy's mouth and leans his head back in frustration as he notices me watching him.

His eyes stay on me for a few seconds as if he's trying to read me, before he turns to Blaine. "Make sure the kid can remember my number by heart. Don't let them leave until he can repeat it back on his own."

"Fucking done," Blaine says with a nod. He grabs the

douchebag by the back of the hair and pulls him up to his feet. "Go wait outside until we send your boy out."

He nods his head, while fighting to catch his breath. "I'll do that and I won't touch him again. Shit, I promise. I mean it. I won't..."

Royal gives him a look that sends him rushing out the door. After the door closes behind him, Royal opens his jacket and puts his gun away, while locking his eyes with mine.

He looks worried, as if he's just done something in front of me that he regrets.

"Go with the boys." He runs both of his hands through his hair, tugging in frustration as he breaks eye contact. "I need a bit."

He doesn't wait for my response, before turning away and walking into a room, slamming the door behind him.

By the time I walk back over to Madison and the guys, Blaine is walking Ian away from the bar and outside to send him off with his loser father.

So many emotions are running through my head that I have no idea what to do or think.

Madison seems just as stunned into silence as I am.

The weirdest part is that I feel like what he did was a good thing. He cares about the boy's safety and that only tells me that his heart is still there somewhere.

It may be broken and in pain, shattered from loss and hurt, but it's very well there and in the right place. I just hope I can find it before it's too late.

I have no idea what this man is doing to me, but I'm afraid for it to stop...

CHAPTER 23

ROYAL

"FUUUUCK!"

Screaming out in frustration and complete hatred, I grab my desk and flip it over, before kicking my chair against the wall, leaving a dent.

I'm so fucking heated and disgusted that I can barely breathe right now from the anger that is running through my veins.

I never meant for her to see me threaten a man's fucking life, but when I saw the kid all bruised up and beaten, my head filled with rage and I lost it. It's not the first time I've seen it either.

It's fuckers like that abusive piece of shit out there that provoke me and eat at me, creating the dirt that I've become.

Pressing my hands against the wall, I hang my head low and take a few long, deep breaths, before I end up going back out there and pulling the fucking trigger.

There's too much darkness inside my head to stop it if I get one more look at the kid.

Standing here, my whole body stiffens when I hear the door open and see the light spill into the small room, but I'm too tense to pull my eyes away from the wall, so I just close my eyes to the sound of her heels echoing throughout the room.

I tilt my head back and suck in a deep breath, when I feel a set of dainty arms wrap around my waist and hear the sound of her soft breathing as she rests her head against my back to comfort me.

We stay like this for a few minutes, before she slides around my body and into the space between the wall and me.

Avalon's eyes are deep as she takes me in.

Her hands run up my body, opening my jacket to expose my gun. She runs the tips of her fingers over it, while looking me in the eyes.

"You helped that kid tonight, Royal." She grabs my face, pulling it closer to hers as I stiffen. "Someone needed to protect him. He had a lot of bruises."

"I wanted to kill him," I admit. "I almost did."

Giving me a pained look, she grabs the back of my neck and brushes her lips over mine, calming me. "But you didn't. Instead, you gave him a reason to fear hurting his son again. That's probably the best thing anyone has done for that kid."

Fuck me... this woman.

Closing the distance between us, I tangle a hand into her long hair, crushing my lips to hers.

Feeling the tenderness of her sweet mouth against mine brings me back to sanity, making it easier to see clearly and let go of some of the anger that's burning inside of me right now.

She does shit to me. She makes me feel less like a monster and more like the man I once was; the man I wish I could be.

"Fuck," I whisper against her mouth, while pulling her hair back and tasting her sweet breath against my lips. "I need you..."

With strength, I flip her around, pressing her body against

the wall. She moans out in surprise and places her hands against the wall for support.

Wrapping one hand around her tiny throat, I yank her dress up and pull her panties down below her ass with the other, before undoing my pants and reaching inside to pull my hard cock out.

Her breathing picks up and she cusses under her breath, as I rub the length of my erection across her ass, before reaching in my pocket for a condom.

I hold my cock against her ass; working her up as I stroke it a few times, before ripping the wrapper open with my teeth and rolling the condom over my length.

Gripping her waist, I brush the head of my cock over her slick pussy, teasing her and making her whimper, before entering her in one deep thrust.

"Ah... fuck... fuck..." she screams against my arm, before biting it. "Holy shit... that hurt."

I yank her neck to the side and graze it with my teeth, while repeatedly pulling out and thrusting back into her, making her move up the wall and bite me harder with each hard thrust.

"Harder," I demand, causing her teeth to dig into my arm. "Hurt me as much as it hurts you to have me inside you."

"I can't," she says, while fighting to catch her breath. "Nothing can compare to what it feels like to have you inside me, Royal. It hurts more than you know." She leans her head back and moans as I push in deeper and stop. "But I want to feel you so badly," she whispers.

Her words cause me to yank her head to the side and suck her bottom lip into my mouth, while fucking her hard and fast; so fucking hard that all you can hear are the sounds of her screams, mixed with our sweaty bodies furiously slapping together.

I'm so fucking close to losing it, her cries of pleasure only bringing me closer to the edge.

Grabbing her tightly, I hold her up as her pussy clenches hard around my dick, causing my own orgasm to fill her throbbing pussy as I push in as deep as her body will allow.

Our ragged breathing mixes together as I swallow her moans and claim her mouth as mine, just wanting another moment to feel her again.

In this moment all I feel is her in my arms and taste the sweetness of her mouth against mine.

The darkness around me slowly fades and a new fear takes over as I realize that she's my calm after the storm. She's like a poison to my heart, slowly leaking her way inside and killing me in the worst way possible. She's the salvation that I seek but know that I can't keep forever, and that's what scares me.

Closing my eyes, I lean my head back and wipe the sweat out of my eyes, before leaning in close to her ear, breathing heavily. "Come home with me tonight."

Without hesitating, she nods her head and whispers, "Yes. I don't want to sleep alone tonight."

Slowly pulling out of her sensitive pussy, I moan out and grip my dick, pulling the condom off and tossing it into the trash while keeping my free hand on the back of her neck.

I look her beautiful slick body over, before bending down and pulling her panties back up while running my lips along her slender legs on the way up.

Her body shudders from the feel of my beard against her flesh, and her head tilts back as she bites her lip. "Your mouth hurts in the best way possible," she breathes as I pull her dress down to cover her ass.

"Come here."

Turning her around, I pull her into my arms and gently kiss her mouth, showing her just a sliver of the gentleman that I used to be.

"Let me grab my shit and we can go."

"Alright," she says gently. "Let me go say bye to Madison

and make sure one of the guys will take care of her. I don't want to leave her alone."

"They both will," I answer her, while opening the door for her and guiding her out to where her friend is enjoying herself with my guys.

Her friend looks up and waves her over as soon as she notices us walking toward them, so I release her waist and let her walk away.

Jax pushes a shot of whiskey my way and silently watches as I tilt it back. "Fuck!" I shake my head and slam the empty glass down. "Everything taken care of with the kid?"

"Hell yes," Blaine chimes in. "I doubt that kid will have to worry again."

I nod my head in contentment and watch the girls talking by the end of the bar.

"You boys good to take care of Madison? I'm taking Avalon with me."

"You know it," Blaine says. "She's in good hands."

"We're about to close up here anyway," Jax says. "Blaine and I will keep her company."

"I bet you will," I mutter, while pushing away from the bar. "I'm out."

Walking over to the girls, I silently place my hand on Avalon's waist, letting her know that we're good to go.

"Text me later," she says to her friend.

"You know I will," Madison responds with a smile.

Taking off my jacket, I slip it over Avalon's shoulders, right before opening the door for her to walk outside.

She snuggles up in it and lets me place my helmet on her head, before climbing onto my bike and holding on tightly as I take off.

Now all I want to do is get her in my bed and hold her until she falls asleep, knowing that she's safe in my fucking arms.

I'm not ready to let anyone else get hurt...

CHAPTER 24

AVALON

I'VE BEEN LYING AWAKE FOR the last hour, running my fingers over Royal's sweaty, tattooed chest, and watching him sleep.

It's cold down here, yet he's completely drenched, looking as if he's battling something inside his head. I hate seeing him looking so pained, even *in* his sleep, and a part of me wants to wake him up and save him from whatever is haunting him.

Last night when we arrived at his house, he immediately brought me downstairs, undressed us both, and pulled me into his bed and into his arms, holding me tightly against him as he buried his face into my neck.

He held me close, not moving or talking the whole night, and I have a feeling that he just needed someone to hold onto. I was happy to be that for him, because the thought of it being anyone else kills me.

It may be wrong of me, but I don't want anyone else touching this beautiful, pained man but me. I want to pull him close, caress his flawless face, and let him know that he's not evil and that I think he's just as good or even better than most people I know.

I jump and let out a surprised scream as Royal grabs my wrist, stopping my hand from rubbing him. "Crap... I thought you were sleeping."

He looks down at my wrist in his hand and loosens his grip, gently rubbing his thumb over it. "Sorry," he whispers. "Did I hurt you?"

I shake my head and pull my wrist out of his grip so that I can touch his still slightly bruised face. "No... you just scared me. Sorry if I woke you up."

He lets out a small breath and looks me in the eyes as I continue to rub his face, showing him that I care. Being able to touch him this way sends my heart soaring and I never want to stop. I want to sit here all day and freely touch this man.

"I needed to wake up anyway," he says in a husky voice. "I should get you home before work."

I pull my hand away from his face and watch him as he tiredly sits up and stretches. "I don't work until one today. I just planned to stop by and visit my uncle on his day off, but I'm in no rush."

Royal closes his eyes and shakes his head, as if trying to shake his sleepiness off. "You guys close? What does your uncle do?"

"Yeah... we're close," I admit. "He's the closest person I have to a parent."

Answering this next part makes me nervous. I still have no idea if it was Royal's bar that my uncle got called to that day, and I'm nervous that he'll want to stay away from me once he knows my uncle works with the law.

"He's a cop," I say with a forced smile. "He moved us here about two years ago when he got word that they were looking to fill some positions."

His eyes are unreadable as he stands up and starts getting

dressed while looking at the wall. "What's his name?" he questions tightly, while still looking straight ahead.

"Officer Knight," I reply, while hopping to my feet and grabbing for my dress to slip it on.

He stops in the middle of doing his belt and runs a hand through his hair before turning to me. "And does he know about me?"

I shake my head. "Not exactly. He just happens to know that I jumped onto the back of some guy's bike a couple weeks ago." I laugh at the thought of Madison and her big ass mouth. "Madison told him that while shamelessly flirting with him."

"I'll come with you." He reaches for a red flannel and pulls it on over his white shirt. "I'll take you by your house to change first. Let's go."

Before I can respond he's walking out the bedroom door. A few seconds later, I hear the bathroom sink turn on and the sound of him brushing his teeth.

"Oh shit... this might not be good." I grab my shoes and sit on the edge of the bed, quickly slipping them on. When I look up toward the door, Royal is gripping the doorframe, watching me.

"Your uncle needs to know who you're going to be spending time with." He exhales and releases the door. "Especially when it's me."

Standing, I meet him at the door and walk up the stairs as he grabs my waist and guides me up them.

My insides are going crazy at the thought of the two of them meeting, but it's not because I'm ashamed of Royal. I'm far from it. Him wanting to meet my uncle fills me with warmth, knowing that I mean enough to him for him to even bother.

It's the fact that I'm worried Royal has possibly had a run in with Mark in the past and there's a chance that things might turn out ugly. The last thing I need is Mark telling me to stay away from Royal. That's the last thing I want to deal with.

When we get outside, I'm a little surprised to see him walking us toward his motorcycle instead of his truck. This dress is not easy to work with, although I did somehow manage to make it work last night.

Sensing my hesitation, he picks me up and swings my leg over his bike, while holding it up for me. "I'll take care of you," he says firmly. "Don't worry. Never fucking worry when you're with me."

Facing me, he throws his leg over his bike and grips my thighs, pulling me up to straddle his strong lap. His eyes meet mine, before he captures my lips with his and gently bites the bottom one, growling as he pulls away. "Hold on, Darlin'."

He grabs his helmet and gently slides it over my head, before throwing his leg back over the bike and turning to face the front, starting the engine.

Burying my face into his back, I wrap my arms around his waist and hold on tight, ready for the ride.

* * *

I'M SO DAMN NERVOUS BY the time we arrive outside of my uncle's house that I can barely even think straight. I'm a bundle of nerves, as Royal grips my hips and helps me to my feet, being sure not to hurt me.

Mark has always given me a hard time about guys that I've dated or messed around with in the past, and that was before he even became a cop. He's always looked out for me the best he could.

His protectiveness is going to come out full force now, especially if he's had to deal with Royal and his bar in the past, which I know there's no way he hasn't. Face it... they're wild. People get hurt and things get broken, especially with Blaine around.

After pulling my helmet off, Royal grabs my face with one hand and presses his lips against mine, as if it's such a normal thing to do now. "Loosen up," he breathes against my lips. "There's nothing to worry about."

"I hope so. Let's just hope that he's in a good mood today," I say as he grabs my hand and walks me to the door, reaching out to ring the bell before I can.

It takes a few minutes, before Mark swings the door open while tiredly running his hand over his face. "Shit, it's early, kid. Don't you..."

His words trail off as he finally opens his eyes enough to see Royal standing beside me. He lets out a small huff and then looks down at Royal holding my hand. "Well damn, you're full of surprises for being so damn early in the morning." He steps aside and motions for us to come in. "I definitely need some fucking coffee now."

I swallow hard, walking inside and following Mark to the kitchen as he pours himself a coffee and mumbles a string of curse words to himself.

"Anyone?" he questions while pointing at the cupboard where he keeps his mugs.

"No," Royal responds, surprising me. "I'm good, Mark."

I swing my head around to look at Royal, surprised as hell to hear him call my uncle by his first name. "You two know each other?"

"Yeah," Mark says tiredly. "I see a little more of him than I should, and my day off is not supposed to be one of them."

"Well, it is now," Royal says firmly, while opening the fridge and pulling out a beer. "Do you mind?" he asks, holding it up.

"Whatever, man. Go ahead." Mark watches me over his mug as he takes a sip of his coffee. "So Royal is this 'Harley guy' that Madison mentioned the other day, huh? Fuck if that doesn't surprise me."

I shake my head and go from looking at Royal leaning against the counter as comfortable as can be, and then to Mark who is looking as if he's just ready to fall over from lack of sleep.

"I'm taking it you guys know each other well?"

Royal tilts his beer back and nods his head toward Mark's arm. "Where do you think he gets all of his ink from?"

A small laugh escapes me as I picture Mark going to the bar on his days off to drink with Royal's crazy friends and get tatted. "I guess we're alike when it comes to that."

Mark pulls his mug away with a surprised look. "No shit! And you couldn't even tell me that you got a tattoo? Anything else I should know?"

"Two," Royal adds. He raises a brow at me and takes another swig of beer, giving me a confident look. "And more to come. Soon."

"Well, you chose the right tattooist. I'll give you that." Setting his mug down, Mark walks toward the kitchen door, stopping before walking out. "We need to have a chat," he says stiffly.

I get ready to walk, but he shakes his head at me. "Not you."

Royal sets his empty beer down and follows my uncle out of the kitchen, leaving me to wonder what the hell they could be talking about.

I spend the next ten minutes walking around the kitchen, poking my head out the door every few minutes to see if I can hear them talking, but nothing.

I hate the feeling. It makes my stomach twist with uneasiness. I want to know what they're talking about so fucking badly.

A few minutes later, Royal and Mark return to the kitchen, looking tense; especially Royal.

"Everything good?" I question. "Do I need to separate you boys?"

"Things are fine," Mark says. "Let's hope it stays that way too. I'd hate to have to put my cuffs to use."

Royal's jaw clenches as he leans over the counter and grips it. "You haven't had to yet," he says sternly, before turning to me. "Want a ride back to your house or are you staying here? I got an appointment to take care of soon."

I look over at Mark to see him yawning again, while reaching to pour more coffee. "Going home. This guy can barely function right now."

Mark sets his mug in the sink and walks over to me, grabbing my shoulder. He looks like he wants to say something, but is fighting hard to hold it back.

Letting out a frustrated breath, he releases my shoulder. "I'll check in with you soon. If you need anything, let me know. I don't care what time of the day it is."

He turns to Royal and runs both of his hands through his hair tensely. "Keep her safe, dammit. I mean it."

Royal grabs my hand and pulls me to him, as if to show Mark that he will. "You know I fucking will. Don't ever fucking question that." He looks Mark over, before turning away and tightening his grip on my hand. "Let's go."

He doesn't say anything the whole ride back to my house and his body seems tighter than it did before visiting my uncle's house.

"What did my uncle say to you?" I question, while handing him his helmet. "Did he tell you to stay away from me?"

He grits his teeth and his grip on the handle tightens. "No."

"And if he did?" I question, needing to know if he'd listen like others have in the past.

He grips his hair, before running a hand through it to smooth it back and out of his face. "Fuck no. I'm the only one that can keep me away from you."

My heart sinks from his words. Even the thought of him leaving me alone makes my chest hurt. "Do you want to?"

Standing up, he grabs me by the back of my neck and pulls me to him. His heated eyes roam over my face, sending chills down my spine, before they stop on my eyes. "Not today."

Before I know it, he releases his grip on my neck and revs his engine, sliding his helmet on.

He looks back at me one more time, but doesn't say a word, before driving off, leaving me to wonder what he meant by *not today.*

Please don't let it be tomorrow either...

ROYAL

TWENTY MONTHS AGO...

"HOLD THE FUCK STILL! DON'T fucking move!" the pig yells in my ear. "Leave this piece of shit with the fucking rookie while we check the rest of the house. There's no way one man took all three of these scums down." I feel officer Payton's knee press harder into my neck, before slapping the back of my head and whispering, "You broke my partner's nose, scum. Huge mistake. It's losers like you that deserve to rot in prison, Royal." He presses into my neck again and digs his knee in until I can't breathe. "Knight, over here," he demands. "Don't let him fucking move. Use your gun if you have to."

I feel the pressure of the officer's knee leave my neck, before an arm presses down on the back of my head, but a lot gentler than the last asshole cop. "I got him. He won't go anywhere."

The rookie waits until the other officers' footsteps retreat down the hall before releasing the back of my head, as I shake his hand off in rage. He doesn't even fight to restrain me, which surprises me. The cops in this town are assholes.

I feel him lean in close to my ear as I sit straight up on my knees and look at her. "These assholes murdered your pregnant fiancée," he whispers in a pained voice. "I would have done the same thing. They deserved to suffer for that shit. I know that for sure." His hands grab at the cuffs, before I feel my left arm fall free. "Say bye to her. That's all I can give you."

Looking at her lying there, I crawl over to her on my knees and immediately feel the tears sting my eyes as I rest my face on her swollen tummy. I've never felt such pain in my life. Nothing can ever compare to the misery running through my body right now, and it's eating me alive.

Fighting the feeling to lay here and die along with her, I pull her lifeless body into my lap and bury my face into her cold neck.

"I'm so fucking sorry, baby. I'm so fucking sorry," I cry. "I failed to protect you and Hadley and I'll never forgive myself for that. I love you," I whisper. "Fuck, I love you so fucking much. I've loved you my whole damn life and I'll never stop. Not for one fucking second. I'd die for you, Livie. I'd fucking die for you."

I run a hand down my face in frustration at myself. "Fuck! Fuck! Fuck! I did this," I cry against her neck. "I should have known to be here. I should have gotten here sooner."

With tearstained eyes, I pull her closer against me, not ready to let go yet, when I hear the footsteps of the other officers approaching again. They're close enough that I can hear them talking now.

"The house is empty. This loser is more lethal than I gave him credit for." It's silent for a few seconds, until the officers come into view, looking surprised, yet pissed as hell to see me down on the ground holding Olivia in my arms.

"What the fuck, Rookie? You looking to lose your job already?"

"His cuffs were too tight," Officer Knight says stiffly. "My bad. Maybe you should learn to put on cuffs better. Just let him say goodbye to his family. He's not going anywhere. He's the one that called us."

"Fuck you, Knight. We'll discuss this with the Chief later."

The sound of ambulance sirens causes the whole room to go quiet and for the officer with the broken nose to finally take a second to look around him at the mess I made.

"Shit, this is going to be a mess to clean up." When he looks over at me again, I see a small glimpse of sympathy, before it's replaced with fear. "Let's get him out of here."

Paramedics rush in and past us, going straight to Olivia as they begin dragging me away.

I can hear them screaming for supplies to work on her and the baby, but those fuckers are too late. Just like I was...

The only thing on my mind as they drag me away is how the fuck I'm going to find Brian when I get out.

Four lives for two... that's the way it has to be.

CHAPTER 26

ROYAL

MY CONVERSATION WITH MARK KEEPS running through my head, messing with me and making me question just what the hell I'm doing with Avalon.

He was right about a few things, one of them being the fact that if she's going to be around me she needs to know what happened in my past.

She deserves to know that she's spending time with a killer; a man that is willing to take the life of anyone who hurts the ones he loves. I killed those men without even an ounce of remorse, and watched as James' life drained from his eyes. I wanted to kill them. I didn't only want to, but I needed to.

The fucked up part is that I'm still out for blood from the fucker that put my family in that position to begin with. I'm not even close to being done yet. Brian has no chance once I get my hands on him and I won't even think twice before putting my bullet straight through his fucking head.

What kind of demented monster does that make me? Can a

human with a beating heart really just take another man's last breath and not be considered cold, dark, and depraved? Does that even make me human at all?

I'm not so sure myself, and the thought of revealing the true monster inside me to Avalon has had me tense and on edge all night. I even attacked Blaine and slammed him against the wall when he asked me about Avalon. Just her name was enough to set me off.

My head is completely fucked up right now and I can't put any rational thoughts together enough to function.

I thought I wanted Avalon to feel me, to see the monster in me, but the thought of her walking away makes my chest ache and my blood boil.

I'm not ready to let that happen yet. That's exactly why I'm parked outside of *Stylin'* right now, waiting in my truck for her to walk out that door.

The "Open" sign has been turned off for over twenty minutes now, and the only car in the parking lot is Avalon's jeep. I hate the thought of her leaving the salon at night without any kind of protection.

That knowledge makes me want to sit outside every night that she works and take her home myself. Her boss is stupid for not having any kind of safety for her employees; either that or she's just a bitch.

Regardless... here I am.

Leaning my head back, I take a long drag of my cigarette and slowly release it.

A few minutes later, I look out my window and toss my cigarette out when I hear Avalon and Madison talking animatedly.

"That's just fucking crazy, Ava, and you know it. Of course I didn't sleep with both of them. We just... you know... had a little fun. I just wanted a small taste. For now..."

"You're one feisty little whore. You know that?" Avalon comments while slowly walking to her jeep without even bothering to check her surroundings. "But hell if I don't want to know the details. Well, maybe not *all* of them."

It makes me angry that she hasn't even noticed my truck sitting in the back of the parking lot, facing them. I could be some crazed fucking maniac... Well, one dangerous to her at least.

This just proves to me that I have something to worry about and makes me glad that I chose to sit out here and wait.

"What can I say?" Madison says excitedly, while playfully snapping her teeth at the air like an animal. "I'm wild and those boys bring out the animal in me. No fucking shame, sweets, none at all. You should try it sometime. Maybe Royal will let one of the boys join. Jax can eat your pussy while Royal fucks your mouth. Hot!"

Alright, I've had enough of this shit.

I crack my neck in annoyance and hop out of my truck, walking straight at them.

Madison is the first one to see me coming. She instinctively jumps back and screams, causing Avalon to turn around and face me.

Avalon's eyes widen in fear for a small second before she realizes that it's me.

"Holy fuck!" Madison screeches, while grabbing her chest. "Where the fuck did you come from?"

I growl and point behind me to my truck. "That massive fucking truck over there. That's where." I stop in front of Avalon and place my hand on her chin, bringing her eyes up to meet mine. "Always be aware of your surroundings. Got it?" I say firmly. "Shit! Someone could've hurt you."

I release her chin and grip my hair in frustration. My heart is racing at even the thought.

"Is everything okay, Royal? Why are you so tense?" Avalon

places her hand on my arm and pulls it down from my hair, while looking me in the eyes. "It's fine. I've been doing it for almost two years now. No one has bothered us."

I grab her face with both hands and roughly caress her cheeks with my thumbs. "Do you want to find out what it's like once it's not okay? I will fucking kill someone if something happens to you. Don't make me do that."

Her hands reach up to cover mine, as if to comfort me. "I'm sorry," she whispers. "I'll talk with Claudette about having someone here at night. Until then, I'll be more careful when closing."

The tone in her voice tells me that she cares about what I think. It's one of the things I love about her. She fucking listens, and doesn't just look at me as a bad boy to fuck the good out of her like most girls do.

It reminds me a lot of Olivia, which is sort of painful and breaks me down a bit. It makes me somewhat vulnerable to her. That's why I need to be more careful with her.

Before Olivia, all the girls ever wanted out of me were a good fuck and someone to rebel against their parents with. It was fun for a while, but always left me empty, until her...

"Good," I reply, satisfied with her response. "I'll just pick you girls up from work until then."

"You don't have to do that," she says gently. "Then our cars will be sitting here all the time and Claudette might freak out."

"We'll worry about car arrangements and shit later. That shit doesn't matter to me. You do."

Feeling my face heat, I turn away and press my hands against the side of the jeep.

It's silent for a few moments, before Madison finally speaks. "I can drive your jeep home if you want to ride with this protective hottie. No worries, sweets. I fucking like him." She turns to me and looks me over in approval. "A whole lot."

"I'll follow you girls home. Get in the jeep." I push away from the jeep and open the door for Avalon.

She keeps her eyes on me, while walking between me and the door, and then hops in. "Come here," she whispers.

Without hesitation, I lean in close.

My heart jumps in surprise when she grabs my face and kisses me hard and deep, running her tongue across my lips for access.

Getting lost in the moment, I tangle my hands into the back of her hair and suck her tongue into my mouth, moaning as my cock hardens.

"Holy shit, that's hot," Madison says, while practically leaning into Avalon's lap.

Laughing, Avalon pulls away from our kiss and elbows her friend out of her lap. "Back up, woman. It's called personal space."

"Looks like you have a Blaine," I mutter.

"Now that you mentioned it," she says, while still elbowing Madison out of her space. "I can see the similarities."

I run my hand over my beard and start backing up. "Alright. Let's go."

When we pull up outside of their little red house, I park my truck and jump out to meet the girls by the jeep.

"Thanks for following us," Avalon says with a small smile while closing her jeep door. "And thanks for waiting outside for us at the salon. No one has ever done that before."

"I'll be inside," Madison yells over to us from the door of the house. "You're a pretty awesome guy, Royal. Tell your friends hello for me." She winks and then disappears inside.

Once it's just the two of us, I back Avalon against the side of her jeep and run my hand up her neck, before gently wrapping it around her throat. "That's just who I am."

She closes her eyes and breathes against my lips. "And I like who you are, Royal. You make me feel safe; yet fill me with excitement at the same time. I like not knowing what to expect next from you." She opens her eyes to look at me. "You're special. So fucking special. Fuck what others think and fuck what you think, dammit. Your heart is good. There's no monster inside of you." She whispers the last part.

"What makes you so sure of that?" I question tensely. "There are things you don't fucking know about me."

"Then tell me," she snaps. Her hands reach up to squeeze my arm. "Tell me something about you that I don't know; anything at all. I just want to know about *you.*"

I swallow hard and lower my head, brushing it against the side of her face. "You know why I hate this world?"

She shakes her head.

"Because my fiancée was fucking taken from me," I choke out. "I wasn't there and she was taken from me. Fuck!" I slam the palm of my hand into the side of her jeep. "I..." I shake my head, unable to get the next words out.

"Oh, my God. I'm so sorry," she whispers. "You don't have to keep going. Royal..." She grabs my face in both hands and forces me to look up at her. "I'm always here if you need me. You don't have to tell me what happened today, but know that when you're ready I'll be here. I promise."

Her words cause my heart to race, and an overwhelming feeling to be close to her takes over, causing me to fist her hair and bury my face into her soft neck.

She doesn't ask questions or choose to speak in this moment. She just holds me as if she knows what I need... and she's right.

We stay like this for a while, before I finally get my shit together and pull away. "I need to go," I say tensely, while removing her hands from me. "Go inside, please."

"Royal..." She reaches for my face, but I pull away and run my hands over my face.

"Avalon, just go inside. I'm not leaving until you do, dammit."

She stands firm and looks at me. "Then I'm not going inside. I want you to stay. Royal —"

"No, the fuck you don't," I bark out. "Just take my word for it. Now go."

"Fuck you," she replies. "Don't tell me what I want. That's my job."

Growling out in frustration, I pick her up and throw her over my shoulder, storming my way up to the front door.

With one hand I reach out and open the door, before walking through the house in search of her bedroom.

"What are you doing?" She slaps my ass repeatedly. "Are you serious?"

"Dead serious."

Madison appears in the hallway, looking at me in confusion.

"Where's her bedroom?"

"Don't tell him, Madi," Avalon says quickly.

"Ooohhh... this looks fun." Madison points out Avalon's room. "Right there. Sorry, sweets, but this game looks fun."

Hurrying to her door, I push it open and toss her onto the bed, before stripping her down to her panties and bra.

"What the fuck?" Avalon sits up on her bed as I start walking toward the door.

"It's fucking late. All I wanted you to do was go inside so I could leave." I look her body over, fighting with everything in me not to take her right now, burying myself so deep that it fucking hurts. "Goodnight."

Before I can lose my willpower, I slam her door closed behind me and rush out the door and toward my truck, getting in.

Gripping the steering wheel, I race out of the driveway before she can get dressed and come try to stop me.

I was so fucking close to telling her everything. She has no idea what kinds of emotions that stirs up for me.

Then she held me. She fucking held me, and it felt so damn good. I needed to get out of there before I lost myself to her.

Fuck! She's slowly breaking me down and making it hard for me not to want to keep her...

CHAPTER 27

R OYAL

I'VE BEEN SITTING IN MY truck for the last twenty minutes, just staring over at Olivia's headstone, while practically fucking talking to myself and hoping that she's listening.

It hurts so bad to think that I could care for another woman the same way that I cared for her. I promised her that I'd only ever love her. I fought every day to show her that, and now look what the fuck I'm doing.

I'm letting another woman into my heart and letting her cloud my thoughts, breaking down my rage, and quieting some of the demons in my head... the demons that are supposed to lead me to Brian.

Getting to Brian has been my sole purpose for two fucking years, and now that Avalon's entered my fucking life, it's second to wanting to be close to her and keep her safe.

"What the fuck is wrong with me, Olivia?" I grip the steering wheel, squeezing so hard that my knuckles turn white. "I know I promised to always love you and Hadley and that's a promise that I will keep until my very last breath. Never doubt that. But..." I lean my head back into the seat and close my eyes, before running my hands over my face. "She's getting to me, baby. She makes me feel peace in my darkest moments and understands me when others don't. It's like she sees some sort of good in me and isn't willing to let that go. Avalon is strong like you and doesn't back down from what she believes in. She's the only light in my darkness besides you and Hadley; a small taste of heaven in this hell I've been living in without you two."

I swallow hard and pull out the CD that Olivia and I used to listen to together. This song was always our way of showing each other how much we loved each other when we were at our worst moments and just needed a reminder.

"Wild Horses" by The Rolling Stones starts to play.

Lighting a cigarette, I close my eyes and listen in silence, letting the tears slide down my face.

My chest aches so fucking bad that I can barely even manage to smoke my cigarette, but I fight through it, letting my feelings consume me until the song finally ends.

Then I play it on repeat.

It's another twenty minutes before I finally shut the CD off and look back over at her grave, feeling overcome with my emotions.

Usually I would get out and go see her, but I needed her to hear our song to show her how much I still care and miss her. I love that fucking woman. Always will.

Gathering my emotions, I pull out of the cemetery and head for the bar, knowing that nothing else needs to be said right now.

I left Jax and Blaine there when I left to wait for Avalon to get off work.

When I get about three blocks away from *Savage & Ink*, a cop zooms past me with their lights flashing.

I instantly know there's trouble from the direction he's heading. It's not hard to figure out.

"Fucking shit! What did you do now, Blaine?"

Stepping on the gas, I run the fucking red light and fly past the cop, quickly turning down the next street to beat him.

As soon as the bar comes into view, the first thing I notice is Officer Knight's car outside and see the boys brawling outside in the parking lot, with Mark trying to get it under control.

Parking my truck, I jump out with my adrenaline pumping and rush over to where Blaine is on the ground with Kane on top of him.

I rush into action, kicking Kane in the face hard as fuck when he reaches for his gun and points it at Blaine's head.

Scrambling to grab Kane's gun that he dropped, I get it in my reach before he does and smack him in the side of the head with it, repeatedly, letting my anguish get the best of me.

Then I lean in close to his face and shove the barrel into his big mouth, about two seconds away from pulling the trigger.

"Don't ever fucking threaten my brother's life. I won't hesitate to fucking blow your brains through your skull."

"Fuuck oue," he mumbles over the gun.

"Fuck me!" I scream, while shoving the gun deeper; so deep that he starts gagging and choking for air. "Test me motherfucker. Go ahead. Do it!"

"Royal!" Mark yells from behind me, drawing my attention away right as the second set of flashing lights arrive, parking next to Mark's car. "Drop that fucking gun. Shit, man! Don't be stupid. Now!"

Grinding my jaw, I look Kane in the eyes, while dropping his gun and standing back up to my feet. "Don't fuck up, motherfucker. I'll be watching."

When I look over, Jax is backing away from some drunk asshole that rides with Kane and his crew.

They're both bloodied and Jax's black shirt is lying beside his feet. Watching me, he nods his head and reaches for his shirt.

Blaine steps beside me and cracks his neck, while looking down at Kane as he struggles back to his feet.

"Put your fucking hands up! Now!"

Letting out an angry breath, I throw my hands up to show him that I'm not holding any weapons. Not anymore at least.

The new officer at the scene lines us all up and drops us down to our knees after patting us down for weapons.

He stops in front of me and grabs the top of my hair, forcing me to look at him. "You're the fucker that—"

Standing up, I shake his hand free and slam my head into his face, causing him to stumble back and reach for his gun.

"Fucking piece of shit! Fuck! Back down to your knees."

"Calm the fuck down, Ryan," Knight growls out. "You deserved that shit." He points at his gun. "Put that shit away. He's good."

Officer Ryan flexes his jaw and slowly puts his gun away. "He fucking flew past me to get here and then he was on top of a guy when I arrived. He needed force."

"The fuck he did," Mark argues. "He's been here the whole time. Your mistake." Mark glances my way and narrows his eyes, before turning away. "Let's just get these two out of here. That one pulled a gun." He nods to Kane. "It was self-defense for these three. They were protecting their bar."

"Fuck!" the dickhead cop yells out when I smirk at him. "Whatever. Let's just get this shit over with."

"We're talking later," Mark mouths at me, while grabbing Kane.

Turning away, I grip my hair in frustration and stare at the building. That's when I notice the fucking window.

"Blaine, you fucking dick," I mutter.

"I told you, motherfucker," Jax says to Blaine. "He's pissed as fuck. Good luck." With that, he steps through the window, leaving Blaine to take my wrath alone.

"Tell me," I say stiffly. "I'm in need of a good fucking story right about now."

"The motherfucker called my cock small." He shrugs and pulls out a cigarette. "So I showed him who had the bigger dick."

I clench my jaw. "By throwing him through my window?"

Blaine grabs his dick and thrusts it at the police cars as they pull off. "Fuck yeah, small dicked bitch. How you like it?" he yells.

Pissed as shit, I slap him upside the head. "You're a fucking idiot." I grip his shoulder and get in his face. "You'll always be like a brother to me and I'll always have your back no matter what, but don't be so fucking stupid." I release his shoulder and walk away. "Clean that shit up."

I hop in my truck and head in the direction that I need to be.

The only place I want to be right now...

CHAPTER 28

AVALON

AFTER ROYAL STORMED OFF AND left me, Madison decided to let herself into my room and hit me with a bunch of annoying questions that only made me want to throat punch her ass.

After about the fifth one, I finally pushed her out the door and shut it in her face. That was me being nice. I wanted to do a lot more. Her giddiness had me twitching to slap her.

I'm beyond annoyed right now and upset at how Royal just tossed me into my bed and left me after the moment we had outside. All I wanted to do was be there for him and he wouldn't fucking let me.

It hurts how he just pushed me away, especially when I can see how much he's dying inside, and all I want to do is ease some of his pain.

I've been sitting here in bed for the last hour now, playing with my phone and fighting with myself on whether or not I should text him. I wasn't ready to say goodbye yet, but every time I get ready to start typing a message out, my heart starts racing so hard that I can feel my fingers throbbing around my phone and I end up tossing it down in anger.

The more I think about what happened though, the more I feel like I need to say something.

"You know what... screw you. You just threw me here and fucking left me."

I unlock my phone for the tenth time and start typing really fast and hard, determined to get my message across before I can change my mind.

AVALON

I can't believe you just undressed me, tossed me into my damn bed, and left. Who does that, Royal?

It's a few minutes before I get a response. My fingers almost can't move fast enough as I work to open the message.

ROYAL

I did what I needed to do at the time. You wouldn't listen to me, so...

AVALON

So... that's what you do when someone wants to spend time with you? You just toss them aside and leave?

I really wish you were here right now.

I'd...

I stop typing and look up as my door flies open to Royal staring me down. He looks a mess, as if he's just walked through a damn storm to get here. "Yeah... what would you do?"

Tossing my phone aside, I sit up straight and crawl over to the end of the bed, keeping my eyes on his dark ones as he sheds his shoes and socks. "You really want to know?" I question with my pulse racing.

He walks closer, stops right in front of me, and places his hands at his sides, showing me that I'm free to do as I wish. "Yeah. Show me."

Feeling like I'm going to explode if I don't touch this beautiful man, I wrap my arms around his neck and pull him down, slamming my lips against his, hard; so damn hard, and it still isn't enough to satisfy my hunger for him. I feel as if I can never get enough of him and the feeling scares the shit out of me.

His arms roughly grab at me, lifting me up to wrap my legs around his waist. He breathes fast against my lips as he speaks. "You want me here, baby? Huh?" His voice sounds pained, causing an overwhelming feeling of sadness to fill me. "How do you feel when I'm around?"

I close my eyes and tell him exactly how it makes me feel when he's close. Exactly how I feel at this very moment... "Safe. Warm. Needed. Whole. Sexy. Alive. More alive than I have felt in a long time, Royal. You make me feel a lot of things. Sometimes I feel like it's too much and it's hard to breathe, but it's a good feeling."

He growls against my lips, before slamming me against the wall and ripping my shirt off over my head.

With his lips against mine, he grabs the back of my neck and starts walking us through the house until we're in the bathroom.

Holding me up with one hand, he quickly turns on the shower water. "Can you handle it hot?" he questions with heated eyes.

I nod my head and grab at his hair. "Scalding," I say, before pulling on his long hair.

The thought of taking a shower with this man is the hottest thing in the world to me. Fuck if I don't want to see his naked, inked body, soaking wet as the water drips down his tight muscles.

Setting me down, he reaches for the top back part of his shirt and slowly pulls it over his head, making my damn legs feel weak as he tosses it at the wall.

Royal is like a beautiful, broken angel: hard to look at, but utterly impossible to turn away from.

He comes at me slowly, yet it's so powerful and intoxicating that the air gets sucked straight from my lungs. Every muscle in his body is tense, his tattooed flesh moist with sweat as he stares down at me with an intensity that has me gripping at the wall behind me. He's breathing heavily, his lips slightly parted as his powerful eyes meet mine and capture them. I'm lost in his darkness, wanting to be right there with him... just like in my damn dream.

He doesn't say a word as he scoops me up, and in one swift movement he bites onto my neck and carries me into the hot shower water.

I moan out in desire, just wanting to touch him, to feel my hands on him in any way I can.

"Kiss me, Royal," I whisper against his lips as the water drips down between them. "Please," I plead. "You have no idea how good they feel against mine."

"The fuck I don't."

He crushes his lips to mine and slams me against the shower wall, grabbing and fisting my hair as if he's just as desperate as I am.

Biting my bottom lip, he sets me down against the wall and places one hand on my waist while working the string on my wet shorts with the other.

His hands are working fast and hard to pull my shorts down my legs and lift my feet out of them, but it still doesn't seem fast enough. I *need* this man inside of me.

Standing here watching his hard eyes, I feel myself panting

as he balls my thong in his inked hand and yanks. The thin strings rip apart, baring my throbbing pussy to him.

Lowering his body, he brushes his lips along my stomach while gripping my hips and squeezing. "You're fucking breathtaking, babe." I feel my legs shake below me as he runs his hands lower down my body, brushing between my thighs to spread them. "I want to taste what I do to you. Fuck... I need this."

Gripping my waist, he picks me up until my legs are wrapped around his waist, and slides me up the wall until he's standing up straight, pulling my legs over his shoulders to support me.

"Oh shit, Royal..." I grip his hair with both hands, and hold on for life when he runs his tongue up my inner thigh, grazing my flesh with his teeth. It has my heart jump-starting, just waiting to feel his tongue where I need it the most.

An aching pleasure runs throughout my body, causing me to tremble above his shoulders as he inches his mouth up to my inner thigh, right beside my pussy, and bites down onto my skin.

The vibration of his growl against my thigh causes me to scream out in desperation and position my pussy against his lips. "I can't take it anymore," I pant. "I want you, Royal. I want you more than anything in this damn world. Touch me. Now."

He runs his lips over my folds, before roughly sucking my clit into his mouth and releasing it. "Then I'm fucking yours."

My back arches and I moan out, biting my lip as his tongue swipes out and runs up and down my pussy, making my whole body jerk in pleasure.

Knowing that he's standing here soaking wet and still in his jeans tells me just how much he truly needed me right now. That does things to me that I can't even begin to explain.

Royal Savage...

He's hazardous to my health, mind, and body, yet the only thing that I crave.

I yank his hair to the side and he sucks my clit so hard that I scream out in pleasure and almost lose my balance, but he catches me. I can feel him growling against my clit and it deepens the pleasure and makes me want more as he holds me steady.

"I need to be inside of you," he says against my pussy, before sliding his tongue in and squeezing my thigh.

Before I can say anything he's lowering me down the wall.

He presses his hands against the wall and shakes the water out of his face. "Take my jeans off."

I drop to my knees and quickly undo his jeans, yanking them roughly down his legs, before biting his hard dick through his wet boxer briefs.

He growls out and grabs my arms, yanking me to my feet and wrapping one of my legs around his waist.

I can feel him working on lowering his briefs with his free hand and a surge of excitement surges through me at the thought of him being inside of me. It feels like it's been forever, and my body is aching for him to fill me.

Running his hand over my breast, he stops on my throat and squeezes, while thrusting into me at the same time, filling me completely.

"Oh fuck!" I scream out from the intrusion and dig my nails into his back in shock. "No condom, Royal? Are you sure you want to do this?"

He closes his eyes and slowly pulls out of me, before filling me again and stopping. "Oh shit..." He leans his forehead against mine and grabs my face, letting the water wash over us while we both stand here breathing heavily. "I never want to use a condom with you again," he breathes.

I place both of my hands on his face and lift it to look into his eyes. "You're the first person to be inside me this way, Royal. Only you," I whisper.

He looks at me for a few seconds, just staring into my eyes as if he's slowly letting my words sink in. His eyes fill with an emotion that I've never seen from him before: pride.

His lips desperately seek mine as he rolls his hips, fucking me deep and hard, as if my words set him off and he can't feel enough of me around him.

The only sound around us besides the water hitting us is the sound of our heavy breathing and our wet bodies slapping together as he takes me so deep that it hurts.

It feels as if he's claiming me, making sure that I'll never want another man inside of me this way.

It's working... oh is it working.

Lowering his face, he bites my neck and grips my hair, while continuing to claim my body.

Before I know it, I'm digging my nails into his arms and screaming as my orgasm rolls through me in strong waves, making my whole body tingle.

"Fuck..." He pulls me away from the wall and turns our bodies sideways, holding me up as he pounds into me fast and hard, getting close to his own orgasm.

As soon as I feel him releasing himself inside of me and hear him growl out, another orgasm hits me hard, causing me to grab onto the shower curtain and pull.

The whole thing breaks down, falling into the tub with us.

"Holy shit, Royal," I pant, while holding onto him. "That was..." I take a second to catch my breath. "Amazing." I grab his face and smile. "I'm glad you're my first this way. There's not a better feeling in the world than having you inside of me."

He smiles against my lips and then laughs as we both turn around to look at the mess we made.

When the curtain fell water went everywhere, soaking the sink, toilet, mirror, and walls.

"I'll clean this up in the morning."

With his arms holding me up, he steps out of the tub and starts walking us toward the door, naked.

"Whoa!" I hold onto him tighter. "What if Madison is out there?"

He cups my ass and holds me as closely as possible. "Then she'll see our asses." He smirks and opens the door.

I peek over his shoulder as he walks down the hall, looking for Madison, but she's nowhere to be seen.

It's not until we reach my door when I hear her screaming and things banging off the walls from her room.

"Holy fuck!" My eyes widen. "Looks like she has some company of her own."

Royal opens my door and drops me onto the bed, crawling in next to me and covering us both up. "I have a pretty good guess at who too."

"Oh yeah?" I question, while straddling his lap and playing with his wet hair. "Who?"

He lifts a brow and runs his hands down my arms. "You'll see in the morning."

He kisses me hard, before rolling me over beside him and burying his face into my neck.

We lay in silence for a bit, but I can't seem to fall asleep. A nagging feeling of wanting to know more about Royal and his fiancée has been making me feel tense.

"Ask me," he says, scaring me. "Then go to sleep."

I turn around in his arms and bury my face in his neck like he always does me. "Are you sure? I don't know if I should ask this."

"Yes," he says sternly.

Running my fingers over the smooth flesh of his arms, I kiss his neck and let out a small breath. "How did Olivia die? You said she was taken from you."

His whole body stiffens and I'm afraid he's going to push me away, but instead he pulls me closer. "She was murdered."

"Holy fuck," I whisper to myself. I feel a tear slide down my face at the thought of him going through such a tragedy.

"She was pregnant with our baby girl. I was at work and I was too late to get to her." He turns his face away and lets out a long breath. "Now let's go to sleep."

God, my heart aches so bad for him. I want to say something. Anything to tell him how sorry I am, but I know that's not what he needs to hear. There's nothing that can make his pain go away and nothing that can make him feel complete again.

Not even me...

CHAPTER 29

AVALON

THE BRIGHT MORNING SUN HITS me hard, blinding me and causing me to groan and cover my eyes as I step out front in search of Royal.

"He's gone," Blaine says from the porch step, grabbing my attention.

I cup my eyes from the sun and look down at him to see him toss his cigarette to the ground and look up at me. "Oh..." I respond softly. "When did he leave?"

"He was gone before I woke up." He reaches his arm out and grabs my hand, to pull me down next to him on the steps. "I'm sure he had something important to do. Don't look so down, you gorgeous ass woman. Sit with me."

I take a seat next to him and pull the band from my wrist, tying my hair up on the top of my head. "So you and Madi? I had a feeling it was you when things started falling off the damn walls." I smile up at him to see him smirking. "Wild Blaine."

"Yeah well..." He stops to slick his hair back and get in a

more comfortable position. "Royal had me text your girl to let him in the house last night. What can I say; your fine as hell friend wanted a ride on my Harley. So..." He fixes his shirt as if he's all slick. "I took her for a ride on my dick instead."

I laugh and nudge him in the side. "That you did. And I'm sure she won't be asking to ride anything else *but* for a while now."

We sit here in silence for a few minutes, before Blaine wraps his arm around my shoulder. "You know... you remind me a lot of my sister for some reason. You're strong-willed and say what's on your mind, without giving a crap about what others think. I like you and I can see why Royal does too."

I smile and lean into him. "So your sister is pretty fucking cool then, huh?"

He nods his head and his amber eyes go dark. "Yeah... she was pretty fucking awesome."

My heart stops as soon as the word *was* leaves his mouth. That's not at all what I was expecting to hear. "Was?" I force out the word, unsure if I should ask the next part. "What happened to her?"

He looks away and exhales, before answering. "Some assholes took her from me. They took the best person in my life and left me with no other family." His left hand grips the top step and I can see his jaw clenching as he takes a moment, before continuing. "She was fucking raped and killed by three lowlifes. You better fucking believe that if her fiancé had not killed those pieces of shit first, I would have. There's nothing I wouldn't have done for her. She was older than me by a year and took care of me growing up. Through the endless bouncing between foster homes, she was the only solid, certain thing in my life. Now she's fucking gone and there's not a damn thing I can do about it."

His words cause my heart to hurt for him and I find myself

reaching out to comfort him as he drops his arm from my shoulder and rubs his hands over his face.

I can't stand it right now. I don't want to see these boys hurt. It's not fair. Not at all. "That's fucking horrible, Blaine." I lace my arm through his and lean my head against his arm. "I'm so sorry that happened to your sister." I swallow hard, trying to keep my emotions somewhat under control. "What happened to her fiancé?"

He pulls out a cigarette and lights it, quickly taking a long drag and blowing out away from me. "He's around."

"He's not in prison for what he did?" I ask in surprise. "How long ago did this happen?"

"Almost two years ago." He shakes his head. "And nah. Self-defense. Those assholes broke into his home and murdered his future wife. He had every right to fight back and he did. Some people look down on him for it, but not me. He's the most badass, loyal, dependable motherfucker that I know."

"So a lot like Royal," I ask. My chest tightens with need at just the thought of him, and I can't help but to wonder where he is.

Blaine's eyes meet mine and for a split second he looks surprised. "Yeah." He desperately takes another drag of his cigarette and slowly blows out. "A lot like Royal."

Sitting in silence, I hold onto Blaine's arm, wanting to somehow comfort him and show him that I'm there. I may not know Blaine very well, but I know that Royal cares about him. That makes me care about him as well. He makes me smile. I like that about him.

The thought of the loss these boys have suffered through the years breaks my damn heart and makes me realize just how rough they've been living.

Royal lost a friend recently, his fiancée at some point, and Blaine has lost his sister. I've known these men for less than a month, yet I ache so hard for the pain they must be feeling and holding inside.

"I'm really sorry again." I squeeze his arm and he wraps his arm back around me. "I'm here if you need me, okay."

He smiles. "Really?"

I nod my head and look him in the eyes. His eyes really are quite beautiful, and I find myself getting lost in them for a second. "Of course. And I'm a pretty good listener too."

"No shit." He pulls me closer and rests his head against mine. "I'll remember that, babe."

We both look up as Royal pulls up in his truck.

"Don't make me break your fingers off, asshole," Royal says to Blaine as soon as he walks around his truck toward us. He holds up a plastic bag from some restaurant I've never been to. "Went to pick up some breakfast. Thought you'd still be sleeping when I got back."

Blaine stands up and Royal eyes him over while grabbing my hand to help me up. "You two sure did seem nice and fucking cozy out here."

I clear my throat and rub Blaine's arm. "Blaine was just telling me about his sister, so you're damn straight we were nice and cozy. I was comforting him."

Royal looks at Blaine. Blaine quickly shakes his head, silently answering whatever the hell that look he's giving him is asking. "Good." Royal grabs my chin with his free hand and presses his soft lips against mine, gently breathing against them when he pulls away. "I don't expect any less from you. Thank you."

"You're welcome," I whisper. "Now what's in that bag? I'm starving."

Royal lifts a brow and smiles. "Everything."

Once we get inside, Royal opens the bag and starts emptying its contents onto the counter.

Bagels. Pancakes. Waffles. Eggs. Bacon. Sausage. Burritos. Fruit.

"Holy shit," I say with wide eyes, about to tackle the food. I'm that excited. "A damn breakfast buffet. I think I might just love you."

"You better," he says, making my damn heart skip a beat from the tone of his voice.

Pulling my eyes away from his, I reach for one of the paper plates and dig in, before I can think too much on his response and take it for something more than what it is.

Madison finally joins us in the kitchen about ten minutes later, looking like she got hit by a damn bus.

Holy shit, Blaine tore it up...

She looks around the kitchen at the three of us eating. "How damn rude. You dicks couldn't shove a bagel in my face and wake me up?"

"I thought about shoving something else in your face," Blaine says. "But then you wouldn't have wanted to get the hell out of bed." He winks.

Madison tears off a piece of her bagel and grins. "So damn true."

Everyone gets quiet, sitting in their own little random spots around the kitchen and eating. It's a comfortable silence and I find that I like it. I could get used to this being my mornings.

"Come on, Blaine." Madison jumps to her feet and walks over to straddle Blaine in his chair. "I have a few hours before work. You up for round five?"

Blaine quickly stands to his feet, picking her up with him. "Oh, fuck yeah." He tosses his piece of sausage down and grips her ass, before spanking it hard. He turns to Royal. "I'll catch your ass later at *Savage,* yeah?"

Royal nods his head.

Then Blaine carries Madison out of the kitchen and we hear her bedroom door slam shut.

"Go get dressed while I clean up." Royal pushes away from the counter and walks over to me. He places both of his hands on my hips and squeezes. "I've got to go help a friend with something real fast."

Smiling, I wrap both of my arms around his neck. "Oh, yeah. And what makes you think I want to go with?"

Royal leans in and brushes his lips against mine, before grabbing my bottom lip in his teeth and gently tugging. "What?" he whispers. "You don't want to?"

I nod my head and suck my bottom lip into my mouth as he releases it. "I'll get dressed," I say, while rubbing the back of his head.

"That's my girl," he says against my lips, before kissing me and walking away to clean up.

I exit my room fifteen minutes later to find Royal standing on the front porch, texting on his phone.

He looks up when he hears me open the screen door. "You look fucking sexy in an old pair of jeans with your hair pulled back." He hits end on his phone and puts it away, before even finishing his message. "Fuuck me." He cups my face and presses his lips against mine. "How the fuck do you always taste so good? I'm pissed that my brother ever got to taste you. No more of that shit. Not as long as I'm breathing. Got it?"

"Yeah," I barely get out, through my heavy breathing. "Your lips are so much better than his anyway," I say with a smile.

His face softens and I'm surprised when he pulls me into a hug and buries his face in my neck. That always gets me.

I could never get tired of the way he makes me feel, and I suddenly feel emotional as he holds me close, as if he *needs* me. It makes my heart go crazy in my chest and causes my stomach to do flips, making me want to scream out that I love this man and I never want him to let go.

I want to always be what he needs. I want to always be his

comfort and to be the neck that he buries his face in; no one else.

He finally pulls his face away. "Let's go." Grabbing my hand, he walks me to his truck and opens the door for me. Like always, he helps me in and shuts the door behind me.

"What about your text?" I ask once he's inside the truck with me.

"I'm with you right now. Jax's text can wait."

My heart swells and my breath hitches when I feel Royal's hand grab mine. He pulls it into his lap and runs his thumb over it.

"What if it's important?" I can't help but to ask.

"Then he'll call when I don't text back." He glances over at me, before turning the radio up and relaxing into his seat as if he's comfortable and content for the first time in a long time.

I spread my hand out on his thigh and smile as I watch him drive.

How can one man be so damn beautifully broken and breathtaking?

We drive for a good twenty minutes, before pulling down a dirt road that leads us to a big white house.

"Cole is an old friend of mine. He was Riley's brother."

I squeeze his thigh. "What happened to Riley?"

He parks the truck and looks over at me, while pulling the keys out of the ignition. "A motorcycle accident. Someone in a van ran the stop sign and hit him. He died on impact."

"Oh, my God." I look at him, now worried for his safety. "I don't know what I'd do if that ever happened—"

"Don't worry," he cuts me off. "That will be the last thing that takes me."

He releases my hand and grips the door handle. "Come on."

I jump out of the truck and meet up with Royal at the front. He grabs my hand and starts walking toward the barn.

"You out here, Cole?" he yells when we get closer to the front of the barn.

"Yeah, man," Cole yells in return. "This shit is pissing me off. Can't get it to start for..."

His words trail off as he steps through the door to see Royal and me.

"Hi," he says to me, looking a bit shocked. He wipes his hand off on a rag and reaches it out for me to grab. "I'm Cole."

"This is my girlfriend, Avalon," Royal says while squeezing the hand he's been holding. "I thought you guys should meet."

I look over at Royal, trying to contain my surprise at his word choice: *girlfriend.*

His girlfriend?!? Am I his fucking girlfriend? Oh, God. Please say yes. I just need to hear it one more time.

I look at his lips, silently willing them to move again and repeat the word.

Royal must sense my hesitation, so he pulls me to him and presses his lips against mine. "Yes, you're my fucking girl. I can't share you with anyone and I don't have any plans to. Got it?"

I swallow and turn around to grab Cole's hand. "Nice to meet you, Cole. Sorry to hear about your brother."

Cole gives me a weak smile. "Thanks. It's good to meet you as well." He looks me over, as if he still can't believe that I'm standing here. "I never thought I'd see the day that this guy brought another girl here."

Royal releases my hand and runs his hands through his hair. "Alright, man. Let's just get this shit looked at."

Cole smiles at me. "Feel free to take a seat anywhere you want or walk around and hang out. It won't take long. Royal is a fucking genius when it comes to getting motorcycles running."

Royal plasters on a cocky smile while stripping out of his black flannel and bending down to work on the bike.

Finding an empty crate, I take a seat and watch Royal as he works.

I find it so damn sexy watching him get dirty from the motor and I can't help but to beam as I watch him move and work so easily, as if it's nothing to him.

Twenty minutes later, the motorcycle is running and Cole is slapping Royal on the back, thanking him.

"Holy fuck. Good shit." Cole straddles the bike and revs the engine. "I'm going to take this shit for a test run," he yells over the loud roar of the engine. "Be back."

Royal backs up to let Cole drive past him and out the side door of the barn.

I smile at Royal as he cleans his hands off. "You did a great job."

He tosses the rag aside. "My father used to work on bikes. He taught me everything he knew about them."

"Well, he did a damn good job," I say.

"Thanks." He smiles and nods his head for me to follow him.

We walk around to the back of the barn and stop when we reach an old tire swing. Holding it, he calls me over. "Come here."

I laugh. "Alright. You going to push me on the swing?"

"Yeah," he responds. "Now get your beautiful ass on before I bite it."

I pause to look back at him after getting one leg through it. "Is that supposed to scare me?" I stick my second leg through and grab onto the rope. "Because nothing in the bedroom can scare me after what you did to me in the middle of the night." I smile from the memory of me waking up in the middle of the night to him finger fucking me. We didn't sleep much after that.

"It got you turned on though, didn't it," he says while giving me a push. "And I can do a lot more fucking damage to your body than I did last night. Never doubt me."

I laugh and grip onto the rope as Royal starts spinning the tire, winding the rope up.

"Whoa! That's tight enough."

He stops spinning the tire to look me in the face and laugh at me. "Hold on, babe."

He releases the tire and it starts spinning so fast that I can barely hang on, yet I can't stop laughing as I fight to keep my head up.

As it slows down, I catch glimpses of Royal watching me in satisfaction.

"Did you enjoy me screaming my head off?" I tease when it stops.

He grabs the top of the rope and pulls me to him. "Oh... you were laughing your head off. You loved it." Leaning in, he runs his tongue over my lips, before slipping it inside my mouth and swirling it around my tongue.

The indescribable feeling of my heart about to beat out of my chest takes over and I find myself gripping the rope even tighter, afraid that I'll faint and fall off.

This man truly has no idea what he does to me. I don't even know what he does, but I love it.

"Hey!" Cole runs out from the barn. "She runs like a beast. Damn, man. I owe you."

Royal grabs my hand and helps me out of the tire. "You want to meet me in the truck? I want to check on him before I leave."

I nod my head. "Of course." I smile over at Cole. "It was great meeting you."

"Hey, you too." He watches me as I walk away, before turning back to Royal.

I'm in the truck for about five minutes before Royal jumps into the driver's side and instantly grabs for my hand, pulling it into his lap.

"Is everything okay with Cole then?"

"He's good," he responds. "He's getting by."

We're halfway to my house when Royal's phone starts

ringing in his pocket. "Shit. Can you grab that for me?"

"Yeah, sure." I dig into his pocket as he leans up for me to be able to get my hand inside.

I hit connect and hold it out to him.

"Take the call for me," he says. "I'm not going to talk and drive when I have you in my truck."

Feeling a bit awkward, I hold the phone to my ear. "Hello."

"Hey," Jax says into the phone. "Royal driving you?"

"Yeah," I respond. "We just left Cole's."

"Good," he says. "That's real good. Hey. Tell Royal that his appointment is here and I have them set up in his chair already. Kay?"

"I'll let him know, Jax."

"Thanks, babe."

With that, he hangs up.

"Jax said your appointment is waiting on you."

"Oh fuck!" He grips the steering wheel. "I forgot all about that shit." He grabs his phone from my hand and tosses it in my seat. "You good for the day?"

I smile and nod my head as he grabs my hand. "Yeah, I'm good. I could use some rest before work. The stupid owner stops by every Thursday. She's sort of a cunt sometimes."

Royal looks over at me and smiles. "I love that dirty mouth." He pulls up in front of my house and shifts the truck into park. "I'll pick you up from work, alright? Don't walk outside until you see me."

I lean in and run my fingers over his face. He grabs my hand and his eyes meet mine. "I'll wait for you," I say. "Thanks for breakfast."

He grabs my hand and kisses it. "Alright."

I jump out of his truck and stand on the porch, watching as he drives away.

What am I going to do about this man? I've completely fallen for him...

CHAPTER 30

AVALON

How's work, baby? You busy?

SMILING, I SET MY HALF-EATEN chicken sandwich down and respond to the message that Royal sent about twenty minutes ago.

I wanted to check my phone as soon as I felt it vibrate in my pocket, but Claudette has been around all day watching us all like a hawk. I'm doing my best to stay on her good side so hopefully she will cut her visits down to twice a damn month.

AVALON

It's been pretty boring. The customers know to stay away on Thursdays when the evil bitch is lurking around. I'm actually ready to pull my hair out from boredom. You?

I pick up my sandwich and continue to eat it, while waiting for his response. This damn sandwich has been the most action that has happened since I walked through the door four hours ago. Madison is lucky she got the morning shift. What I wouldn't have done to switch with her.

ROYAL

You know the boys. Never a dull moment here. No windows broken yet, and no one has gotten choked out. Pretty fucking tame compared to some days.

I respond to his message, while laughing to myself. I almost feel sad that I'm not there with them... like I'm missing something. I've found myself wanting to hang around his friends more and more with each day. I feel like they're the norm for me now.

AVALON

Yeah, well I'd much rather be there than stuck here for the next three hours. I miss you and the boys. Especially you...

It takes about five minutes before his next response comes through.

ROYAL

Who is this crazy lady with the Ronald McDonald hair that is looking at me as if I've just robbed a bank?

"Holy shit!" I drop my sandwich and jump to my feet, rushing to the door. "There's no way..."

I open the door and look outside to see Royal sitting at my station, looking at the break room door, as if he's been waiting for me to appear.

He instantly raises a brow and smiles at me when his eyes meet mine. "Come here, baby," he demands.

I close the break room door and glance over at Claudette,

who is giving me a disapproving look. She's probably never seen a man that looks like Royal and his friends around here. She almost looks nervous for the first time ever. "Avalon? You know this man?"

"Claudette," I say with confidence, walking past her to get to Royal. "I do. Very well. He's pretty amazing to know."

Royal stands when I reach him. Locking eyes with me, he cups my face in his hands and leans in to press his lips against mine. His kiss feels hard and desperate, as if he's telling me that he missed me too. "So you miss me?" he questions with a grin.

I laugh against his lips and place my hands over his, not caring what Claudette thinks. I fucking love this man. It's becoming clearer with each time I see him. The way my heart reacts to him is undeniable. "So damn much. How do you always know the right time to show up? You truly amaze me."

He leans in closer, intimately brushing his lips over mine. "Because it's always the same time that I'm needing you," he answers. "Which is way too fucking much."

Claudette clears her throat from beside us, looking appalled. "Perhaps you two can take this unwanted show outside." She looks down at her watch and then looks up, avoiding any eye contact with Royal. "For the last six minutes of your break. You know better than this, Avalon."

I tilt my head and narrow my eyes at her. I've never, and I mean ever, questioned her in the entire time I've worked here. "Do I, Claudette?" I grab Royal's hand and lace my fingers with his, causing her eyes to lower to our hands. "Better than what?"

"To..." She swallows hard and looks up at my intense stare. "I would just appreciate it if you would take that outside. We'll talk later before I leave."

Her pen accidentally falls from her hand, landing next to her feet as she begins to walk away.

Without hesitation, Royal bends down, picks it up, and

hands it to her. "Ma'am. I don't normally bite. Only if you ask nicely." He winks and lifts a playful brow.

Claudette cautiously grabs the pen and sucks in an uncomfortable breath. "Thank you." Smiling weakly, she walks away without another word, leaving us with the clicking of her heels.

"Let's take it outside before Red's heart stops on her. That's the last thing I need to add to my list of shit."

He places his hand on the small of my back and guides me outside to the back of the building.

As soon as we're out of sight, he wraps my legs around his waist and presses me up against the brick building.

Before I know it, his lips are pressed against mine and he's reaching in between our bodies to undo the top of his jeans.

"Fuck, I can't stop thinking about being inside you this way. You do things to me, baby." Pulling my skirt up and my panties to the side, he sinks me down onto his erection and holds me still, while I adjust to his big size. "You okay?" he asks softly, while brushing my hair out of my face.

I nod my head and lean in to run my lips over his. "More than okay. I'm always more than okay when I'm with you, Royal. Never forget that."

He places one hand behind my neck and gently kisses me, while rolling his hips and moving inside of me.

It feels so good to have him inside of me that I couldn't care less about the fact that we're outside of my work right now and that Claudette or anyone else could come around and find us at any second. I need this beautiful man to be with me like this. I'd gladly say goodbye to this job and move on if it meant getting this moment with him.

He moves slowly, being sure to sink in as deep as he can with each thrust. His breath is soft and controlled against my lips, causing me to lean in and taste him.

My heart swells at the thought that this is the gentlest he's ever been with me. No choking. This is new to me.

"You're fucking perfection," he whispers against my lips. "And you're mine. No other man gets to be inside you this way." He gently runs his hand up the front of my neck, stopping when he reaches my lips. "You make me want to live again," he whispers.

I tangle my hands in his hair and gently bite his bottom lip, causing him to growl out in desire. "You've made me feel alive from the very first day I walked in on you." I brush my lips over his. "Let's help each other live."

"Fuuuck, baby." He runs his hand up the side of my head, before moving to the back and gripping my hair. "Hold on," he breathes.

I grip his shoulders, digging my nails in as his movements pick up. With each quick thrust, I find myself digging deeper as I get closer to climax.

"Royal..." I breathe hard against his lips as I lose myself to him yet again.

Holding me tight, he slams into me three more times, before I feel him releasing himself inside of me.

He presses his forehead to mine and holds my face still. "Why the fuck are you so perfect for me?" His eyes search mine as he rubs his thumb over my face. "I never thought I'd meet someone that could make me fucking feel. You do, and it scares the shit out of me."

I hold onto him, not ready to let go yet. "Royal... I..." Stopping myself from possibly making a huge mistake, I bite my tongue and rephrase what I was about to let slip. "You make me feel too. Please don't ever stop. Please."

Not saying anything, he presses his lips to mine and gently sets me back down to my feet. Quietly, he yanks his shirt off and cleans me off.

"Royal," I call out as he turns away. "Are you okay?"

He runs his hands through his hair, but stays facing the other way. "I don't know yet."

Balling his shirt up, he turns around and faces me again. "You should get back to work. I'll be back to pick you up in a bit." He walks over and gently kisses me on the forehead. "Bye..."

"Bye," I whisper as he walks away.

I wait a couple of minutes after I hear his truck pull off, before I walk around the building and go back inside.

As soon as I walk through the door, Claudette is watching me. "In my office."

"Just great," I mumble under my breath, while following her.

She waits for me to walk in first and then closes the door behind us. "You're late from your break. You're never late."

I nod my head. "Well, I needed a few extra minutes to deal with my personal life. It won't happen again."

She walks over to her desk and starts gathering up her things. "Can I still trust you to run this salon in the same manner now that you have that man in your life?"

"Are you seriously asking me this right now?" I ask, pissed off that she's treating Royal as if he's some kind of dog.

She looks up from gathering her things. "Yes. I am. I've seen what men that look like that are capable of."

"Is that right?" I give her a hard look. "And I've seen what men that look like your husband are capable of. That mustache is a bit creepy and suspicious of pedophile activities if you ask me?"

She huffs. "Are you accusing my husband of being a criminal?"

"I don't know," I reply. "Are you accusing my boyfriend of being a criminal based on his choice of tattoos and clothing?"

She shakes her head. "This conversation is not going in a direction that is looking well for you, so I suggest that you sleep on whatever else you plan on saying to me and we'll be talking again next week."

Grabbing her bag, she heads for the door and reaches to open it, but I slap my hand on the door, stopping her.

She looks over at me in surprise.

"Royal is a good person with a big fucking heart. You don't know him. I do, so I suggest that you keep your fucking mouth shut before you think of speaking to me about him again. Got it?"

Her mouth opens in shock and for once, she looks stunned speechless. "Consider yourself lucky that you're well desired here. You only get one second chance, missy." She runs her hand over her dress, smoothing it out. "Don't blow it."

She waits for me to back away from the door, before she pulls it open and stomps out.

I wait until the bell dings, indicating that she's left the building, before falling against the door and running my hands over my face.

I was so fucking close to losing my job, yet I didn't even have to think twice before defending Royal.

I'm beginning to see that Royal comes first to everything else. He's all that truly matters to me at the moment and I'm not afraid to make that known.

This man completely consumes me and there's nothing that could make me want to stay away from him. Nothing...

"Yo! Woman!" Madison's voice screams from the front, making me smile. "Get the hell out here."

Feeling relieved that she's here to keep me company I pull the door open and walk out.

I'm surprised to see my uncle here as well.

"Well, this is weird," I say awkwardly. "Did you two come together or something?"

Mark laughs and takes a seat in my chair. "Not exactly. We just shared a stoplight together on the way here."

Madison shrugs. "Close enough."

"Hi, Officer Knight," Ellie says while looking up from her phone.

"How's it going, Ellie? Staying out of trouble?"

Ellie pops her gum and nods her head. "Of course I am. You'd be the first to know if I'm ever in trouble, gorgeous."

Rolling my eyes, I toss the apron on Mark and grab for my scissors. "You're every woman's favorite officer. How does that feel?"

He looks at me through the mirror. "What can I say? I've still got it."

"So, Mark..." Madison says from her chair. "What do you think about Ava over here spending time with Royal? Have you arrested him before? I want the scoop."

Mark shrugs. "I'm trusting him to take care of her. I've known Royal for almost two years now. Doesn't mean that I won't be creeping around a damn corner ready to arrest him if he fucks up my trust."

"So you haven't arrested him yet?" Madison asks with wide eyes, pushing for an answer.

"Only once," Mark says stiffly. He sits up and takes the apron off. "Follow me outside real quick."

"Alright," I say nervously. I turn around to look at Ellie. "I'm going outside for a minute."

"All good," Ellie says while playing on her phone.

I follow Mark outside to stand by his car. "What do you know about Royal and his past?"

I get a bit choked up just thinking about what I've learned about him. "I know about him losing his pregnant fiancée. Is that what you're asking?"

Mark looks up from his phone that starts going off. "Is that all you know? He hasn't told you how?"

I shake my head. "No, I haven't asked. I didn't want to make him feel uncomfortable."

He holds up his finger and huffs as his phone goes off again. "Give me a sec."

I watch him as he walks away and takes his call. He returns a few minutes later with a look that tells me he isn't happy.

"Look. We need to talk later tonight. I'll come by your house when I get off work."

"Okay," I say confused. "What is going on? Is there something that I should know?"

Mark opens the door to his car and gets ready to get inside. "Yeah. I definitely think you need to know this. I don't have time to explain right now. I hate to tell you this way and I'm sorry, but I can't hold it in. His fiancée was raped and murdered. You need to know the whole story, and if Royal isn't going to tell you I am. I've given him time." He pauses and looks down, frustrated. "Gotta go. Be home later and I'll swing by."

Before I can stop him, he jumps into his car and slams the door shut behind him.

I stand here and watch him drive off as the information slowly starts to sink in and I piece the puzzle together.

My breath escapes me and I feel sick to my stomach at how stupid I was to not put this together when Blaine told me about his sister the other day.

"Holy fuck. No..." I cry.

I cover my mouth as the tears come pouring down. Gagging, I fall to my knees with my hands on the pavement as I empty my stomach in front of me, while fighting to catch my breath.

Royal killed those three men after they murdered Olivia: Blaine's sister.

CHAPTER 31

ROYAL

SITTING HERE, MY THROAT FUCKING burns from the pain and hate that is building up inside of me and eating at me as I sit here in this darkened room, looking around me.

I should be holding my baby girl in my arms, loving her and giving her everything that her tiny heart desires. Anything that girl would've asked for would've been hers. I'd give her the world just to know that my baby was happy and well.

I should be able to see her tiny fingers and toes, and be able to smell her soft little baby hair as I hold her close to my chest and remind her over and over that nothing in this world will harm her as long as her daddy is here.

God, it fucking hurts so bad to know she'll never have that.

Everything is so different from what I expected it to be when I first found out the news of Olivia's pregnancy. I thought I had life figured out; that we would live happily in our big home, have the guys over for dinner and watch games on the TV while Hadley laughed and played with her uncles.

None of that is my reality. None of that will ever happen.

Fucking ever. She'll never have the love and security that she deserves and I'll never forget how I've failed her and Olivia.

I'm royally fucked up. My head is fucked up. My past is fucked up. My future is fucked up. Nothing about me is what Avalon wants or needs in her life, yet I'm slowly letting her break me down and force her way into my heart.

My memories and loss of the past will always fucking consume me; therefore, fueling the monster that I've become and making it impossible for me to love her the way that she deserves. It will always lead me back to this room full of baby stuff that will never get touched.

This is my fucking life.

Screaming out, I clutch the half bottle of whiskey in my hand and toss it at the wall. The bottle shatters into sharp pieces that land at the foot of the wooden crib I put together just days before Olivia died.

I numbly watch with tears stinging the back of my eyes as the amber liquid spreads across the floor, running to my feet and wetting my boots.

Leaning my head back, I squeeze the gun in my hand and let my eyes close as my whole chest begins to burn. I can barely fucking breathe right now and I'm not sure if I even deserve to.

"Whoa! What the fuck!" Blaine yells from the open door. "Put that shit down."

I sit up and open my eyes to look at Blaine. "Relax. I'm not going to shoot myself. Fuck, I'm not that fucked up. Not yet at least."

"Good. Now get the fuck up!" Blaine says in a rush, while painfully looking around the room. "I've been looking for you for over a fucking hour and have been calling your ass nonstop. We've got to go. Now."

I reach into my pocket and pull out a cigarette. This motherfucker has bad timing. Always. "My phone died. It's downstairs on the damn charger. What the fuck do you want? I'm busy drowning in my fucking sorrows." I motion around the room with one hand, while placing the smoke between my lips. "Can't you see?"

Blaine's jaw clenches as his eyes meet mine. He looks extremely pissed and anxious. "It's Brian, dickweed." My heart fucking stops at the mention of that name, and suddenly I'm done drowning in my sorrows. "Cole said he spotted him an hour ago over at *Happy's Lounge*. Cole is there now, keeping his eye out for him to leave. We need to be prepared before he fucking skips town again."

"Fucking shit!" With my head spinning, I jump to my feet and rush past Blaine. "I need to call Jax."

"We don't have time for that shit," Blaine points out. "What the hell." He grabs at my arm in an attempt to stop me from going downstairs for my phone. "That's not important, dammit!"

I turn back and growl at him, before pushing past him. "The fuck it isn't. Avalon, man. Fucking Avalon."

His face changes, finally understanding what the hell I need my phone for. If this shit is going down, I need Avalon in the safest hands I can get her in. I don't trust anything not to happen to her.

Yanking my phone off the charger, I run up the stairs, while giving Jax's phone a call. He picks up on the second ring.

"I need you to get to Avalon's work and pick her up. Take her away for the night. Got it."

"Oh fuck," he says, fully aware of what's about to go down. "What time can she get off?"

I pull my phone away and glance down at the time. "A little over an hour, but I don't give a shit. Make her leave now."

"On it. You just take care of what needs to be done."

"Plan to."

Rushing outside, I slam the door behind me and jump into Blaine's truck.

He offers me a quick glance, before pulling off and heading for *Happy's*.

I look down at my phone in my hand and take a second to look through my phone to see four missed calls from Avalon.

"Shit," I mutter, while calling her back. I don't like that one bit. She's never called me. Ever.

Avalon picks up on the first ring. "Royal? I've been looking for you. We need to—"

"I need you to go with Jax," I blurt out, cutting her off. "Don't ask any questions. Just get on his bike and leave when he picks you up."

"Royal. What is going on? Are you okay? Are you hurt?" she asks in a panic. "Tell me where you are. Please. I need to see you."

I shake my head. "No. You can't. Not for a while. I just need you to go with Jax."

"I know," she blurts out. "I know what happened to those men that murdered Olivia and it doesn't matter to me. You didn't do anything wrong. Please just see me. I need to see you. Royal. Royal."

"I'm sorry," I whisper. "Just fucking go with Jax. That's all I'm asking you. Trust me. Please promise me you'll go with Jax."

She's silent for a few seconds and it almost sounds as if she's crying. "Dammit, Royal. I promise."

"Thank you."

Before I let myself get too wrapped up in Avalon, I hang up the phone and look over at Blaine. "Let's do this, brother."

Blaine grips my shoulder and turns back to the road.

Now all there is to do is wait...

VALON

I FEEL COMPLETELY SICK TO my stomach as I gather my belongings in a hurry.

I have no clue what is going on or why Royal asked me to leave with Jax when he gets here, but my gut is telling me to listen to him and hope that nothing is going to happen to him.

"Ellie, I need you to close up for me tonight. I'm suddenly not feeling well. Can you do that?"

She looks away from her customer and nods her head at me. "Yeah, I can take care of it tonight. Go home and get some rest."

"Thank you. I appreciate it."

I open the door when I see a set of headlights outside, thinking that maybe Jax drives a car that I don't know about.

Slowly walking closer, I finally see that it's Colton's car.

"What the hell?"

Gripping my purse, I walk up to the driver's side window and lean my arm over the top of the glass. "What do you want, Colton?"

His eyes look pained as he looks my face over, stopping when his eyes land on my lips. "I can't stop thinking about you. I miss you so damn much, babe."

"Now is not the time for this," I say softly. "Please don't do this right now."

He reaches out the window and grabs my hand. "Will you give me two minutes? Please. I just need to talk to you and find some kind of closure. That's all I'm asking."

Sucking in a frustrated breath, I look around me to see if Jax is anywhere. The small parking lot is empty besides who's inside the building. "Fine, Colton. You get two minutes."

I hear the sound of his doors unlocking as I walk around to the passenger side and jump inside.

He smiles weakly and places his hand over mine. "You look beautiful."

"Let's just talk about what you came here to talk about. Got it?" I yank my hand away. "Okay?"

"Yeah, alright."

He shifts the car into drive and slowly starts driving through the parking lot.

"Colton," I warn him. "I didn't say I would go anywhere with you. I said we could talk."

"It's fine," he says, while pulling out into traffic. "We're just going around the block. Sitting here is making me nervous. The last thing I need is for Royal to show up."

"Dammit, Colton. Just hurry so you can drop me off."

"Don't you miss us?" he questions, while glancing over at me. "Do you think about us and what we had at all?"

I shake my head and answer him honestly. I won't lie to make him feel better. That's not me. "No. I don't think about you, Colton. We didn't belong together. I don't understand why you think we do."

"We were good together," he snaps. "I gave you six fucking months and you just walk away for my brother." He punches the steering wheel, before fighting to catch his cool. "Sorry."

"Colton. Pull back into my work now," I demand. "I don't like this." I reach for the door handle when he goes right past the entrance of the parking lot. "Let me the fuck out."

"Not yet, Marie." He grips my hand and holds it away from the door, while swerving through traffic. "We're not done talking. Just give me time."

"Yes the fuck we are!" I yell, while trying to break my hands free. "Now stop the fucking car. Stop right now. Stop!"

"I said no. Fuck! Please just look at me. You have no idea how messed up this is for me. It's keeping me up at night."

My heart starts racing and I begin screaming at the top of my lungs, and trying to roll down the window, when I hear the sound of a motorcycle close by.

Colton quickly locks the window, making my stomach knot up with anxiety. "Stop screaming. Shit, woman."

"Jax!" I take my free hand and slap at the window. "Jax!" I turn back toward Colton when I realize I'm getting nowhere with my pointless screaming and that the man on the motorcycle isn't even him. "Pull the fuck over and let me out. Now!"

My head slams into the side window as Colton quickly makes a right turn when the car in front of him suddenly slows down. He knows damn well that if I get the chance I will jump the fuck out of this moving car. He's smarter than to slow down.

Cussing, I push and punch at his side as he continues to speed up and ignore me.

"Sit the fuck still. What is your problem? You're scared of me now? Huh?" He grabs my arm and pushes me away. "You're not afraid of a fucking murderer, but you're afraid of me. How the fuck does that make any sense to you? It doesn't! Open your pretty little eyes."

"Fuck you!" In a panic, I grab at the steering wheel. "Don't you fucking talk about him like that. I love him, asshole. Not you. Fucking him! Now stop the car!"

"Let go!" He reaches his hand out and slaps me hard across the face, sending me flying back into my seat. "Oh shit. Fuck! Look what you made me do," he yells as I cover my face and back away from him as far as I can.

"Asshole!"

Colton reaches out and grabs at my face once he realizes that my lip is bleeding, but I push his hand away, not wanting him anywhere near me. "Stop the car," I demand. "I don't want to be with you. I love your brother and I don't care what you say or think. I'm *in* love with him. Hit me all you want, but that won't change. I promise you that."

Colton grips the steering wheel and slams his head into the back of his seat. "Shit! What the fuck am I doing?"

He turns to me, and attempts to grab my face again. "I didn't mean to hit you. Avalon, I'm sorry."

"Just watch the road," I yell. "Get me back to my work. Now. I'll get Jax on the phone so fucking fast—"

Colton suddenly slams on the brakes, sending me flying forward, hitting my head so hard on the window that tears instantly sting my eyes as I reach out and cradle my head in my shaking hands.

I lean back and look out the window to see a silver truck blocking us.

Before I know it, my door is ripped open and Jax is reaching inside to pull me out to my feet. "Shit! Are you okay?" He quickly looks me over, before running his thumb over the bump on my forehead. "Get in my truck and lock the door. I'll be right there."

Holding my head, I walk around Jax and hurriedly jump into his truck, locking the door as I watch to see what Jax is going to do.

All I can make out is Jax leaning halfway inside of Colton's car and grabbing at Colton.

I jerk back in shock when I hear the car horn sound, scaring the shit out of me. Colton's face must be making a new friend. It goes off three more times, before Jax makes his way over to his truck, mumbling and gripping at his hair. He looks completely heated and ready to kill someone.

Happy to see him returning so quickly, I unlock the door and watch as he jumps inside. "Damn, Avalon. I was scared as shit when I showed up at your work to find you gone." He grips the steering wheel and takes a deep breath, before leaning over and checking on my head again. "Fuck, I'm sorry. I shouldn't have done that, but I needed to stop Colton. I need you with me. Let me look at it." He leans in closer and examines it. "I should've told you to look out for my truck."

"I'm fine," I whisper, while covering my head in my hands and closing my eyes. "I just need to rest. You drive and I'll rest my eyes."

"Nah, fuck that. I'm not risking anything. That bump looks pretty bad. It's bleeding too. Royal won't hesitate to kill my ass if something happens to you. Trust me." He quickly pulls off, being careful to avoid oncoming traffic. "I'm taking you to the hospital. I'll let Royal know where we're at."

"I guess I have no choice," I mumble.

We drive for about thirty minutes before we pull up at a hospital one town over. I have no idea what is going on right now, but this is really making me nervous. I need to know what is going down tonight.

"Jax." I lean up and grab his arm. "Tell me what the fuck is going on. Please."

Jax parks his truck and shakes his head. "I can't. Don't ask me again because you will get the same response. All I can tell you is that Royal has everything handled."

"Jax—"

"Don't worry about Royal. Got it?" he snaps. He grips the steering wheel and I can tell that he's just about as worried as I am. "I'll text him once I get you inside and taken care of. Now let's go."

I wait inside the truck as Jax jumps out and walks over to help me out. The thought of anything happening to Royal has me fighting for air. "You better not fucking lie to me, Jax." I try to fight back my tears, as I look him in the eyes. "I can't lose him."

Jax closes the door behind me and rubs his thumb over my chin. "You won't," he says with more confidence this time. "Everything will be fine. *He* can't lose you. So let's get you the fuck inside."

When my head begins to spin, I grip onto Jax's arm to keep my balance, as he walks me through the parking lot and toward the building.

As soon as I get checked in, you better believe that I'll be calling to check on Royal. I don't care if Jax tells me otherwise.

Nothing can happen to him. I don't know what I would do...

CHAPTER 32

ROYAL

WE'VE BEEN WAITING IN BLAINE'S truck for an hour now and my patience is really fucking starting to run thin. Any second now I'm going to lose my shit and drag him out of the bar my damn self.

"Any word from Cole yet?" I ask stiffly, while staring at the rain through the window.

Blaine shakes his head. "Nah, not yet." He looks up from twirling his phone. "You still want to do this, man? His death is going be another weight on your shoulders that will never fucking go away. I'm not sure if you can come back from this." He pauses for a second and reaches for a cigarette. "I can do it and you can go about living your life and move on with Avalon. You two could have a life together. She's good for you."

"It's not that fucking simple," I grind out. "He took my family from me. There's already no way to move on from that. Having that fucker pay is just a small step closer to the relief that I will never fully get. I'm fucked up, Blaine. You know that shit. Too fucked up already to care."

"He took my family from me too, brother," he points out. "I know how much that shit hurts. I know how it fucking eats at you, making you feel empty inside and full of rage. I've been here through it all, and it kills me every fucking day."

I swallow hard and look over at him. I can see the pain swallowing him whole, just as much as it is me. It only gives me more reason to kill that fucking cunt: for all of us. "I know, man. I'm sorry." I grip his shoulder and squeeze it. "You're my brother, Blaine. You don't need this shit on your hands. Got it? This is on me to do. It always has been."

He shakes his head and grips the steering wheel. "Fuck! This shit... It's so fucked up." His eyes widen as his phone goes off in his lap. He reads the message and then turns to me, his amber eyes dark with rage. "This couldn't be anymore fucking perfect." He throws his phone down and starts his truck. "Cole overheard dumb-fuck say that he's headed to that old warehouse off Twentieth and Teasdale to pick up a drop. No one in their right mind goes over that way after dark. Looks like the devil is on our side tonight."

Closing my eyes, I take a deep breath and anxiously run a hand through my sweaty hair as he takes off in the direction of the warehouse.

This is the fucking moment I've waited almost two years for. It's happening, and I can finally find peace knowing that Brian is rotting in the fucking ground. Right where his wrongdoings put Olivia and my unborn child. He's going to feel my wrath tonight and understand the pain he's brought to my family.

When we reach the warehouse, Blaine turns off his headlights and parks in the alley out of sight. It's hard to see through the rain, but there are two vehicles parked out back and three men standing around talking. One of those fuckers is Brian. I've only ever seen him in a photo, but as soon as my eyes seek out his tattooed face in the small lighting and crooked ass nose, I know that it's him. My heart will never let me forget that fucker's face. It's been haunting my dreams for far too long.

They talk for a few minutes, before the other two guys jump into a red car and pull off. Brian waits after they leave, and then jumps into his dump as their taillights disappear, turning on the light and just sitting there, most likely testing out his shit.

"Get out of the truck," I demand, keeping my eyes straight ahead.

"What? Are you serious?"

"I'm dead serious. I'll buy you a new one. Now out."

Blaine shakes his head, but doesn't say another word as he jumps out of his truck and softly closes the door behind him, being careful not to alarm Brian.

I crack my neck, start the engine, and slam on the fucking gas, driving right into the side of Brian's car.

The impact causes me to slam my head into the windshield, but with my adrenaline pumping I don't feel shit. I shake it off and focus on what I came here to do, to finish this.

Kicking the door open as hard as I can, I jump out of the truck and rush over to Brian's side of the car. "You fucking piece of shit." I punch my fist through his window, watching him jump back and cover his face as the glass shatters around him.

"What the fuck!" he screams. "Take my shit. You can have it. Please."

I reach through the broken window and grab him by his hair, slamming the side of his head into what's left of the window. Then I pull his head up so that he can look into my eyes. "I'm here to take much more than that."

With both hands, I yank him out through the window and throw him down onto the ground, before yanking him up to his knees.

I lean in close to his face as he grabs at his wounded flesh, trying to stop the blood from his cuts. "You took everything from me!"

"Royal," he stammers.

I raise a brow and choke him up against the side of his car. "You were stupid for coming back here. You know that, right?" I squeeze his neck tighter and slam him against the car again. "Answer me!"

"I'm sorry! I'm sorry!" He grips my arm with both hands. "I didn't know he would come after you and your family. You have to believe that."

Releasing his throat, I punch him across the face, causing him to fall over and grab at his busted mouth. "You think that shit matters to me? Huh!" I place my boot on his back and force him flat down on the gravel. "I lost my world that night. Those fuckers came into my home and raped and murdered my fiancée... and my child. They were fucking innocent. Do you know what I did to them when I walked in and had to watch that? I saw it with my own fucking eyes! Did you know that?"

He shakes his head and grips at the gravel, as if it's going to somehow save him. He's wrong. Nothing will now. "No. No. No," he says quickly. "I didn't know!"

With my boot on his back, I pull out my knife and kneel down close to his face. "Well, good thing you're here so I can tell you then."

I flip him over on his back and kneel over his shaking body, shivering from the cold rain and fear of what's about to happen to him. "I shot them each in the dick." I bring my knife down to his dick, putting pressure on it. He closes his eyes and shakes his head. "Then I shot them in the head." I bring the knife up to the side of his skull and pierce the skin with the tip. "And I watched as they bled out."

"Shit! No! Please," he begs. "I have a baby girl. She's almost two!"

My heart stops from his confession and my throat feels as if it's closing up. I'm losing it. I'm fucking losing it.

"That's why I did it. I needed money to get my wife out of

here and somewhere safe. She was already nine months pregnant and I did what I had to do to get the money. It wasn't safe here for my family."

I lean my head back and shake it, letting the cold rain drip down my face. "Shut up!" I bring the knife down to his throat and slightly puncture the flesh, twisting it. "Don't fucking talk! I don't want to hear that shit."

"Please! She's sick and she needs her father. She has leukemia. Her name is—"

"Stop!" I quickly stand to my feet and kick him back over to his stomach, not wanting to hear another word from his mouth. I place my boot on the back of his head and shove it into the dirt, pissed as fuck about what I've just learned. "Fuck! What did I say? One more word and I'll cut your fucking throat out!"

I drop to my knees and grip at my hair, before running a hand down my face. So much shit is running through my head that I can't decide what to do next. This is not how the fuck I planned this.

"Please don't kill me. I only came here to visit my mother and get some more money for my daughter's treatments. She's so sick," he cries. "Please. Her mother can't work. It's only me."

Guilt overwhelms me to the point of suffocation. I feel like ripping his fucking heart out the more he talks, but the thought of Hadley being here, sick and losing her father, eats at me, making me vulnerable and sick to my stomach. I would die for my family.

"I'm sorry! If I could take back what I did I would." He crawls up to his knees and laces his hands together, begging me. "Please don't take her father away from her. She's just a little girl."

"Fuck!" I scream out. "Shut the fuck up!"

We both look over as Blaine comes rushing over, soaking wet and out of breath. "Shit, man. I got a message from Jax. Some shit went down."

Fear consumes me at the thought of anything bad happening to Avalon, and suddenly all I can think about is rushing to her. I can't fucking let anyone hurt her. The thought has me quickly rising to my feet. "Fucking hell!"

My eyes land on Brian on his knees pleading. All I can see when I look at him is a man begging and doing anything in his power to provide for his child. I'd do the same thing.

Walking over to him, I take my knife and cut his shirt open, before placing the knife to his fast rising chest. "Never fucking forget the lives that were lost because of you. Every time you take off your shirt and look in the mirror, you will remember them. It will fucking haunt you like it does me."

Grabbing his neck, I dig my knife into his flesh, causing him to close his eyes and scream out as I slowly carve an O on the left of his chest and then move over to carve an H onto the right side. It's so deep that there's no doubt in my mind that he'll be hurting for a while, before scar tissue forms making it permanent.

When I'm done, I stand back and look at his bleeding chest as the rain mixed with his tears runs down his grateful face. "If you do anything to fuck up that little girl's life, I will come after you and I will fucking kill you. I will carve your fucking heart out and watch as your life slowly drains from your lifeless eyes. That is a promise."

He nods his head and falls forward, gripping the ground as I walk away.

"Let's go," I say, while brushing past Blaine.

Blaine nods his head. "Give me one sec."

I nod my head in understanding and jump into Blaine's truck. Worried about Avalon, I power my phone back on. I turned it off to get rid of any distractions. I usually do that when I need to keep my head together.

When it finally turns on, multiple messages and missed calls pop up from Avalon, making my chest fucking hurt in fear.

I feel like fucking exploding as I call her phone and it goes straight to voicemail.

Blaine hops in the truck, grabbing at his fist. I grab him by the shirt and shake him. "What the fuck did Jax say? Where is she?"

He releases a breath. "Your brother practically fucking kidnapped her. Jax got her out of the car, but she has a pretty bad bump on her head that is causing her some pain. They're at the hospital about thirty minutes away from town."

"Fucking bastard. He finally grew some fucking balls all of a sudden." I quickly back away from Brian's car and hit the road, with my hands shaking and my heart racing out of control.

All I can think about is getting to her and making sure that she's safe in my arms; no one else's.

My brother will be seeing my ass later...

MY BLOOD IS FUCKING BOILING the whole way to the hospital. Between thoughts of letting Brian live for the sake of a precious little girl and thoughts of choking my brother out, my mind has been consumed the whole thirty-minute drive.

That piece of shit will learn to never fuck with my girl again. He was lucky as shit to even get his chance with her when he did, but she's over him now and has moved on with me. I have no problem with beating that info into his pretty little head.

"What floor is she on?"

I pull into the hospital and hurriedly search for an empty space to park. There's so many damn parking spots here that it's making me anxious. She could be anywhere in that fucking building.

Why in the fuck are there so many cars here?

CHAPTER 33

AVALON

AFTER COMPLETING THE BRAIN SCAN THAT the hospital recommends I get done, I rush back into my room in hopes that Jax has heard back from Royal or Blaine.

I could barely lie still when they took the X-rays because all I could do was worry about Royal, scared shitless that he may have gotten himself into some kind of trouble. Between that and my nerves from being in the hospital, I was a complete shaking mess.

Jax has been in my room throughout the whole thing, trying to keep me calm and assure me that Blaine would never let anything happen to Royal. I want to believe him, but it's hard without any solid proof. It's driving me insane.

"Have you heard from them?" I ask, causing Jax to look up from his phone. "Please tell me they're okay. I need to hear something."

Jax immediately stands up from his chair beside the bed and helps me get comfortable beneath the sheet on the shitty mattress. "Fuck, you're shaking, girl." He sits on the edge of the bed and starts rubbing my shoulders and arms to warm me up. "You really care about him, don't you?"

I nod my head. "Of course I do. He's all I ever think about, Jax. I haven't been able to get him out of my head since that night I walked in on him in the basement. It hurts me so much to ever think about losing him. He's special to me. I don't care what he says about himself. He's good to me." I grab his handsome face and pull him toward me so he can look me in the eyes. "Now, please tell me something before I rip your balls off, Jax."

He smiles at me and leans in to kiss my forehead. "You've definitely been spending too much time with Royal." Releasing my shoulders, he lets out a small satisfied laugh. "They're on their way here. They should be close now."

Feeling relieved, I throw the sheet off of me and sit up. "How long ago did they leave?"

"I don't know. About thirty minutes ago."

"Good."

I hop out of bed and quickly rush past Jax, making my way down the hall. A few nurses try talking to me, but I brush them off, leaving them throwing their arms out in frustration and looking after me. Whatever it is they want out of me can wait.

I can hear Jax calling my name from close behind, but I ignore him as well and keep on walking. He knows better than to attempt to stop me from getting to Royal right now, so he's keeping a small distance.

All I can think about is the fact that I need to be with Royal right this second, and he could be pulling up right now, looking for me too. I've waited too long to hear that he's okay. I'm not waiting another second longer to see it with my own damn eyes. I have no idea what it is that he had to do tonight, but right now all that matters to me is that he's alive and safe.

Once I reach the exit, I rush through the door, running barefoot across the wet parking lot in search of Royal.

There's too many damn parking lots surrounding this hospital, but by some kind of freaking miracle I spot Royal and Blaine in the parking lot that is on the other side of the huge fountain, exiting a silver truck with the front smashed in.

"Royal!" I scream out. My heart goes wild in my chest as I take a step forward and shield my face from the rain. "Royal!" I scream again, but louder this time.

Our eyes meet from across the fountain, and without a second thought I take off running in the direction of the water, needing to get to him as fast as I can. Fuck going around it. That will take entirely too long and I can't handle that right now. I need to feel him in my arms. I need to run my hands over his beautiful, flawless face and taste his fucking mouth.

I need this man like I fucking need air and no small bit of water is going to keep me from him. Nothing can right now.

As soon as he sees me moving toward him, he rushes toward the fountain as if he's just as desperate to get to me as I am him. His face looks lethal as he walks with power, moving much faster than my legs will allow me.

Gasping from the shock of the cold water splashing against my legs, I run through the frigid water and he catches me in his arms, squeezing me tightly.

Gripping my face with both hands, he leans down to my height and desperately presses his lips against mine, while moving his hands up to grip at my hair, as if he just needs any and every part of me.

His tasty mouth is on mine. His strong, inked hands are in my hair. Our bodies are molded together as we desperately hold on to each other. I almost can't breathe right now.

When he finally breaks the kiss, he wraps one hand behind my neck for support and places the other on my chest, while looking into my eyes. What I see behind his makes my heart stop mid beat: love. "I'll never let that piece of shit near you again. I fucking promise you that. No one will *ever* hurt you."

His eyes move up to land on the bandage on my head. "Fuck," he breathes. "I'm so sorry. Shit. Come here."

He pulls me in as close as possible, burying his face into my neck and holds me as if he can't bear to let go of me, and truthfully, I never want him to.

We stay like this for a while, him holding me in the fountain as the water splashes down around us. It's cold. So damn cold.

He doesn't seem to care though. He just holds me close, comforting me as if he knows that I need him this way right now... and he's right. This right here is all I need: him.

Finally pulling away from my neck, he rests his forehead to mine and cups my face in his shaking hands. "Tell me you're okay, Avalon. Please..."

I grab his hands as he rubs his thumbs over my face and closes his eyes, waiting for my response. "I was scared something bad was going to happen to you, Royal." I move my hands up to grip his wet hair and pull it out of his face. "Tell me that I'll never lose you," I whisper. "Then I'll tell you that I'm okay."

His jaw tightens and he turns his face to the side, as if to hide it from me.

"Royal..." I pull his face back to mine and brush my lips against his. He sucks in a small breath, but stays where he is. "Can you promise me that? Say it. Please... say it."

Breathing heavily, he crushes his lips against mine, before pulling away and grabbing my hand to walk us out of the water. "Let's get you back inside and changed. All that matters to me right now is that you're taken care of. I'm not letting you get sick because of me."

He quickly wraps his arms around me and picks me up to cradle me against him, before I can say anything more. Releasing a long breath, I wrap my arms around his neck and press my face against the side of his as he carries me past Jax and Blaine and back into the warm hospital.

He asks Jax where my room is and he carries me there, shutting the door behind us, before undressing me from my wet gown and helping me back into my clothing.

The nurse comes back in a few minutes later, shakes her head at me, and gives me my discharge papers.

"The doctor has cleared you to go. That's what I tried telling you as you were rushing past me down the hall." She looks to Royal, standing there dirty and wet. "There's instructions on what you need to do overnight. I'll just let you read it yourself since y'all seem to be in a hurry."

"Thank you," I say, while flashing her a weak smile. "Sorry about the puddle."

She looks down at the floor where my wet gown is laying in a huge puddle. "Mmm hmm. I'm sure you are."

Grabbing my hand, Royal leads me out of the room, motioning with his head for the boys to follow. "I have a pit stop to make on the way home. You good with that, Blaine?"

Blaine squeezes his shoulder. "Hell yeah. I'm always down."

After Royal helps me into the backseat of Blaine's truck, he closes the door and walks over to talk to Jax.

"Hey," I say to Blaine as he jumps in the driver's side. "Should I worry about this little pit stop?"

Blaine grins. "Nah. This is going to be good. Trust me."

Royal jumps into the truck a few minutes later and wraps a blanket around me, before pulling me into his arms. "Get comfortable, but I need you to stay awake for a while." He leans in and kisses the top of my head. "Can you do that?"

I squeeze his hand and bury my face into his chest. "Yeah, I'm fine. I'm not tired yet."

"Good," he whispers.

The drive back into town is quiet. I'm suspecting it's due to my head injury, and neither one of them want to give a reason for my head to hurt even more. I'm thankful for the silence, but I won't be for long.

I want to find out what happened with Royal tonight, but tonight probably isn't the best time to talk about it. I'll wait until the morning.

"This is going to be fun," Blaine says, while shifting the truck into park.

Sitting up, I look around to see that we're parked outside of Colton's house.

"Stay here," Royal demands. "I'll be out in a few minutes."

"Oh trust me... I never want to step foot in that house again," I mutter.

Royal quickly kisses my forehead and then jumps out of the truck, slamming the door behind him.

I hear Royal digging in the back of the truck for something, before I see him toss a rope down beside the truck and rush up to Colton's door.

Without even bothering to check if the door is unlocked or not, he kicks at the door three times before it flies open and he rushes inside.

"That's always fun to watch," Blaine says, while lighting a cigarette and rolling down the window. "At least he won't need to break any of my shit now."

I don't say anything. I just stare at the door, waiting for Royal to come back out. A part of me even wishes that I could see the scared look in Colton's eyes as Royal kicks the shit out of him. Maybe Madison will get her wish and he'll piss his pants and ruin his damn perfect carpet.

We wait patiently for about ten minutes, before we hear Colton cussing as Royal drags him out of the house, naked, by his neck.

"You're fucking crazy! What are you doing, you, crazy son of a bitch?"

Royal slams him face down into the grass, grabs the back of his head and slams it into the ground, repeatedly, before grabbing his left arm and snapping it in half with his boot.

Colton cries out from the pain, snot bubbles running down his face.

Grabbing the back of his hair, Royal pulls Colton's head back and presses his knife to his throat. "Come by her again, brother... and you'll see how fucking crazy I can get."

"Fuck!" Colton yells. "I'm done. I'm done."

"Good," Royal seethes.

He turns toward the truck to look at Blaine who is now sitting out his window. "Bring me that fucking rope."

Blaine laughs and throws down his cigarette, while climbing out the window. "Hell motherfucking yeah."

I place my hand over my mouth and watch as Royal ties Colton up to his porch, naked, his face now covered in dirt, grass, and blood.

Royal stands back so that he can get a look and reaches to light a cigarette. "If you scream loud enough, maybe one of your neighbors will come untie your fucking ass." He flicks his lit cigarette at the side of Colton's head.

"Fuck you!" Colton screams while pulling at the ropes. "I'm calling the cops."

Blaine disappeared into the house a couple of minutes ago, but steps back outside, smirking as he looks down at Colton. "With what?" He holds up a cell phone. "This?" He shakes his head and then leans down to set the phone down in front of Colton where he can't reach it. "Good luck, bitch."

"Fuck you! Fuck you! Come back here and untie me! I need to go to the hospital."

Royal and Blaine walk back to the truck, ignoring Colton as he continues to yell at them, cussing and pulling at the ropes.

Blaine pokes his head inside the truck and smiles at me. "Told you it'd be fun to watch."

I look back out the window at Colton struggling, naked, and tied to his porch. I have to admit that it somehow makes the night worth it.

I smile and grab Royal's face as he hops back into the truck. "How did you get him naked? Did you undress him?" I ask with a laugh.

Royal smiles against my lips and then kisses me. "Caught his ass in the shower. Now let's get you home to rest."

I nod my head and then lean back into him as Blaine pulls away from Colton's house. With this neighborhood, I'm pretty sure that the cops are already on their way to untie him, but just knowing that they'll find him naked, baring his little dick to the world, makes me a happy girl. Maybe he'll learn to stop being such an ass to everyone.

We pull up to Royal's house.

"You two good for the night?" he questions over the seat.

"Yeah," Royal responds. "I'll let you know if she needs anything."

"Alright, brother." Blaine smiles at me. "I got your back, girl. If you need some ice cream, a chick flick, or a full body rub..." He playfully lifts his brows. "Call me."

Royal palms his face and pushes him away. "Don't push my ass tonight."

Laughing, I pull Royal's hand away from Blaine's face. "Take it easy on dirty Blaine. He means well."

"She totally gets me," Blaine says teasingly, before becoming serious. "Now get your ass inside and take care of her."

After Royal helps me out of the truck, he takes me downstairs to his bedroom, undresses us both, and crawls into bed, pulling me under the blankets with him.

Every once in a while I doze off, but Royal wakes me up to check on me, before rubbing my head while I fall back to sleep again.

This goes on for most of the night, as he is now, but this time, it's with him on top of me and between my legs.

When I open my eyes, I reach up and grab his face as he slowly enters me.

He's extra careful with me, slowly thrusting in and out, while leaning his forehead against mine and breathing gently against my lips.

Looking into his eyes and seeing the passion inside of them as he buries himself deep inside of me, has me about ready to break. All of my emotions take over and suddenly I feel as if I'm going to suffocate if I don't get the words out.

I lock my feet together behind his ass and close my eyes as he makes love to me, touching and kissing every single place on my body that he can get to at the moment.

He's so quiet; too quiet, and I don't know what to make of it.

"Royal," I whisper.

"Shhh..." he says against my lips.

I shake my head and grab onto his hair as he starts moving a little faster. "I need..." I whisper. "I need to tell—"

"What," he asks, cutting me off. "Am I hurting you? Does your head hurt?"

I shake my head.

"Then close your eyes, baby." He leans in to whisper in my ear. "I need you to feel this right now. Just feel me..."

I grip onto him tighter, closing my eyes and letting him slowly take me. He's moving so slowly that I can barely handle it. It feels too good. I can feel every single inch of him each time that he pulls out and moves back in. It's the most intense pleasure I've ever felt in my life.

"Come with me," he whispers into my neck. "I want to feel you squeeze my dick."

"Okay," I whisper. "I feel it."

He thrusts in a few more times, before we both come undone, holding each other as we ride out our orgasms, both of us breathing heavily against each other's mouths.

His hands move up my neck, to push my hair out of my face. "I think you're okay to sleep now. It's been close to six hours." He leans in and kisses my forehead. "I'll let you get some rest."

I move my hands to cup his face. He closes his eyes as I rub my fingertips underneath them. "Royal..." I brush my lips across his face, stopping to whisper in his ear. "I've fallen in love with you. I love you and I'm hoping one day you can learn to love me back."

He pulls away from me. "Avalon... don't..."

"I know," I say. "I know it's not easy for you. It's okay," I whisper. "It's okay."

He rolls over and sits up on the side of the bed. "Fuck," he whispers. He runs his hands over his face, before standing up and getting dressed. "I shouldn't have let it get this far."

He starts pacing around the room.

"Royal." I sit up and cover myself up with the sheet. "I'm sorry, but I couldn't keep it inside anymore. I. Love. You. You're good. You're so good to me. No one has ever made me feel this way. I wish you could see that."

He stops pacing and stops next to the dresser, gripping the edge of it. "You can't," he growls out. "I need to go."

Fear rushes through me as soon as he mentions leaving. "Please don't say that. Don't leave."

"I have to," he whispers.

I quickly jump to my feet and grab his arm to make him look at me. "No you don't, Royal. You don't have to go anywhere. Stay here. Stay here with me."

"You don't understand." He yanks his arm away from me and zips up his jeans. "Dammit, Avalon. It's not that fucking easy." He backs me up against the wall and pins me in. "You make me feel. I never thought I'd feel again, but here you are, making me think that maybe there's a chance for me to be human; a chance at me being me again. Do you get that? Do you get how impossible that is?"

I shake my head and wrap my arms around his neck. "It's not impossible," I say. "You're not some fucking monster like you say you are. You're capable of love."

He yanks my arms from his neck and backs away from me, gripping at his hair. "No, I'm not."

I rush over to the bed and yank the sheet off, wrapping it around my body as Royal heads for the door. "You are, dammit!"

I follow him up the stairs, not willing to give up on him.

"I need this," he says when he reaches the front door. He stops and grips the door handle, but doesn't turn to look at me. "I can't fucking hurt you," he says firmly. "I can *never* fucking be who you need or want me to be. I'm too fucked up!"

He turns to look at me, and rushes over to grab my face when he sees the tears flowing down my face. "Don't fucking cry. Please don't cry. Fuck!" He brushes his face over mine, while gripping at my hair. "I need you to understand why I need to do this."

"No." I grip his hands and push him away from me. "I can't, because I don't want you to leave me! I don't want you to leave here. I need you!"

He shakes his head and grips at his hair again, as he starts backing up toward the door. "I can't be that right now. I don't know if I ever can."

He runs his hand over his face, looks me in the eyes, and then walks over to kiss me. "I'm sorry," he whispers. "I let everyone down. This will hurt the least... I promise."

With that, he turns and walks away, leaving me standing here in shock.

I can't move. I just stand here and stare at the door, as if he's going to turn back around and run at me, pulling me back into his strong arms.

He doesn't...

I finally force my legs to work and run out the door, just in time to see him pulling away.

I run after the truck, screaming as the tears run down my face. "Don't fucking leave," I cry. "Please! Don't leave me."

He's already too far gone, and the reality starts to set in at the fact that I have no idea when I'll see him again; if I'll see him again.

I fall down to the ground and grip at the sheet as the tears fall and I fight to breathe.

I feel a set of arms grab at me from behind, before I hear Jax whispering things that I can't manage to put together.

"He needs time," he whispers. "He'll be back. He won't leave you for good. He can't, and the only reason why he's leaving you at all is because he knows I'll take care of you. I'll take care of you, girl." He pulls me into his arms and covers my head so that it's buried into his chest. "We just don't know when he'll get his head together and come back. We never do…"

I grab onto him and cry.

It's all I can do…

CHAPTER 34

AVALON

TWO WEEKS LATER...

WALKING TOWARD THE DOOR TO leave, I feel a strong ache in my chest over the absence of Royal and the fact that no one has heard from him yet.

I never thought it would hurt this much to lose someone. I never thought I'd be one of those lucky people to find and care about someone so much that it would kill me if I ever lost that person.

Royal has opened my heart to him, made me fall madly in love with him, and then took off, taking my crushed heart with him.

I'm not going to lie; eating and sleeping has been a hard task since that night, and I've been checking my phone about every damn minute, waiting and hoping that he'll respond to one of my many calls and messages and put me out of my misery.

The boys tell me not to worry. They tell me that he's

strong... that he'll be okay, and that he just needs time to get his head straight.

Well... what if he never gets it straight? What if he realizes that he can't open his heart up to me? What if...

I can't stop wondering about the what-ifs, and it's slowly breaking me down little by little, making me lose hope that I'll ever get to feel his lips against mine, feel the warmth of his arms around me, or the feel of his soft breath against my neck... All of these things I miss so much that it hurts to breathe.

Madison looks up from the couch as I walk through the living room, past her. "You okay, honey? You want me to go with you?"

I shake my head. "No, I'm not okay, but I will be." I grip the door handle to open it, but then stop to look back at her. "I'm going to see Mark. He's at work but wants me to meet him at that foster care place." I blow a strand of loose hair out of my face. "I can't remember the name, but I know where it's at. I'm fine to go alone. I'll just see you later. Thanks though."

"Always, sweets. I'm always here if you want to talk about it. Please remember that."

I nod my head. "I know." Turning the handle, I pull the door open and step outside.

I jump back in surprise when Jax pushes away from the railing and uncrosses his arms. "Jeez, Jax. You scared me," I mutter. "Any word from him yet?" I ask in hope.

He gives me a sympathetic smile and shakes his head. "Not yet. Sorry." Walking over to me, he wraps his arms around me and pulls me in for a hug, placing his mouth close to my ear. "Royal cares about you. I have no doubt that he will be back, but you need to understand how hard this is on him. He had a fiancée and a baby on the way at one point..." He stops and lets out a small breath. "He lost all that. Then he found you. There was never supposed to be anyone else but her. He needs time to wrap his head around that and come to terms with the fact that someone else besides Olivia has his heart."

Feeling my heart breaking from his words, I squeeze him as tightly as I can and hide my face in his chest. "How do you know that I have his heart? I told him that I loved him..." I stop to swallow back the pain. "Then he left."

Jax pulls me away from him and looks me in the eyes. "Because the only message I've received from Royal was the day he left. You know what that message said?"

I shake my head.

"It said *check on her every day. Let me know she's okay.*" He shakes his head as if his emotions are getting to him. "I've done just that. He didn't ask me to update him on his fucking bar, or to update him on his house and make sure everything is taken care of. He pretty much told me to take care of you, so that's what I'll do until the day he returns. Give him time. Don't give up on him."

I lean in and kiss him on the cheek. "I need to go. My uncle is waiting on me." Without another word, I turn and walk away before the dam can break and I find myself helplessly crying in his arms like a fool.

I'm so confused and hurt that I honestly don't know what to do at this point. I just need to take every day for what it is and see how I feel. I want to wait for him. I do... but I'm scared. I'm so fucking scared.

When I get to the foster care place that my uncle asked me to meet him at, I park on the street behind his car and walk up to the building.

As soon as I open the door, I spot Mark standing around, talking to some older lady with long, white hair.

He nods at me and holds up his finger when he notices me watching him from afar.

I nod my head in understanding and take a seat in one of the chairs by the entrance.

Looking around, I start to feel sad, but for a whole new reason. The thought of these kids not having any parents to tuck them in at night or read them a bedtime story breaks my heart. Some of these kids have probably even been passed around from home to home, feeling as if no one loves them.

It really makes me wonder why Mark asked me to meet him here. I never even knew that he came here, but the way he's talking to that lady makes me believe that he comes here often.

"Avalon."

I look up at my uncle.

He nods his head. "Come on."

Standing up, I walk over to my uncle and smile at the lady, as I follow him through the building and outside to the back, where there's a bunch of kids playing.

I look at Mark to see him smile as his eyes land on a little girl with long, blonde hair.

It causes me to smile. "Who's she?" I pause. "That look on your face tells me she's somewhat special to you."

He pulls his eyes away from the little girl and turns to look at me. "Her name is Kylie. She's two years old and has been with two families since she was born. She's special to me all right."

"Oh," I whisper, not knowing what else to say. "Why is she back here? What was wrong with the families she was with?"

He shakes his head and pulls his eyes away from me. "They weren't good enough. There's always something not good enough and I'm not going to just leave her with anyone. She deserves so much more than someone who doesn't even give a damn that she's breathing. At least here she has friends and the staff has practically become her family."

I follow him as he walks through the playground, toward the little girl. He stops beside her and kneels down. "Kylie."

As soon as Kylie looks over and sees Mark, she throws her

arms around his neck and holds on, as if she's been waiting for days to see him.

I get choked up, but quickly try to hide the tears that unwillingly slide down my face as I watch them. I've never seen Mark hold someone so close in my life. You would think it were his own daughter.

"I heard you've been good," Mark says as she pulls away from the hug. "You're always good, right?"

The little girl smiles and nods her head.

"I knew it," Mark says excitedly. "I have someone I want you to meet, okay? She's important to me just like you are."

Mark grabs her hand and stands up. He looks over at me, and motions with his head for me to come closer.

I smile nervously and walk over, stopping right in front of them. I'm stunned speechless when she looks up at me and my eyes meet her wide, curious ones.

"Oh, wow," I whisper.

Her eyes are the brightest shade of green I've ever seen, and in the upper right side of her left eye is a patch of gray. They're absolutely the most beautiful sight I've ever seen.

Mark smiles. "Kylie, this is Avalon." He stands behind her and pulls her long hair out of her face. "She's very special to me. She's like a daughter to me."

Keeping my eyes on her wide ones, I kneel down in front of her and give her my best smile, fighting through all of my many emotions. "Hi, Kylie. That's a beautiful name."

She laughs and then turns to hide her face in Mark's leg. Every few seconds she turns back to me, and laughs before hiding her face again.

I can't help but to smile at her, and before I know it, I'm playing peek-a-boo with her, moving around Mark's legs to get her.

"I'm going to get you!"

She lets go of Mark's legs and takes off running in what

looks like slow motion. She's so darn cute and tiny that her small legs don't take her very far.

We play for a good fifteen minutes, before she runs back over to Mark and he tackles her in a hug.

He looks up at me from the ground. "It's about her dinnertime." Standing up, he grabs Kylie's shoulders and looks down at her. "Would you like Avalon here to come back and visit with me next week?"

Kylie looks up at me. Her eyes meet mine and she laughs, while nodding her head.

"Alright. Why don't you go have Lynn clean you up for dinner." He looks over at the white-haired lady as she appears next to him and grabs Kylie's hand. "Thank you."

She nods her head and grabs Mark's shoulder. "Thank *you*. We'll see you next week."

With that, she walks away, pulling Kylie along beside her.

The look in Mark's eyes as he watches them walk away tugs at my heart, but I have no idea what to say to him. This is a side of him that I've never seen before. It makes me wonder what got him here in the first place.

The walk back out front to our vehicles is silent, but I can't help but to notice the pain etched across his face.

I watch as Mark leans against his car and runs his hands through his messy hair. He keeps looking over at the building as if he wants to go back.

"Why did you ask me here? What is going on?"

He turns around to grip the top of his car. "There's something you should know." He turns to face me, and swallows before speaking. "I'm not sure what all Royal has told you..."

"Don't stop there, dammit," I growl out when he stops. "You can't mention his name and then stop. Tell me," I push. "What does this have to do with Royal?"

"I need you to listen and I need you to listen close." His voice cracks. "I was there the night his fiancée got murdered."

He slaps the top of his car and hangs his head low. "I was just a rookie then; had only been on the job for a few weeks at that point and I had no idea what to expect." He pauses, but doesn't look over at me before continuing. "We got the call that a man's pregnant fiancée was raped and murdered, and that the man killed the three men that did it to her. We showed up at the house as he was saying goodbye to her. It was a sight that would break any good man down."

I grab onto my car and watch Mark as the tears slide down his cheeks. "I'll never forget that moment for the rest of my life. The pain he was feeling... The look of pure agony and loss in his eyes ate at me and made me realize that if I were in his position that I'd do the same. I'd kill for my family too." He releases his car and turns to me. "He's not dangerous. He's not a bad fucking guy. He fights for the ones he loves and does everything in his power to protect them. That makes him a good man that was in the wrong place at the wrong time. He was thrown a shitty hand and he dealt with it. All of these people in this small town don't see it that way. They're twisted here in some ways, and want to believe that they know who are the good civilized people and who are the bad, uncivilized savages that are nothing but a waste of space and a disgrace to their town. To them... Royal became a savage that night. Even to his own fucking family."

"Oh, my God," I whisper, while wiping the tears from my eyes. "I never knew you were there that night. I'm sorry. I know how hard it must have been to witness such a tragedy. And Royal..."

He shakes his head, trying to pull it together, but I can see how much this truly still hurts him. "It was the hardest thing that I've ever had to witness, and to top it off, Royal went to jail that night. He assaulted a police officer; broke that son of a bitch's nose for trying to keep him away from his dead fucking fiancée. He deserved it, but the court didn't see it that way. Officers Payton and Cooper made sure of it, and also made sure that he didn't get to see the light of day until his justice was served. They couldn't get him on murder because it was self-defense, so the asshole cop whose nose he broke, charged him with assault. Royal spent five weeks in jail after losing the love of his life. It was total fucking shit and I felt helpless that I couldn't do a damn thing to help him. He didn't utter a word for weeks.

"His parents took care of everything on the outside to make sure Olivia had a proper burial, but they stayed far away from Royal and didn't even bother to visit him."

I cover my face and shake my head so hurt by all that Royal has been through. I had no idea the extent of things and I hate hearing this. It makes me angry. "So Royal was in jail when they buried Olivia? Those assholes kept him away?"

He nods his head. "Yeah... he was. He was a fucking mess, but refused to speak to anyone. He shut down, so I went and visited him every few days just to let him know that he wasn't alone and that I stood behind him. Small towns like this work different from larger ones, Avalon. It's the only thing I hate about being here."

"Fuck," I whisper. "All of that, and on top of it he lost his baby girl. He doesn't deserve all of this pain. He doesn't..."

"Yeah," he says softly. "He couldn't handle all of the shit that was going on, so during his time behind bars papers were signed to give up his daughter. It's the one and only time that his stepfather went to visit him. I was surprised at first, but then realized that Royal was broken at the time. He'd been through more than any one person should have to go through. I could see how keeping his daughter would be hard on him, so I tried my best to keep my opinions on the matter to myself and support his decision."

He breathes out. "She's the little girl you just met. That's Royal's daughter," he continues. "That's why she's so important to me. She lost everything that night and I was there to see her last bit of family break down."

My hearts stops and I find myself fighting to breathe. The more I fight, the less air I seem to be able to get. He has to be wrong. This can't be... "What did you just say?"

"I'm sorry that I told you this way, but you needed to know. That little girl is Royal's child. I've been visiting her since she was a baby. I've been protecting her and looking out for her. I know Royal won't speak of her. He never does."

I shake my head and fall against my car, suddenly feeling weak. "No. That can't be true. She's dead," I say softly. "There has to be a mistake. Royal said she was dead. He said..."

Mark rushes over and grabs my arm, pulling me back up straight when I about fall over. "What are you saying?" he screams, while supporting me against the car. "What do you mean Royal said she's dead?"

"He said they both died," I cry. "Blaine told me the same thing. They both think they lost her."

Mark pulls me into his arms and holds me as I cry into his chest. "Royal thinks she's dead. He thinks she's dead and now he's gone. He's fucking gone and I can't tell him that she's here."

"Fuck. This cannot be happening. Payton is a dirty fucking piece of shit cop, and I'm willing to bet he was in on this shit along with Royal's fucking parents. I knew that son of a bitch was fucked up in the head."

"What are you saying?" I question. "What does that mean? Why would they do that to him?" I pull away and push at Mark's chest, feeling overwhelmed. "How could you think that Royal would give his daughter up? He would never do that!"

He punches the top of his car a few times, before gripping it again. "It means that Royal's parents forged his signature, and Payton and them made Royal believe she was dead. It also means that it would be Royal's word against Payton's. He stands no chance at fighting him in court. I never fucking talked about her to him because I didn't want to bring up the memories and pain of that night. I always suspected that he gave her up because it hurt him too much. I was a fucking idiot. You're right. I should have known he wouldn't give her up. Fuck!"

"I want her," I say without hesitation. "Tell me what I need to do to get her out of there and into my home."

Mark nods his head. "I'll do everything that I can." His eyes meet mine. "Are you sure you want to do this? Don't take on something that you can't handle. This is a little girl that we're talking about here. I need to know that you really want her, and will take care of her and love her as your own."

"Please," I say firmly. "I love him. That is his child in there and I'll love her too. I've never been more certain of anything in my life. Help me."

"Alright," he says softly. "Just don't let that little girl down. If Royal doesn't come back... it's the two of you against the world. You're her family. You need to know that."

"I know..." I whisper.

That's something he'll never have to worry about. That little girl has just become part of my life now. Royal has the other part and I'm not giving up until I'm whole.

CHAPTER 35

ROYAL

ONE MONTH LATER...

IT'S PAST MIDNIGHT, AND JUST like every other night in this shithole motel I can't sleep for shit. There are so many fucked up thoughts running through my head that almost none of it seems to make sense anymore. It pisses me the hell off. It's been a whole month since I left her, and I'm no closer to having my shit together now than I did the night I took off.

The thing that seems to be haunting me the most, though, is the look in Avalon's eyes as I left her in tears, running after me in *my* sheet that night. Fuck, it shoots right through me and straight to my heart, weakening me from the one spot that I thought no one would be able to reach again... but she has. She has my heart in her grasp and I'm willing to let her keep it as long as I can't hurt her.

I never wanted to have that power over someone else again: to be able to hurt another or let her down. Not like I did Olivia. I was doing so fucking good, keeping everyone at a distance, until she walked through that door, knocking me on my fucking ass and making me want her.

I gave her the opportunity to see me. To see the real me, giving her the chance to run before it was too late... but she didn't. Instead she did the exact opposite and fell for me.

She fell in love with me. She told me she wanted me and needed me.

Every time I think about it, I tell myself that she has to be just as fucked up as I am to believe she's in love with me.

Time...

With time she will see the truth and her eyes will start to open up to the fact that there's nothing good about me. I'm not a good fucking man that will bring her flowers and plan romantic candlelit dinners and then make love to her, whispering in her ear that she's my one true love. I can't be what she deserves. I'm not sure I can be anything.

She just can't love me. I need enough time and distance between us for her to see that so I can't fucking hurt her.

Reaching over beside me to the sticky table, I grab the bottle of whiskey and bring it to my lips, while powering up my phone and watching as it lights up.

It's that time of the night that I know Jax or Blaine's text will be waiting for me, letting me know the same thing they tell me every day: Avalon is good and safe.

That's all I asked from both of them when I left. I don't want anything else at the moment, and I know that Jax and Blaine are the only two that truly understand how my head works.

Every other message that I receive throughout the day gets deleted without even a second thought, because I know if I allow myself to read any messages from Avalon I will break and only drag her down with me.

It's not safe yet. Not until I can get my head straight and figure out a way to move on.

Setting down the bottle, I rub my hands down my face and

release a deep breath. "I need to know that what I'm doing is the right thing, Olivia. I need to know that these feelings I have inside are true. I need a sign from you. Please."

I shake my head and look around the dark, stale room, wishing that things didn't have to be this way. I hate it here and I hate that I can't be with her. It makes me feel less alive more and more each day.

"I love her," I say in a pained voice, hoping that Olivia understands. "I love her so fucking much, but I'm scared. I don't want to hurt her. Can you tell me that I won't... because I can't?"

I turn on our song for the hundredth time tonight and close my eyes, pretending that everything will be okay.

That I somehow can remember how to live again...

CHAPTER 36

AVALON

FIVE MONTHS LATER...

"KYLIE! WHERE ARE YOU, GIGGLES?" I yell, while opening up the lower cabinets in the kitchen and pretending to look inside. "Hmm, I wonder where Kylie could be? Somebody sure is good at disappearing! Must be magical..."

I hear her tiny, high-pitched giggle coming from under the kitchen table, but I continue to play along and look everywhere else except the place I know she is hiding.

She laughs again as I walk over to the table and shake my head, as if I'm disappointed that I can't find her.

"Oh man... she must be gone. Shucks! Too many magical Skittles today." I reach for her favorite pink plastic bowl. "I guess I will just have to eat this macaroni and cheese all by myself."

Laughing, she runs out from under the table and dives at my leg, squeezing it in her little arms. "Mommy! Mine! Mine!"

Feeling overwhelmed, I smile big and pick her up, hugging

her tightly as tears form in my eyes. With each day I get more and more attached to this beautiful little angel, and there's no better feeling in the world than to hear her call me mommy.

My heart hurt the first few times she said it. It made me feel guilty. There was an ache in my chest that made me feel for Olivia and hurt for her. She should be the one being called mommy. She should be the one seeing her running around and laughing and holding her at night while she falls sleep. Not me, but her and Royal. They were supposed to be a family, but this little girl had it all taken from her. It kills me, but makes me happy that I can be here for her now.

I set Kylie down in her highchair and turn and wipe the tears away as they continue to fall down my face and wet the top of my shirt. She looks so much like Royal that it hurts, knowing he's gone.

I try my hardest not to think about Royal and how much he's missing out on with his little angel here, but as hard as I try, I can't force myself to stop. He means more to me now than ever, and I want nothing more than for him to be here, especially after having his beautiful little girl in my life.

Not a day has gone by that I haven't sent him a text to let him know that I need him to come home. He needs to know about his daughter, but I refuse to tell him over the phone. He's been through too much already. I can't do that to him over a phone call.

That's exactly why I haven't told Jax and Blaine the truth yet. As far as they know, Kylie is just a little girl that I adopted and fell in love with. She's been with me for two months now thanks to my uncle's connections. Every single day with her is special.

I knew that if I told the boys there's no way they wouldn't tell Royal. Just the thought of him reading it over a text or hearing it in a voicemail breaks my heart. He needs to be here. He needs to see her with his own eyes.

This little angel is life changing. As much as it hurts me not to have Royal here, I need him to come back on his own. I need him to be ready to be in his daughter's life, whether that includes me or not. He's got a lot going on in his head. Only he can choose to let go.

I just don't know how much longer I can hold out on telling him about her, or how much longer I can have hope that we will be together again. There has to be a time that I allow myself to move on with my life.

"One more month," I whisper to myself. "Just one more month."

The tears fall harder, because honestly... I've been saying the same thing for the last four months now. Those words haven't done shit to make him appear in front of me and into Kylie's life.

"Hey girls! I'm starving." My uncle walks through the kitchen, still dressed in his uniform, and kisses Kylie on the forehead. "Is this for me?" He teases Kylie while grabbing her spoon and pretending to eat her food.

I quickly wipe my face off on my shirt, before he has a chance to look at me. "Hey, Uncle Mark. I'm just pulling the food out of the oven now." I walk over to the oven and pull out the lasagna. "How was work?"

He stops teasing Kylie long enough to pull out the chair beside her. "Unfortunately, it's not over yet. Some teen punks keep causing trouble in the parking lots of the convenience stores around town. Been getting a new call about those kids about every hour. Let's just say they're lucky they can run fast."

"Gotcha," I say with a laugh. "Hey... just look at it this way: old men need exercise too. Don't be too mad." I look up to see him giving me a dark look.

"Watch it, young lady." He turns to Kylie and pokes her nose. "Uncle Mark isn't old. Right, baby girl?"

She shakes her head and then points at me, as if to say that I'm the old one.

"I sure feel that way, baby girl." Pulling out a chair, I take a seat across from Mark and start making my plate.

"Any word from... you know..."

I shake my head, but keep my eyes on my plate, afraid to let Mark see how much it still hurts me. "Not a thing. Even the boys are starting to worry about him. I'm not liking it one bit." I look up from my plate. "What if something happened to him?"

Mark shakes his head and forces a smile. "Nah... Royal can hold his own. Not many men are capable of taking him down. I'd worry more about him getting in trouble with the law than anything else."

"Yeah, I suppose."

Mark stops eating and reaches over to place his hand on mine. "Hey..." I look up. "Everything will work out like it's supposed to in the end. For now you just continue to focus on yourself and that little girl. You're everything to her. Got it? Just be patient. After Olivia passed away, Royal left once he got released from jail. No one saw or heard from him for six damn months. He has a lot to work through."

I clear my throat and quickly wipe my wet face off. "Yeah... I didn't know that. Didn't realize that he left for that long before."

"He's had a rough life, Ava. I don't blame him for being caught up in his head right now." He clears his throat and smiles over at Kylie as she pokes his arm with her spoon. "Eat. You're looking too thin. Don't let stress overpower everything else good in your life."

I nod my head and eat in silence, letting his words sink in. All there's left to do now is to be strong for Kylie. That's what I intend to do... with or without Royal.

We eat dinner and clean up, just in time for Mark to get called out to check on those teenage kids again. It's late and the little one is getting tired.

Kylie is cuddled up in my arms on the couch and her favorite cartoon is playing on the TV, making her force her eyes to stay open. It's a losing battle. She'll be out in less than five minutes now.

"Hey," Madison whispers, as she walks in the front door. She nods down at Kylie wrapped in her blanket, fluttering her eyes. "Someone looks like they had a long day."

I rub the top of Kylie's head and smile. "A very long one," I say softly. "This little booger has more energy than anyone I've met in my life. She's special."

Madison tilts her head and smiles down at her. "That she is..." Quietly, she walks over and takes a seat beside me on the couch. "You doing okay, babe?"

I pull Kylie in tighter as she squeezes my arm in her sleep. "Yeah... I think so. It's still hard, but I think time will help. This little angel keeps me busy."

"I'm sorry," Madison says in a soft voice. "You love Royal and I know you're hurting really bad right now. I can see it in your everyday activity. You can't hide it from me, sweets." She leans in and kisses the side of my head. "Just know that I'm always here for you. Kylie is too."

"I know." I watch as Madison stands up from the couch. "You going out again tonight?"

She shakes her head. "No, ma'am. I'm exhausted. I hate to admit that there's no way I'll be able to keep up with Blaine tonight." She lifts her brows and smiles. "I'm choosing to stay away from him so I won't have to. Night, babe."

"Night..."

Being careful not to wake Kylie, I stand up and carry her to my bed, before changing into a pair of shorts and a tank top, and crawling into my warm bed beside her.

I lay here, holding her for the longest time, not able to fall asleep, so I just close my eyes and listen to the steady rhythm of her breathing. I find that it somehow calms me at night. It's about the only thing that keeps me sane in the middle of the night when I'm lonely and missing him.

Picking up my phone with my free hand, I send a goodnight text to Royal like I do every night, before placing my phone back on the bed beside me, and snuggling Kylie tightly in my arms.

"I love you, baby girl," I whisper. "You're the most precious thing in my life." I kiss the side of her head, before snuggling up close behind her and closing my eyes. She's so soft and warm in my arms, making me feel warm inside.

You give me peace when I feel that it's all lost...

OYAL

I'VE BEEN WAITING ON BAXTON for the last twenty minutes, and I'm beginning to grow impatient as fuck. I can't be here for one second longer without losing my shit.

Four months is way too damn long. This place has kept me from the one place I want to be and I despise myself for ending up here in the first place.

Pulling out a cigarette, I light it, and start walking down the dirt path in hopes of meeting up with Baxton along the way.

He was with me that night at the bar when I landed my ass in this shitty, small town jail. He watched from the background as I beat the shit out of that no good, redneck, woman abuser. If it weren't for him stopping me at the end, that guy would be dead, but he's known me for years and knows how much I've been through after losing Olivia.

I wouldn't have cared at that moment either. My head was

still filled with rage and fucked up thoughts. His face was the stress reliever that I needed at the time, and I took it further than I should have.

Being behind bars has given me time to truly clear my head and realize what's most important to me: Avalon.

Not a day has gone by that my chest hasn't ached to get back to her. Thinking about getting to her had me pointlessly trying to rip the fucking bars off of my cell. All it did was fill me with more rage and want to choke whichever guard came to check on me first.

I'm out now, and there is nothing that is going to fucking keep me from getting to her. I know that I have a lot of apologizing to do and a lot to make up for, but I'm willing to do everything in my power to show her how much I love her.

That woman is my fucking life and I'm willing to give mine to her. I'm ready.

Looking up, I toss my cigarette aside when I hear an old beat up truck coming around the corner.

I would know the sound of that old thing from anywhere. He's had it since back when we were just teenagers.

"About fucking time," I mumble.

Baxton pokes his head out of the window and slaps his truck when he sees me walking up. "Damn dude... what the fuck were they feeding you in there? You're a fucking beast. Get your crazy ass in here."

Opening the passenger side door, I jump into his old piece of shit and slam the door shut behind me. "I've had a lot of frustration to work out. What the fuck took you so long, dick?"

"Is my ass ever on time?"

I run my hand over my face and hold my hand out. "Give me your phone."

Reaching between his legs, he grabs his phone and tosses it at me, before taking off in a hurry, squealing his damn tires. "I got your truck and shit at my house. It's gassed up and ready to hit the road, man."

I look up from dialing Jax's number. "Appreciated, brother."

Jax answers his phone on the second ring.

"Yeah," he responds. "Make this shit quick because I got shit to do, Bax."

"What the fuck shit do you have to do?" I say with a small smile, happy as fuck to hear his voice.

It's silent for a moment, before I hear him walking through a crowd of people. "Fucking Royal. Fucking shit." He slams a door shut, which I'm assuming is my office door at *Savage*. "You have us all worrying and shit. What the fuck are you doing there with Bax?"

"It's a long story. Bax just picked me up from the county jail and I'm heading to my truck now."

"Why the fuck didn't you call one of us and let us know?" he asks, pissed as fuck. I don't blame him. I'd be pissed too if it were him or Blaine.

I let out a long breath and lean my head back against the seat. "I needed time to clear my head. Didn't need you guys trying to show up and visit; especially Avalon."

"You're damn straight my ass would've been there. Glad your ass is still alive. Shit."

"I know you would have." I pull the phone away and rub my fingers over my eyes, dreading this last part. "Is Avalon still around?"

"Yeah..." He pauses for a second. "She's around. She's been rough, but she's pulling through. Things have changed, man."

Feeling stressed, I pull out another cigarette and take a long drag, before slowly blowing the smoke out. "How's that?"

"I think it's best if you just see for yourself."

"Don't fuck with me, Jax," I growl. "Is she back with my brother?"

"No," he responds instantly. "That girl is madly in love with you; even after all this time. It's bigger than that. Just get your ass back here, and fast."

"Dammit," I hiss. "Don't tell anyone I'm on my way. Got it. Not even her."

"Yeah, man. Got it."

I pull the phone away from my ear and disconnect the call.

My heart is racing at the different ideas running through my head. I need to get my ass home and fast.

"Step on it..."

I just hope it's not too late. I'm not sure I can handle losing her...

AVALON

UNABLE TO SLEEP, I MAKE my way outside to the front porch and lean over the railing, closing my eyes as I inhale a deep breath and slowly release it.

It's nearly four o'clock in the morning and extremely cold out here, but I somehow feel as if being out here is where I need to be at the moment. It helps me think straight and get away from the noise inside when we have a house full, which seems to be often since Kylie has come home with me.

Since waking up an hour ago, my heart has been telling me that something big is about to happen, and no matter how hard I try I can't shake the feeling. It's so fucking scary.

Shivering, I pull my sweater tighter around me and look out at the dark, lonely street. The only light is from a few houses that have their porch lights on.

The more I look around me, taking in the lonely scenery, and letting everything fall into place in my head, I feel an overwhelming sadness take over and begin to lose all hope.

"Why won't you just come back?" I cry to myself, while

running my hand over my face with my free hand. "Your daughter is the most precious thing in this world. I want you to meet her, Royal."

Choking on a sob, I cover my mouth and try my best to stay quiet. "Seeing her beautiful smile every morning numbs all the sadness in the world. I want you to experience that feeling. I want you to know that you have a reason to live. I'm sorry that I wasn't enough for you, but maybe she will be. Just maybe..."

Placing my back against the door, I slowly make my way down to my butt and wrap my arms around my knees to keep warm. I'm angry with myself for thinking that by talking out loud to him that he will somehow just show up. It hasn't worked yet. Why would it now? Why the fuck now?

Burying my face into my legs, I allow myself to cry unrestricted. I've been trying so hard to be strong around Kylie. All I need is just a few minutes to let it all out, so that's what I do. I cry until my throat feels raw and my eyes become so puffy that my vision becomes blurry.

Just as I'm wiping my face off and standing to my feet, a car engine sounds from close by, reminding me of the sound of Royal's truck. I stop, and for a split second... so does my heart.

Something about that sound as it gets closer sends my heart into overdrive, and I find myself clutching at my chest as my eyes stare off into the night, waiting for the vehicle to come into view.

As soon as a huge truck comes into view, I lose it. Every piece of me breaks and I fall down to my knees, crying and clutching at my sweater as his truck pulls up in front of the house. He jumps out in a hurry, barely giving himself time to stop.

"Oh, my God," I cry to myself as his pained eyes meet mine. "You're here. You're really here..."

As soon as the words leave my mouth he rushes across the

yard, not stopping until he's standing on the porch, lifting me up into his strong arms.

"Fuck, I missed you so much, baby. Don't cry. I'm here." Wrapping his hands in my hair, his mouth presses against every inch of my wet face, as I clutch onto him for dear life in fear of him leaving again. I don't know what I'd do if that ever happened again, but I don't intend to give him the opportunity.

"You left," I whisper through a small cry. "You really left."

Grabbing my face, he pulls it up for our eyes to meet. "I had to," he says firmly. "I'm so fucking sorry, but I want you to know that I'm never leaving you again. You hear me?"

I shake my head as more tears helplessly fall down my face. "I was so fucking scared," I say, while squeezing his arm. "I thought I'd never see you again. Do you know how much that hurt me?"

He looks away for a second, as if to hide his emotions. "It hurt me too."

"Did it?" I question angrily. "It's hard for me to believe that when I told you that I loved you, Royal. I fucking told you that I loved you and you left. You still left."

"Look at me," he demands, while cupping my face. "Look at me, dammit."

Letting out a frustrated breath, I finally bring my eyes up to meet the beautiful ones that I've missed so damn much. "I'm looking," I whisper painfully.

"I. Love. You," he whispers. "I love you and it scared me. That's why I left." My eyes slowly close as he runs his thumbs under my wet eyes. "Nothing scares me more than hurting you. I had to clear my head and know for sure that I was strong enough to let you in and fully love you like you deserve. I can never take back leaving, but I can promise you that you'll never have to wake up another morning without me by your fucking side."

He pulls my face up; making me open my eyes again.

"Please tell me that you'll let me love you. Will you?" He whispers the last two words.

Bursting out in tears from his confession, I wrap my arms around his neck and slam my lips against his. Feeling his soft lips against mine wakes something inside of me, making it feel as if I'm truly breathing for the first time in five months.

"Yes," I pant against his lips. "I love you so fucking much." I slap his chest, before grabbing his face. "Don't ever leave me again. I won't survive."

"I'm yours," he says gently, while placing my hand to his heart. "This is yours and has been for a long time now."

I smile through my tears and hold onto him as tightly as I can, as he buries his face into my neck and kisses it repeatedly, while whispering how much he loves and needs me.

I've never felt more whole in my entire life than I do right now, right here, standing in Royal's strong arms... but there's one thing I need to do and there's really no right way of going about this. I just need to tell him.

"It's not just me anymore," I whisper, causing him to look up at me. "There's a little girl in my life and I love her more than this whole world."

His gray eyes widen as they search mine. "You adopted a child? You had one before us? I don't..." He swallows. "It doesn't matter. I'll love you both. You must know that," he whispers. "Nothing is going to keep me away from you. Not anymore. Fuck that. I'm not going anywhere unless it's with you."

Tears stream down my face from his words and I find myself wanting to break down for this man. This is going to be so damn hard to do. He's missed two years of his daughter's life and he doesn't even have a clue that she's in my bedroom in my bed right now.

"She's yours," I say, so softly that it's barely audible. "Hadley is here... in my bed."

His whole body stiffens as he gasps. "What did you just say?"

"Your daughter is alive," I whisper, while wiping the tears off my face. "She didn't die. She's very much alive."

Releasing me, he drops to his knees and grips the back of his head. "I don't fucking understand! Are you fucking with me?" He looks up with tearstained eyes. "Is this some kind of sick joke to get back at me for leaving?"

I shake my head and crouch down before him to grab his face. "I would never do that!" I scream through tears. "I know it's hard to believe, but I promise you that it's the truth. She looks just like you," I whisper. "So much so that it hurt to look at her, knowing that you were gone. Your daughter is here with us, right now, in the house. She's fast asleep, warm and safe."

His fists clench at his sides as the tears uncontrollably pour down his face. Tilting his head, he looks around me to look inside when the door slowly opens behind us, making a creaking noise.

I must have forgotten to close it all the way, because from the look of pure shock and awe on Royal's face, I know that it's Kylie standing there and not Madison. He's seeing his baby girl for the first time.

Wiping at his face, he stands to his feet and stares down at Kylie as she stands there, shivering while holding her blanket.

"Oh, my God..." he cries out, before scooping her up into his arms and carrying her back inside where it's warm.

I've never seen a man hold a little girl so tight in my entire life. His grip on Kylie is fierce, as if he fears ever letting her go, at risk of losing her again. He's gone the last two years believing that his daughter was dead, yet she was living not more than twenty minutes from his home.

The million emotions running through his eyes right now as he realizes that this little girl is his life is almost enough to drop me to my knees and clutch my chest.

Watching this moment unfold right in front of me is the most intense moment I've ever experienced in my life. This moment is worth a million tears and I'm about to shed just that.

"Hadley," he cries, while running his hands over her head and burying his face in her soft baby hair. "Daddy loves you, baby girl; so much. I'm never letting you go. I promise. I promise you that on my life."

My heart aches and a sob escapes me as I watch him cry into the side of Kylie's head. I've never seen Royal so vulnerable, and witnessing all of the pain and suffering finally pouring out of him and freeing him; it hurts. It hurts, but it feels so damn good at the same time.

Kylie's eyes meet mine from over Royal's shoulder. They're filled with confusion as Royal continues to hold her close and cry against her, but instead of her being scared, she holds him back and tears fill her eyes as if she knows this moment is something deep: a special moment between a father and his daughter.

Wiping my eyes off, I reach for Kylie's head and gently kiss it. "Your daddy is here, baby. This man is going to take care of you like I have. He's going to love you, baby." I rub the side of her face. "You're going to have two people who love you very much. Understand, Kylie?"

Royal's grip loosens on Kylie long enough for him to look at her face. "Kylie," he whispers, clearly confused.

I nod my head as Kylie just stares up into his wet eyes.

"Yes," I respond. "That's what she's been going by."

He smiles through his tears when their eyes meet for a moment. "You have her eyes," he says gently. "And a part of mine."

Nodding my head, I smile while wiping my wet eyes off. "She does. They're the most beautiful eyes in the world."

Slowly, he lowers himself to his knees and sets Kylie down before him. "Are you tired?"

Wiping at her eyes, Kylie nods her head and yawns.

He turns to me. "Let me put her to bed. I want to tuck her in. I need to make sure she's warm and safe. I just need to..."

"Yes," I whisper. "I bet she'd like that."

Cupping her face, he gently places his forehead to hers.

I get distracted when the front door swings open again, but this time to Jax and Blaine rushing inside.

"What's going—" Blaine stops and turns to me when I grab his arm to quiet him.

In silence, we all stand here and watch as Royal scoops Kylie back up into his arms and carries her away to my bedroom, holding her as if she's going to break if he moves wrong. She's so precious to him and it's clear to see.

"I need to tell you both something very important." My eyes go up to find Blaine's. Something registers in them that has my heart going crazy. He's going to be so pissed.

"Ah fuck!" Blaine bursts out while gripping his hair and looking at the hallway. "It's true." He starts pacing and looking around with wild eyes. "I had a feeling. Her eyes. Her damn eyes..."

Swallowing, I nod my head. "Yes. I'm sorry. I was going to tell you, but I wanted to wait —"

"I get it," he cuts me off. "You wanted Royal to find out in person. It hurts, but I fucking get it. That's my niece. My fucking niece... Damn."

I nod my head and wipe at my face when Blaine looks over at me with wet eyes. "Yes. She reminds me a lot of you sometimes. She's goofy and fun like her uncle."

"I've been spending time with my niece this whole time. My fucking niece," he whispers. "My family." He crouches down and rubs his hands over his face, smiling through tears. "My niece," he repeats.

"Well I wasn't expecting this fucking twist," Jax says, finally speaking for the first time since he's walked through the door. "I'm not sure if that's a good thing. I mean it is, but it's not."

My head whips around to Jax. "Why not?" I ask worried. "What does that mean?"

"It means that someone fucked Royal over to keep his daughter away. It means that Royal is going to rip someone's fucking throat out. That's what the fuck it means."

Fear sets in at the realization that he's right. There's no way Royal is going to let that little fact slip by him, no matter how happy he is to finally have her back in his life.

"How did you know?" Blaine pushes, while standing back up. "Who the fuck led you to Hadley? Someone had to know this whole damn time."

"My uncle," I whisper. "He said..."

The room goes quiet as Royal walks back into the room and stands with his hands over his face.

"She's asleep," he says, while walking over to the chair and sinking down into it. "She fell asleep in my arms. I should be in there, but I don't want to scare her in the morning when she wakes up in my arms. She..." He shakes his head. "She needs to get to know me first. I need to be here every day; every fucking day until she realizes who I am. I'm not leaving her side until she does."

"And you can be. She will," I say, while walking across the room to be close to him. "She needs her daddy, Royal. She needs you just as much as you need her."

"I'm happy for you, man," Jax suddenly says. "She's an amazing little girl. I know..."

"Two years," Royal growls out. "I've missed over two years of my child's life because someone took her from me. My fucking baby girl."

"I know how you feel, but don't do this, brother," Blaine says while gripping his shoulder. "You need to be here for your daughter now. You can't lose your shit whenever you damn well please anymore. I know what's running through your head."

He pushes Blaine's hand away and jumps to his feet. "Tell me how you knew about Hadley... Kylie. Shit, I need to get used to her name."

I swallow hard, nervous to tell him the story, afraid that he'll go and hurt someone. "My uncle thought you gave her up for adoption this whole time: your stepfather and some officer that was there that night. They said you signed her over. I don't know—"

"That motherfucker," he growls. "That day he came to my cell with papers. He told me they were papers for Olivia. I wasn't in my right mind and I sent him away without my fucking signature. Well now I know what the fuck they were doing. I was never good enough by him in the first place. Now... they look at me like a monster: him, Colton, and my fucking mother. That son of a bitch forged that shit when I refused."

Jumping to his feet, he rushes outside with me taking off after him. I'm so scared of what he'll do.

"Royal!" I yell out to him as he stops by his truck and repeatedly punches the side of it, leaving a bunch of dents, until his hands are covered in blood. "Royal! Stop!"

Finally, he stops and looks back at me, while fighting to catch his breath. "I'll be back." He points to Blaine. "Take care of the girls while I'm gone. Don't leave until I get back."

Stumbling over my feet, I rush down the porch and over to his truck, almost falling. "Don't do it, Royal! Please!"

"Go inside," he demands, while jumping inside his truck and rolling down the window to yell at me. "Take care of our little girl. Go!"

"No! Fuck you!"

Not giving a shit what he says, I make my way around the truck and jump inside, slamming the door behind me.

Growling out, Royal punches the steering wheel, before

gripping it and leaning his forehead against it. "Fuck, Avalon! This needs to be done."

"Then I'm going with you." I pull my seatbelt on and growl over at him. "Go! If it needs to be done... then go, but you're not getting rid of me."

He punches the steering wheel one more time, before yelling out in anger and pulling off.

The closer we get to June and Ken's, the more nervous I become, and my stomach begins to twist up with knots as I watch the houses around us in passing.

I don't say a word though. Not yet. I know that he needs to confront Ken. He won't be able to live with himself if he doesn't. I can't take that from him. It would be selfish of me.

All I can do is be here to support him and hope that I can bring him back to sanity before things go too far.

The truck comes to an abrupt stop, and before I can even look over at Royal, he's out of the truck and running at Ken, who is just coming out of the house.

I quickly jump out of the truck in time to see the look of pure horror on his face when he notices the brick house that is charging at him.

"Royal..." He throws his arms up for protection. "Don't be stupid!"

Ignoring his plea, Royal grips him by the throat and slams him up against the house. "You kept my fucking daughter from me! The only thing left in my life that mattered. You fucking no good piece of shit!"

Pulling Ken away from the house, he drags him across the porch, toward the steps. "Just go home," he chokes out, while trying to pry Royal's hand from his neck. "You'll never understand."

"I'll never understand? Huh?" He releases Ken's throat and swings out, punching Ken in the mouth.

I watch with wide eyes as Ken falls down the steps, scraping his face on the cement. Before Ken can gain his composure, Royal is on top of him, pulling his knife out.

"No!" June screams from the open door. "He's your father. Don't hurt him!"

"He's not my father. He's just someone you dated before dad, then left dad when he fucked up by getting locked up, and decided to get back with and marry. Fuck that! He means nothing to me."

Placing the knife to Ken's throat, Royal leans in and growls in his bloodied up face. "You made me believe for over two years that my daughter died. Do you have any idea what that's like? You and that bitch cop fucked me over."

He presses the knife down, causing blood to drip around the tip. "I should kill you right now. I should take your life, just like you took two years of mine. It could've been more," he screams. "I could've never fucking known. Do you get that?"

"Royal! Stop! You're hurting him. You need to stop!" His mom continues to scream at him from the background, but he tunes her out as if it's just him and Ken.

"Royal!" I scream, as he presses the knife a little deeper. "You can't do this," I say gently. "Your daughter needs you here with her. If you kill that asshole for taking her from you, he's still winning, and you will still end up without your daughter. Do you understand that? Do you get that?"

He tilts his head to the side, his eyes moving up to lock with mine. There's so much pain behind his gaze that I almost want to kill Ken myself.

"Let him go," I whisper. "He has the picture now and you have your daughter at home waiting for you."

Slowly, I walk over and grab the knife out of his shaking hand. Then I bend down and grab his face. "Let's go home... with our true family. Please."

Releasing a breath, he stands to his feet and quickly runs his hands through his sweaty hair.

"I was only trying to protect her," Ken says quietly. "Your head was too messed up after what happened. After Olivia died..."

"Stop it," Royal demands. "Shut the fuck up before I change my mind and cut your throat out."

Grabbing my hand, he stares Ken down, while backing me up toward the truck. "Stay the fuck away from my family. This is your only warning. Fuck with my family and I won't hesitate to kill you. That's the fucking truth."

Relief washes over me as he helps me into his truck and jumps inside, quickly taking off.

The whole ride home is silent. I expect nothing more. He needs this moment to calm down. Any good man who loves his family would.

Once we pull back up in front of my house, he turns the truck off and grips the steering wheel, while fighting to catch his breath.

Crawling over the middle to get to him, I duck under Royal's arm and straddle his lap. "You need to let it go for her. You need to be strong for her. Everything that you do now has to be for her. Your daughter needs you even more than I do."

Releasing the steering wheel, he cups my face and looks me in the eyes. "How can I just let it go? Tell me how I can move on and forget that they took her from me. Tell me! I should have killed him."

Trying to keep my emotions in check, I wrap my arms around his neck and press my forehead to his. "It's not going to be easy... I can tell you that right now, but isn't having her in your life right now better than not having her at all? If you go back and teach them a lesson, you're losing her again... and me. You're going to lose us both."

"Fuck," he says in a pained voice. "Fuck, baby. I love you. I love you both so fucking much. All I want is to be the best for you both."

Letting my own tears spill again, I hold him tightly as he breaks down in my arms.

I close my eyes and whisper repeatedly that I love him and that what's best for us, is to have him in our lives, as he buries his wet face into my neck.

This man will never understand just how strong he truly is right now for not killing that asshole. He had the power in his hands and yet he found it in him to stop. Not getting his revenge will be the hardest thing he's ever had to do over losing Olivia.

"I love you, baby. You belong here with us. Promise me that you'll never fucking leave again."

Gripping his face, I pull it up to look at me. "Promise me," I demand.

He grabs my face and runs his thumbs under my wet eyes, while kissing me long and hard. "I promise," he says gently. "I'll never leave you guys. The only way I'm leaving is dead."

We sit here and hold each other for what feels like forever, before Jax finally opens the door and laughs at us. "Get your asses inside and join the fucking slumber party. I see you kept his ass in check. You're the only one that could have."

I laugh against the side of Royal's face. "Way to interrupt a deep moment, jerk face."

Jax winks at me and reaches inside to help me out of the truck and to my feet. "Sorry, but you did good," he whispers. "Real fucking good."

"That's because she's my woman," Royal says, while jumping out of the truck and shutting the door. "Her and Kylie are my world and I won't do anything to jeopardize that. I just needed a moment to get my shit straight."

Royal's hand reaches out to grab mine, like old times, as he walks me back to the door, and inside where Blaine and Madison are chilling on the couch, surrounded by tons of blankets with a movie playing on the TV.

In this moment, here with my family surrounding us, is the only place I'd ever want to be.

Now that Royal is back, I can see that our family is complete.

I'm complete...

ROYAL

EIGHT MONTHS LATER...

GRIPPING THE BAR, I PULL up for the hundredth fucking time, letting out a relieved breath as I release it and jump down to my feet.

I've been up for the last hour, working off steam and getting ready for the day. I need my head cleared whenever I'm around my family, so I come in here every morning at the ass-crack of dawn and workout until all of my tension is gone.

So far... it's been working, and I hope to keep it that way.

Grabbing for my towel, I run it over my sweaty hair and body, before tossing it aside and quietly jogging past Jax's open room and upstairs to the kitchen to make breakfast.

By the time breakfast is done, I look up at the clock to see that it's about time for Kylie to wake up. She seems to be on a schedule, always waking up at or around the same time each morning.

Grabbing the tray of Mickey Mouse pancakes, I make my way up the stairs, stopping to peek inside Kylie's room.

I smile to myself and look down the hall when I hear sounds of her and Avalon laughing from down the hall.

These two women are what keep me sane from day to day, living the crazy life that I've grown up in. I know it's not an easy life, but I've made sure to keep most of the drama out of the bar now. Things are slowly changing for the better.

These two women are my life now, and the last eight months with them have been the best days of my life. To be able to hear my baby girl laugh each morning and to be able to kiss her goodnight each night is the best thing a man could fucking ask for. There is nothing better in life than having a family to take care of and love.

I know this now...

Leaning in the doorway, I stand here and watch the girls for a few minutes as they play around on the bed, laughing and giggling as Avalon tries to get Kylie to calm down and stop jumping on the bed.

"Okay! Okay!" Avalon yells playfully. "I'm awake. Mommy's not going back to sleep. I promise."

"Mommy awake!" Kylie jumps one last time, before diving into Avalon's arms and wrapping her arms around her neck.

"You're awake," I whisper, causing them both to look over at me.

"Daddy cook breakfast again! Yummy tummy!" Crawling out of Avalon's lap, Kylie jumps down off the side of the bed and runs at me, causing me to set the tray down and catch her in my arms.

"Daddy will always be here to make breakfast for you and mommy," I say happily. "Who else can make damn good pancakes like daddy?"

"Royal!" Avalon scolds. "Language."

"Hey..." I set Kylie down and she runs over to the bed where she usually eats her breakfast on Sunday mornings when we don't have guests. "I'm getting better. I didn't use the F word this time. Progress, baby."

I pull Avalon into my arms and look over to see Kylie getting lost in cartoons.

"Easy, buddy," Avalon laughs against my ear as I cup her ass and squeeze it. "It's going to be a long day before that can happen."

"Oh yeah..." I run my bottom lip up the side of her neck, before biting her ear and growling. "Uncle Jax is downstairs and Uncle Blaine is only a call away."

"Nice try." She slaps my chest and walks away, leaving me gripping my hair. This woman has never turned me on so damn much. She's so sexy, and she still has no fucking idea how much.

"Why don't we go downstairs and eat at the table this morning." Avalon turns off the TV, making Kylie throw her head back and whine. "Come on."

With a pouty lip, Kylie huffs and jumps out of bed, grabbing for my hand. "No Mickey Mouse," she cries softly.

Bending down, I scoop her up into my arms and distract her by blowing against her belly and walking fast down the hallway.

She begins laughing and squirming in my arms, being so loud that I wouldn't be surprised if Jax came running up the stairs soon.

Once we get to the kitchen, I plop her down into her booster seat and grab the tray of pancakes away from Avalon so she can get out the orange juice.

"Mmmmm... Mickey Mouse never looked so fucking good," Jax mumbles tiredly from the doorway.

"Language, asshole," I complain.

"Both of you," Avalon scolds while giving us the evil eye. "You two are hard to tame."

I bite my bottom lip, before gripping her face and roughly pressing my lips against hers. Fuck... I love her to death. She puts up with so much from us. "I warned you, babe. Now eat your food."

She narrows her eyes at me and shakes her head, before turning to Kylie. "You better eat up before Uncle Blaine shows up and eats Mickey."

"Already here, gorgeous."

"Of course," I mumble, while reaching for more plates and pulling the pan of extra pancakes out of the oven. "Where there's food there's Blaine and Madi."

"You know it," Madison says with a smirk, before walking over and snatching the pan from me. "Every Sunday, sweets. Get used to it. We don't wait for invites anymore."

"Oh you were waiting for them, babe. That's why you stacked that pan with pancakes," Avalon says with a smile, happy we've all become so close lately.

I may not admit it out loud, but I've grown used to the gang showing up at our house for breakfast. I sort of like it, even though that means seeing Blaine's hyper ass so early in the morning.

"Get your ass over here and sit down, brother." Blaine throws a pancake, hitting me in the side of the head.

"I give up," Avalon growls. "I'm going to have to start smacking you all in the mouth." She points to Kylie, eating her food. "Little people ears here. Do I really have to remind you she's like a sponge?"

"Shit! Got it!" Blaine says, clueless that he just fucked up again.

Avalon gives him a dirty look, but just shakes it off and continues eating her breakfast.

I have to walk behind Blaine to get to my seat, so I make a pit stop on the way there to slap him on the back of the head and drop his pancake that he threw at me on his plate. "Eat up, brother."

Laughing, I take my seat between Kylie and Avalon, where I belong.

I feel Avalon grab my leg from under the table and squeeze it. "I love you," she whispers.

I place my hand over hers and squeeze it. "Love you more, baby." I kiss her on the side of the head, before leaning over to kiss Kylie on the side of the head as well. "Love you, baby girl."

Kylie eats Mickey's ear and talks with her mouth full. "Love you more, Daddy."

My heart melts from her words; just like they do every single time that I hear them. She has a power over me that no one else could ever have.

She holds my heart in her tiny hand and I wouldn't want it any other way.

IT'S BEEN A WHILE SINCE I've been here; too long actually, and as I stand here staring down at the murky water, my heart aches that I'm standing here alone... without my family.

A part of me wanted to ask Avalon and Kylie to come with me, but a small part of me feared that Avalon's feelings would be hurt that I still need to come here for Olivia. I know that she understands, but I also know that it can't be easy either. I never want to do anything to hurt Avalon again. She and Kylie come first now, and I will protect them both at all costs.

I'll just give it a little more time. Maybe with a few passing years, Kylie will be able to fully understand our situation and I can make it a father-daughter thing each year.

"I'm sorry that I missed your birthday," I whisper. "I've been making up for lost time with our daughter." I stop to collect my emotions before continuing. It's never easy being here. "She's an amazing little girl, and I have an amazing woman to help me raise her. You'd like her. You would also be so proud of the father I've become. I know I am. I'm different because of them. Complete... finally."

Holding up the single calla lily, I get ready to drop it into the water, but stop when I hear some noise behind me. It sounds like feet dragging in the dirt.

I drop my hand down to my side and turn behind me to see Kylie walking, holding a calla lily in her tiny hand. She's dressed in a little aqua colored dress. It makes me smile because it was Olivia's favorite color.

My chest fills with warmth that I can't describe when she walks over and stands next to me, reaching for my hand with her free one.

Then one by one, more bodies join us, each one holding a single calla lily. First Blaine, followed by Jax, Madison, Mark, and then finally... Avalon.

With her eyes on me, and filled with love and understanding, she smiles and takes a spot between Kylie and Blaine.

Seeing them all here makes my chest ache with so much emotion, as I look down the line to see them all looking down into the water.

There's no need for words right now. Nothing said out loud could make this moment any more special than it already is.

It's perfect...

Swallowing back my emotions, I toss the calla lily I was holding into the water.

Then, I watch as each one drops theirs in, one by one down the line.

This is my life. This is my family. This is where I belong and where I plan to stay. I will do whatever it takes to keep it this way...

BOOKS BY VICTORIA ASHLEY

Standalone Books

Wake Up Call

This regret

Thrust

Hard & Reckless

Strung

Sex Material

Wreck My World

Steal You Away

Walk of Shame Series

Slade

Hemy

Cale

Stone

Styx

Kash

Savage & Ink Series

Royal Savage

Beautiful Savage

Pain Series

Get Off On the Pain

Something For The Pain

Alphachat Series (Co-written with Hilary Storm)

Pay For Play

Two Can Play

Locke Brother Series (Co-written with Jenika Snow)

Damaged Locke

Savage Locke

Twisted Locke

ABOUT THE AUTHOR

Victoria Ashley grew up in Illinois and has had a passion for reading for as long as she can remember. After finding a reading app where it allowed readers to upload their own stories, she gave it a shot and writing became her passion.

She lives for a good romance book with tattooed bad boys that are just highly misunderstood. When she's not reading or writing about bad boys, you can find her watching her favorite shows.